ELLE GRAY

BLAKE WILDER

FBI MYSTERY THRILLER

THE
MISSING
GIRLS

PROLOGUE

Caffeine Corner; Annenberg, ND

SHE WAS PERFECT. ABSOLUTELY PERFECT. THE MAN watched her from across the crowded coffeehouse as he had almost every day for the last couple of weeks. He watched her working behind the counter, serving up lattes, mochas, and whatever the hell else people wanted to drink. She always served her customers with a smile and chatted them up a bit. She was sweet. She seemed like a happy person. He liked that about her.

He glanced at his watch and saw that it was a quarter to ten. Emily was off in fifteen minutes. The man felt a jolt of excitement shoot through him. He always got that hit of anticipatory elation when the time came to move on one of his girls. It gave him a high unlike any drug he'd ever taken. It was cleaner. Purer. He was hungry, and his girls were the only thing that satisfied his cravings.

The man finished his drink and left the coffeehouse. He walked down the street and got into his car. He'd parked on a side street that gave him a view of the lot behind the coffeehouse. The clock on the dashboard clicked to ten o'clock, and excitement filled his veins with electricity so strong that he was trembling and couldn't stop smiling.

At five past ten, he squirmed in his seat and drummed his fingers on the steering wheel. Emily would be doing her last-minute chores and was usually out the back door and walking to her car by quarter after ten. He turned on his car stereo and surfed the stations until he came to a classic rock station. He'd always liked some of those moldy oldie bands he remembered his dad listening to. Well, before he died anyway. When his father died— victims of a drunk driver named Evan Bass—the man's entire life changed. And not for the better.

But he made sure his father's death didn't go unavenged. He'd made sure Bass paid the price, even if the damn Sheriff couldn't prove it was him. But he knew. He'd seen his face. And he'd exacted his revenge.

No, he didn't kill Bass. That would have been too easy. Too quick. He did make sure that Bass never forgot him though. He made sure that every single time Bass looked in the mirror, he remembered what he'd done to his father, and that on the outside, he looked like the monster he was on the inside. He'd sentenced Bass to a life of suffering, torment, and loneliness. The man thought it perfectly fitting for Bass's crimes.

The back door to the coffeehouse opened at 10:15, and Emily walked out. One of her male coworkers, a kid named Josh, walked her to her car and waited as she got in and drove off. The man smiled. When she turned out of the lot and headed down the street, he put his car in gear and pulled out, following her at a discreet distance. He knew the route she took home like the back of his hand; he'd already taken measures to ensure she was forced to stop on the long, lonely stretch of road she used as a shortcut home. All he had to do was be patient. All he had to do was wait, and then she would be his.

On a long and lonesome highway, east of Omaha, you can listen to the engine moanin' out his one-note song. You can think about the woman or the girl you knew the night before…

He sang along with Bob Seger's classic "Turn the Page," feeling pretty good about himself. And up ahead of him, as Emily turned the corner to take her shortcut, he smiled as a sense of anticipation and excitement grew inside of him. He was eager and had to force himself to calm down. She would be his soon enough.

The man turned the corner and saw Emily's headlights about a hundred yards ahead of him. The long stretch of road ran behind a row of warehouses, most of which stood empty these days. The streetlights that once lined the road had long since burned out or had been broken, and the city hadn't felt the need to replace them. Which was just fine with him. It worked to his benefit.

Just up ahead, Emily's taillights flared, and her car came to a sudden stop. He watched as she got out of her car, a silhouette in the darkness. Though he couldn't see her details, he knew she was looking at her rear tire on the driver's side. It was flat. And he knew that because he had made sure it would blow on her trip home.

The man slowed as he pulled up alongside her and stopped. He lowered the passenger's side window and leaned over. Even in the dim shadows of the night, she was lovely as she looked back at him. Her eyes were wide, and he saw the fear in her face. He didn't blame her for being scared. It was late at night, and he was a stranger to her. Annenberg was a safe place, more or less, but it was 2022, and there were deviants and monsters who would snatch you away in the middle of the night lurking everywhere.

He bit back the laugh that threatened to burst from his mouth as the thought passed through his mind. That would only alarm her more. Wanting to allay her fears, he held a hand up and smiled at her.

"Hey there," he called out. "Car trouble?"

She hesitated a moment and studied his features. She was cautious. But then the muscles in her face relaxed, and she turned, gesturing to the tire.

"I got a flat," she said. "I must have run over something I guess."

Yeah, the nails I stuck into your tire, the man thought but did not say. Instead, he kept that smile on his face. His heart beat in his chest like a trip-hammer, and his stomach churned with anticipation. He was close. So close. The man subtly blotted his suddenly damp palms on the thighs of his jeans.

"You got a spare?" he asked.

She pursed her lips. "Maybe?"

He chuckled softly then put his car in park and shut it off. He got out of the car, making a show of smiling and being friendly, secretly worried that he was overdoing it. But Emily didn't seem spooked, so he figured he was good.

"Pop the trunk for me?" he asked.

"That's sweet, but I can just call AAA," she said.

"Sure, and then you'll have to wait out here for two hours for them to arrive," he replied. "Art's is closed for the night, and the nearest place to get a tow from is over in Belford. I can change your tire and have you on your way in fifteen minutes. How's that sound?"

A shaky smile touched her lips, and she still hesitated. The man knew none of that was true. There were two shops in town that ran tows twenty-four hours a day. But he was banking on Emily not knowing that. She was a sweet, smart girl, but the one thing he'd learned in the time he'd been watching her was that she didn't know much about car maintenance or things like that. He slipped his hands into his pockets and kicked at a small stone near the toe of his boot.

"I can't just leave you out here. Wouldn't feel right," he said. "So, you either let me change your tire, or we'll sit out here together for a couple of hours until the tow truck gets here."

Emily smiled to herself and seemed to consider his words for a moment. She finally raised her eyes to him.

"If you're sure it's not a problem," she said. "I'd hate to trouble you."

"No trouble at all," he replied. "Just go ahead and pop your trunk."

"Thank you," she said. "I appreciate your help."

"You're very welcome."

Emily did as he asked and popped the trunk of her car. He made a show of looking for her jack—which he knew was not there, since he had removed it three days ago. He looked over at her.

"No jack?" he asked, his expression a perfect mockery of concern.

She shrugged. "I—I don't know. I'm not good with car things. My dad usually—"

He stopped her with a smile. "No problem. I've got one in my trunk."

The man casually looked around as he opened his trunk, making sure there was nobody else on the road. There wasn't. Reaching in, he quickly doused the rag inside with chloroform. Emily had her back to him, so he stepped up behind her and covered her mouth with the rag. She struggled in his grasp, and being a strong, sturdy girl, nearly broke free. But he tightened his grip and kept the rag over her mouth and nose and a few moments later, her entire body went limp.

Smiling to himself, the man lifted Emily's body and put her in the trunk of his car. Working quickly, he put a pair of plastic cuffs around her ankles and wrists, then put a gag in her mouth and secured it. That done, he slammed the lid of the trunk and quickly got back into his car. The man started it up, cranked the volume on Led Zeppelin's "Whole Lotta Love," and drove down the dark street laughing to himself.

The day was bright and unexpectedly warm as Stacy Wilhite walked her dog through the park. She smiled at and greeted the people she passed as the frisky two-year-old golden retriever danced around and pulled at her leash, trying to drag Stacy toward the trees.

"Delilah, stop," Stacy called.

Stacy frowned. Delilah was always energetic and playful, but she seemed agitated today. She didn't normally pull at her leash.

She was always well-behaved and never acted up like this on a walk. Well, not since she was a puppy anyway.

"Hey, Stace!"

She turned to see her friend Desiree walking toward her. She and one of their friends from their book club, Michaela, were out for a run. Stacy raised her hand in greeting, and that momentary distraction was enough for Delilah. The golden yanked at her leash, ripping it out of Stacy's hand, and just like that, she took off.

"Delilah!" she shouted as her dog sprinted for the trees.

Stacy turned to Desiree and Michaela who both waved her off.

"Go get your dog," Desiree called. "We'll catch up later!"

"Sorry!" Stacy shouted back.

She turned and ran for the woods that sat at the edge of the park, calling Delilah's name. She heard her dog barking in the distance. Stacy silently cursed the pup as she picked her way over and around rocks and exposed tree branches. This section of the forest was rocky, and the level ground of the park gave way to a steep downward grade. Her foot slipped on wet leaves and loose dirt, nearly sending her tumbling down the embankment several times as she tried to navigate it.

"Delilah!" she called, feeling perturbed.

The dog's barking echoed to her, the distorted sound bouncing off the trees around her. But Stacy had grown up around there and was well used to the confusing acoustics in the forest. When her father had taught her to hunt when she was a kid, he'd taught her to cut through the echoes and focus on where the sound was coming from. Getting to the bottom of the embankment, Stacy followed Delilah's barking until she stepped into a clearing about a hundred yards away from where she first stepped into the woods.

A small creek ran through the center of the circular clearing, and Delilah was on the other side. She was digging at the soft earth and barking excitedly.

"What are you doing, girl? Stop that," Stacy chastised her dog.

Stepping over the small creek, Stacy walked over to Delilah and picked up the handle of her leash, wrapping it around her forearm. She walked over to the hole Delilah was furiously digging at, and when she stepped to the edge of the hole and leaned down to grab her collar, she froze. She stared into the hole for a long moment; her heart stopped dead in her chest as she tried to wrap her mind around what she was seeing.

Stacy swallowed hard and tried to pull Delilah back. She shortened her dog's leash and yanked her back from the hole. She stared into it as a thick feeling of surreal disbelief settled upon her. Delilah kept struggling and pulling at the leash, desperate to get back into the hole she'd dug and retrieve her prize. But Stacy held her dog tight, not allowing her to get near the nightmare she'd uncovered.

Trying to hold on to Delilah with one hand, Stacy fumbled as she tried to pull her phone out of her pocket with her other. She was trembling so hard, she nearly dropped it twice, but she somehow managed to hold on to it and dial 9-1-1.

"Oh my God," she whispered and pressed the phone to her ear. "Oh my God."

"9-1-1, what's your emergency?" the operator answered.

Stacy stared down into the hole at her feet and tried to speak but no words came out.

"Hello? Do you have an emergency to report?" the operator pressed.

Stacy cleared her throat and stared into the wide, unseeing eyes that although milky white with the glaze of death, seemed to be staring back at her. A gust of wind stirred the coppery red hair, giving her the illusion of movement that turned her stomach. She heaved and doubled over, throwing up on the ground at her feet. Stacy wiped her mouth with the back of her hand and tried to blink away the tears that streamed down her face.

"Is there anybody there? Do you need help?" the operator asked.

"Y—yes. Please. I need help," she said, her voice barely louder than a whisper.

CHAPTER ONE

Hearts & Paws Animal Care Clinic, Beacon Hill District; Seattle, WA

"WHAT HAPPENED?" I ASK, TRYING TO CONTROL my panic. "How in the hell did this happen?"

The woman who'd called me—April Inness—looks at me with more questions in her eyes than answers.

She's a tall, slender woman with a head full of long, dark braids tipped with white beads that click when she shakes her head. Her caramel-colored skin is smooth and flawless, and her eyes are a light hazel.

"I—I don't know," she says, her voice tinged with a soft Caribbean accent. "I got to our meeting place and found her on the ground. Shot. It couldn't have happened more than ten minutes before I arrived—"

"So, you brought her here? To some back alley, shady-as-hell clinic?" I demand. "You're letting her be worked on by a guy who spends his days treating schnauzers?"

April closes her eyes and takes a beat, looking like she's counting to ten. I look at the doors set into the wall across the room from us and feel my heart lurch inside of me. April said Kit has been in surgery for the last couple of hours. The sound of the dozen or so dogs barking up a storm in the boarding facility connected to this small, windowless waiting room is deafening and makes the entire situation seem all the more surreal. I've seen veterinarian clinics double as back-alley trauma centers in movies, but never in real life before.

I know I'm coming at her hard, but it's my sister bleeding on the table in there. Not hers. It's my sister some doctor I don't know has his hands in. Not hers. So, yeah, excuse me for coming in a little hot right now.

"She had a gunshot wound, Blake. If we took her to a hospital, not only would there be questions we didn't want to answer, but they would also be legally obligated to contact the police. We didn't want that—I didn't want that," April says patiently. "And Dr. Jacoby trained as a trauma surgeon. He worked at Johns Hopkins for twenty years before deciding to become a vet. He's handled more than a few shooting victims."

"*We*. You keep saying *we*," I snarl. "Who in the hell even are you?"

"I'm Kit's friend. I—help her with things when she needs me," April replies.

"What kind of things?"

"Those are details between me and Kit," she says, her voice cold.

I throw my hands in the air then fold my arms over my chest and start pacing the small room. I shouldn't be coming at her sideways like that. April Inness may be a complete stranger to me, but she's Kit's friend. Apparently. She did manage to get Kit somewhere safe. She got Kit to a place where her injuries could be treated. I guess I can't discount that. I let out a heavy breath and turn to her.

"Thank you for getting Kit here," I say.

"Of course."

I resume pacing the room, my brain spinning and my heart aching. I've always tried to steel myself for the day I got the call that something happened to Kit. Living the kind of life and doing the things she does, the odds of a long, healthy life aren't really on her side. I know that. And I've tried to insulate myself from the pain that dreaded phone call would bring me. Now that she's lying in the other room with a bullet in her, though, I see that I haven't been able to immunize myself from the pain at all. It's all I can do to keep from sinking to my knees and breaking down right here and now.

I need to focus my mind somewhere else. Need to keep my mind from succumbing to the dark, grief-filled thoughts that are racing through my head. It's not doing Kit or me the least bit of good. What's going to happen to her is going to happen to her. It's completely out of my hands and in the hands of a doctor who may or may not be a surgical expert from Johns Hopkins. Who may or may not be a doctor at all, come to think of it.

Pinching the bridge of my nose hard enough to sting, I push those thoughts away and try to focus on the here and now. On something tangible and concrete. I turn to April, who is sitting in a chair against the wall, her eyes closed, looking entirely Zen-like.

"What was she doing here?" I ask. "What brought her to Seattle?"

April opens her eyes, sits up in her seat, and looks at me. I can tell what happened to Kit is hitting her hard, and it shows me that she and my sister are very close. The look in April's eyes is the look of somebody contemplating how to navigate the world without their best friend.

"I honestly don't know. She called and said she was coming in," April replied. "She said she needed to get to you right away."

"And she didn't say why?"

April shakes her head. "I know she was working on something that had to do with the Thirteen, but what it was exactly—"

"She told you about that?" I interrupt.

11

"Well… yes. I've helped her with a number of things."

"Wow," I say, trying to process this information. "She must have trusted you quite a bit."

"She does," April says simply.

April raises her chin as she looks at me, a glint of challenge in her eyes. It's surprising that Kit wouldn't have ever mentioned somebody she trusts as much as April to me. And to have pulled her into the mess with the Thirteen, she has to trust her every bit as much as she trusts me. So, why wouldn't she have ever said a single word about her?

"How long have you two known each other?" I ask.

"A while," she replies.

"And how did you meet?"

"Our paths crossed on a job we were both working on," she says cryptically.

I can't tell if she's being deliberately vague just to irritate me or if it's because I'm a Fed and she's afraid of saying too much. As I look into her eyes, though, I realize how stupid this is. We both seem to be feeling some sort of possessiveness over Kit, which is just… ridiculous. Even though I don't know her, April is Kit's friend. If Kit trusts her, I probably can too. I run my hand over my face and blow out a frustrated breath.

"Listen, I'm sorry," I say. "I'm just stressed out. I don't mean to come at you sideways like that. If Kit trusts you, that needs to be good enough for me. So… I'm sorry."

"I'm sorry too. I'm probably being a little overprotective. This is a stressful time for both of us," she admits.

I gesture to the room around me. "So, I assume you know about this place because of… work? I mean, I assume you guys have used this Dr. Jacoby before?"

"Not personally. But he's got a good reputation. Does solid work."

I'm not entirely sure how to respond to that. I'm used to going to actual hospitals and not off-book, back-alley veterinary clinics. So, instead of saying anything, I just give her a nod. What I want to know is what drew my little sister to Seattle in the first place. She sneaks into town from time to time—mostly to celebrate holidays with me. And even then, it's usually not for more than a day or two. She stays on the move. Always.

Other than holidays or special occasions, though, she usually avoids the city like the plague because she fears making it too easy for the Thirteen to wipe both of us out. As much as I'd like to say that's paranoia talking, it's unfortunately a valid concern. So, what was it that drew her back here in the first place? What had she learned about the Thirteen that was so important that she risked coming here to tell me in person rather than sending me the usual coded message we use to communicate?

Or had she not learned anything at all? What if this had all been an elaborate ploy by the Thirteen to draw her here just to get a shot at her? What if Kit's life is hanging in the balance because she walked into their trap? That doesn't sound like her though. Kit is careful. She's meticulous. She's spent a lifetime learning how to avoid traps. A lifetime of training to be the hunter and not the hunted. Kit plans her every move. She isn't careless. There is no way she would be so sloppy that she walked into an ambush.

"You're just like her."

April's voice snaps me out of my head, and I look over at her. "What do you mean?"

A faint smile flickers across her lips. "You get that little furrow between your brows when you're concentrating hard and trying to figure something out," she explains. "In this case, I'm guessing you're trying to figure out why Kit came back and how she let herself get shot."

"That obvious, huh?"

She nods. "Yeah. A little bit," she tells me. "But you know she's tough. She's a fighter. If anybody is going to pull through this, it's going to be her."

The swinging doors open and a heavyset, white-haired man steps through wearing black scrubs and a black cap. This has to be the infamous Dr. Jacoby. His face is grim, which sends my heart plummeting into my stomach.

"Dr. Jacoby," I say. "I'm Blake Wilder—Kit's sister. How is she?"

He nods. "She lost a lot of blood before she got here. The bullet nicked a couple of arteries and did a little internal damage that I was able to repair."

His tone isn't encouraging, though, and there's a glint in his eyes that sets my heart racing as I wait for him to deliver the gut punch I fear is coming.

"Unfortunately, your sister is in a coma, Miss Wilder," Jacoby says.

And there it is. My heart feels like it stopped dead in my chest. I'm fighting back both the tears and the waves of nausea battering my insides.

"Wh—why is she in a coma?" I ask. "You said you repaired the damage."

"I don't know why she's in a coma, Miss Wilder. I'm not a neurologist, unfortunately."

"But she's going to come out of it, right? She's going to recover, isn't she?"

He frowns and looks down, seeming to take a beat before answering me. The fact that he seems to be searching for the right words to say sends a ripple of fear through my heart. Jacoby finally looks up at me.

"I don't know, to be honest," he says. "All I can tell you is that the damage the bullet did to her insides has been repaired, and she's receiving a transfusion for the blood she's lost. Aside from that—well—her recovery will be up to her. She could wake up from her coma an hour from now—or never. That's, unfortunately, not something I can either control or help with."

His prognosis feels like a dagger made of ice that just pierced my insides. I feel like I can't breathe. And when I look at April, I can see the same emotions I'm feeling cycling across her face. Her eyes shimmer with tears, and she seems to be at a loss for words. I give myself a shake, knowing I need to start thinking clearly and figuring out what our next steps are going to be.

"All right," I say, my voice shaking. "I—I need to get her somewhere safe."

"Miss Wilder, I would strongly suggest you don't move her. Your sister is in a fragile state right now and—"

I shake my head. "No offense, Dr. Jacoby. But I'd feel a lot better if she were somewhere safer than behind your veterinary clinic. The men who did this to her might come looking for her, and I don't want them finding her here with you."

He held up his hands. "Say no more."

"Do you know someplace safe?" April asks.

I put my hands on my hips and turn in a circle as I roll the question around in my brain. My place is out. Not knowing if there are any open investigations into her for her former career as a Thirteen assassin, I can't go to the Bureau or the Marshals service for help on this one. And I don't trust putting her up in a hotel. Which leaves me only one real option.

Pulling my phone out of my pocket, I dial the number and then press it to my ear. My call is picked up before the second ring has time to stop.

"Hey. It's me," I say. "I—I'm sorry to bother you, but I'm in some trouble, and I could use your help."

CHAPTER TWO

Jade Moon Apartments, Pike Market District; Seattle, WA

"I CAN'T THANK YOU ENOUGH FOR DOING THIS, FISH," I say. "I feel like I'm starting to run up a tab."

He gives me a gentle smile. "Think nothing of it, my friend. I'm simply glad you trust me enough to look after her. I know how precious Kit is to you."

We're standing in the living room of a poshly furnished two-room condo in Fish's building. The open floor plan is very clean and modern. The appliances in the kitchen are all stainless steel and sleek, the entire place done in soothing earth tones. It's a calming place with a fantastic view of the water of Elliott Bay beyond the tall floor-to-ceiling windows.

"Of course, I trust you," I reply. "In a weird way, you're family."

He laughs and nods. "It makes me feel good to hear you say that."

It makes me feel strange to say that. Once upon a time, Fish was one of the most notorious gangsters in all of Seattle. Brutal. Lethal. An immigrant to this country, Fish came from nothing and started his life in America working the docks as a fishmonger—hence, the nickname, Fish. But as a kid, he taught himself to read, taught himself—everything, really—and worked his way up. He carved out a niche for himself in the criminal underworld and then cut a bloody swath through it as he built an empire.

Fish, otherwise known as Huan Zhao, is a tall, slender man with a flamboyant, some might even say, effeminate manner about him. But he's got a spine made of steel and a mind sharper than a razor blade. He's not a man to be trifled with, and the only reason our paths crossed in the first place is that I was working on a case he was tangentially involved in. Strangely enough, over the course of that case, a bond formed between us, and we developed a level of trust. We developed a level of comfort with each other, and he eventually became an informant for me.

I'm not naïve. At the time we were getting to know each other, I knew his help was self-serving. Fish was simply offering up his biggest rivals to me on a silver platter. He was clearing the board to expand his empire. But sometimes you have to make a deal with the devil if you want to have a chance at rounding up all the other demons running loose. In law enforcement, you sometimes need to consider what the greater good is in a given situation. And while throwing Fish in prison would have been quite a feather in my cap, my partnership with him, on a macro scale, has made Seattle a safer, better place thanks to the dozens of bad people we've taken down.

In some ways, Fish has helped make my career. As I got to know him, though, I found him to be something other than a hardened and murderous mob boss. At his core, Fish is a good man. It sounds strange to say about a mob boss, but Fish's goals all along have been bigger. Much bigger. He's used his power and influence—as well as the wealth he's created—as a leading member of the criminal underworld to do some good in the community—a lot of good, if I'm being honest. Especially for the women and children in bad situations throughout the city.

While he's always going to maintain a presence in that criminal underworld, and his name still carries a lot of weight, he's divested himself from many of the industries that he once ruled. As he's gotten older, his big picture has changed. Or maybe, has become refined. Rather than being at the top of the food chain among Seattle's dark underbelly, he wants his legacy to be something different. He's one of the only crime bosses I've seen who has made a successful transition from a life of murder and mayhem to one as a legit businessman.

Take this condo complex for instance—the Jade Moon. It's one hundred percent above board, and Fish has used his own money to revitalize this section of the waterfront. He's put in a couple of restaurants and bars as well as housing—affordable housing at that. He could easily charge an astronomical amount of rent for these units, but he wants normal people to have access to places like this—not just the wealthy. He's also invested in educational programs for poor and underserved kids, encouraging them to lift themselves up and make something of their lives the way he did. Well… maybe not exactly like he did. He encourages education, not murder.

Fish is a rarity. He's come through for me time and time again. And over the years, I've come to trust him in ways I don't trust most people. As he said, I'm trusting him with the care and protection of my sister. That's not something I would trust just anybody with.

"These units are not listed on our blueprints or rental diagrams. Nobody knows they are here," he tells me. "I keep half a dozen units off the books for… special guests."

I smile. He's got a similar setup with some rooms above a restaurant in a mixed-use he owns in Chinatown. I had to make use of those rooms before. The rooms are impossible to get to without knowing how to get them in the first place. Fish takes the security of his special guests seriously and usually goes above and beyond, installing either keycard readers, biometric scanners, or some other form of defensive measure to keep them safe and protected.

"I will make sure she has top-of-the-line care and protection around the clock," he continues. "Nobody will get near her, Agent Wilder."

"Are you ever just going to call me Blake?"

"Maybe one day," he replies with a mischievous grin.

As I watch them wheel Kit's hospital bed into the guest room, my eyes well with tears. Fish puts a comforting hand on my shoulder and gives it a squeeze.

"Come," he says.

Fish leads me to the guest room, and as the care workers hook my little sister up to a battery of machines, tears roll down my cheeks. She looks so small, so fragile beneath the sheets. The sun is slanting in through the windows, casting a glowing nimbus around Kit, who is completely unaware of the warm rays spilling across her face.

The nurse flips a few switches on the machine next to the bed, and the room is filled with the sound of its soft but steady beeping. She turns and gives Fish and me a gentle smile.

"We'll have nurses rotating in eight-hour shifts," she says, then looks at Fish. "They've all been vetted, and they're clean."

Fish nods. "Very well. Thank you, Mrs. Golding."

"Of course," she replies then turns back to me. "Don't worry. Your sister will get the very best care available. And if anything changes, we will be sure to contact you immediately."

"Thank you," I say.

Mrs. Golding pats my arm reassuringly and then walks out of the room. Fish waits until we hear the front door close before he turns to me.

"Don't worry. I've worked with Mrs. Golding for a very long time. If she says we can trust her attendants, there is no question that we can," he says.

"I trust you," I reply, never taking my eyes off my sister.

As I look at the array of machines connected to my sister, I wonder how I'm going to pay for all this care—not to mention the round-the-clock security Fish is providing. It can't be cheap, and I work on a government salary. And then I feel like a jerk for even having the thought. As if reading my mind, he puts a hand on my arm and turns me toward him.

"Don't worry about anything," he says. "Anything."

"Fish, I don't know how I'm going to pay you for this—"

"As I said, you need not worry about a thing," he cuts me off. "Right now, you simply need to focus all your energy on your sister. Be present with her. She's in a dark place right now, but your energy can help lead her back to the light. Your energy can help bring her back to you."

It's the closest thing to a spiritual belief I've ever heard fall out of Fish's mouth. We've talked about a lot of things over the years, but religious or spiritual leanings have never been one of them. It's interesting to hear his thoughts about it.

"Thank you, Fish."

He takes my hand, but I wrap my arms around him and give him a tight hug. He's stiff at first but gradually accepts the gesture. Fish does not enjoy physical contact all that much, preferring handshakes and gentle pats of the hand, but I feel like everything he's doing for me warrants a bear hug.

I slowly step back and wipe the tears from my cheeks. Fish is standing there looking slightly uncomfortable in the wake of my emotional display, but smiles at me. He takes my hand in his and gives it a pat, drawing a shaky grin to my face. But then he lets go and checks his watch.

"I'm going to give you some time with your sister," he says. "The first security detail should be here in five minutes. I would stay, but I have a meeting I cannot miss."

"Thank you, Fish. Truly. For everything," I say.

"As you said, we are family—of a sort," he replies with a smile. "And there is nothing I will not do for my family."

He gives me a slight bow of the head and then leaves the room. When I hear the front door close, I pull a chair to the side of the bed and sit down. I take Kit's hand in mine and gaze at her pale, slack face. I have to fight off another wave of tears that threatens to overwhelm me. Instead, I let my thoughts turn to what Fish said.

"Come back to me, Kit," I whisper. "Don't stay down there in the dark. Come back to me. Come back to the light."

CHAPTER THREE

Office of SSA Wilder, Black Cell Alpha Team Bullpen; Seattle Field Office

"**M**Y GOD, BLAKE. I'M SO SORRY," ASTRA SAYS. "What have the doctors said?"

"That they don't know what's going to happen. He repaired the damage from the bullet, but she's still in a coma," I tell her. "He doesn't know why, and he doesn't know when she's going to come out of it. Or *if* she's going to come out of it."

Just saying those words is like a kick to the gut. It leaves me weak and breathless. I take a deep, steadying breath and try to control the emotions that are roiling within me. There's nothing

I want more than to sit at Kit's bedside until she wakes up. But I know I can't. That will only lead to questions I don't want to answer. I have no idea how much the Thirteen is influencing the current government nor how much they've said about Kit and her—activities—prior to betraying the Thirteen to save me.

After being abducted when they murdered our parents, Kit was trained to be a spy. And an assassin. She spent her adult life hunting and killing on the orders of the Thirteen. Over her career, if that's what you want to call it, Kit has left more bodies in her wake than Fish has. Why she was doing it doesn't matter. And these people are going to use that to leverage her in any way they can. They'll use it to not just destroy her but to get to me as well.

It's why I can't speak my sister's name to anybody other than Astra. I can't admit to knowing where she is. I have to go through life pretending she doesn't exist. Pretending she died along with my parents that day so long ago. At least, outwardly.

"Are you sure this guy's a doctor?" Astra asks.

I nod. "Yeah, I checked him out thoroughly. Everything April told me about him is true. He was a bigwig up at Johns Hopkins."

"And what do you know about April?"

"Next to nothing. She's as much of a ghost as Kit is," I tell her.

"So, she was probably doing the same job as your sister."

"I'm assuming. She was vague and cryptic about it all."

"Where is she now?" Astra asks.

"At the safe house watching over Kit," I say. "She's as protective of her as I am."

"Living the life they're living... I assume it bonded them pretty tightly."

"Yeah, I suppose so."

"You don't trust her."

"I don't know her," I correct Astra. "But if she wanted to do Kit any harm, she could have. But she got her to a doctor and seems genuinely attached to my sister. Kit trusts her enough to bring her into the loop on the Thirteen, so I guess I've got no choice but to trust her."

"Wow. Kit told her about that, huh? They must be tight," Astra says.

"Yeah. Seems that way," I reply. "And speaking of the Thirteen, I think we've got bigger problems on that front than we imagined."

"How so?"

"I saw Hedlund and Stone having a private tête-à-tête in the garage," I tell her.

"Hedlund, huh? What is the good Senator from West Virginia doing here in Seattle? And meeting with our boss, no less?"

"That was my question."

Astra sits back in her chair and gets that look on her face that tells me she's about to say something I'm not going to like very much.

"I don't want to hit you with a cold slap of reality—"

"Yes, you do," I cut in with a wry grin.

"Well, maybe. But just because they were talking doesn't mean either one of them are part of the Thirteen and are actively conspiring against you," she says. "I understand why you're in that frame of mind though. I mean, with what happened to Kit, it makes sense. So, I get it."

"It's more than just what's going on with Kit though. I mean, we've always suspected Hedlund of being part of the Thirteen—"

"But we've never had proof of that. Suspicion and gut feelings aren't proof. And you know that," she counters. "Also, do you think somebody like Maximillian Stone, a man who's devoted his entire life to this country, would be part of a group like that? Or maybe more importantly, do you think he would be?"

"He would be one of the last people you'd ever suspect to be part of the group," I tell her. "That's kind of their thing. Remember?"

"I've only had a couple of brief conversations with the man, but I honestly don't think he's one of them. He just doesn't set off the warning bells," she replies. "Can you sit there and tell me he seems like one of them to you? That he sets the red flags waving in your head?"

I lean back in my seat and pause to consider her questions. Ordinarily, I would never think that Max Stone could ever be mixed up with a group like the Thirteen. He's always seemed like one of the guys wearing white hats to me. I've always believed he's one of the good guys. He's somebody I've always admired.

Somebody I thought so highly of that I've patterned pieces of my career after him.

But seeing him with somebody like Kathryn Hedlund, a woman I know to have dark, possibly even evil tendencies and motives, has made me rethink my position. It's put everything I know about the man—or what I thought I knew about him—in doubt.

"My initial read on him is that he's a straight arrow," I say. "Seems dedicated to the job and doesn't seem like the type who'd be part of the Thirteen."

"There you go," Astra replies. "You're the one who's always telling me to trust my first instincts since those are usually the right ones."

It's true. I've made a point of telling my team to go with their first instincts. Those raw instincts, not run through layers and filters of self-doubt, are usually the ones that cut to the truth. But first instincts aren't always right. I've personally relied on first instincts that have turned out to be very wrong.

"That being said, you're not wrong that Stone meeting with Hedlund in a dark garage is more than a little suspicious," Astra concedes. "And given the timing of it all—Hedlund being in town at the exact same moment Kit gets shot? It raises a lot of red flags."

"Yeah, that thought went through my mind too. About a million times."

"It's not conclusive by any stretch of the imagination. But it's a pretty big coincidence."

"I don't put much stock in coincidences."

"I know you don't. I'm not a big fan of them either."

I run a hand through my hair. "But you're not wrong to give me a little perspective. I know I don't have a lot of that right now."

"As I said, it's understandable."

My mind flashes back to Kit lying in that bed in Fish's condo. I keep thinking about how delicate and small she looks. How fragile. It sends a spear of pain through me again, and I have to fight off the tears that are welling in my eyes. Astra gives me a sympathetic smile.

"Sorry," I say. "I need to get myself together."

"Hey, if you need to take a little time, you should—"

"I can't," I tell her. "Not only will my sitting by Kit's bed obsessing about her not do either one of us any good, but I also don't want Stone or Ayad asking questions about where I am. I don't want them asking questions that might lead them back to Kit somehow."

"Fair enough," Astra nods. "But if you're going to be here, you're going to need to be here, Blake. If we get a case and your head isn't right—"

"I know, I know," I tell her. "I need to keep my head in the game. And I will. You won't need to worry about me if we catch a case."

Astra scrutinizes me for a minute then gives me a firm nod. "All right. Good."

"Speaking of which," I say as I point to the bullpen.

Through the glass wall of my office, I see Ayad coming into our bullpen. He gives everybody a curt nod as he passes through, heading for my office with a black folder in his hand. Astra stands up and gives me a wink as she turns and walks back out into the bullpen, passing Ayad as he steps into my office. I clear my throat and sit up as I get my game face on.

It's time to go to work.

CHAPTER FOUR

Black Cell Alpha Team Bullpen; Seattle Field Office, Seattle, WA

"ALL RIGHT, ALL RIGHT, ALL RIGHT," I CALL OUT AS I step to the front of the room. "Eyes up, kids."

Everybody sits down at their stations and the room falls silent. All eyes turn to me, and I use the remote to power up the computer screens on the wall behind me. On the screens, the photos of four girls pop up.

"Starting on your left, you're looking at Juliette Templeton, age seventeen. Her body was just discovered in a park in Annenberg, North Dakota," I tell them. "Well... kind of."

"Kind of?" Astra asks.

"She was dismembered," I clarify.

A silence falls over the room, and everybody exchanges grim glances. Murder in any form is terrible, but there's something about a dismemberment that's especially disturbing. People do the most awful things to each other. But at least going through the grisly details of the crime gets my mind off my sister as well as the Stone and Hedlund situation and lets me obsess over something else. Small victories.

"The next girl is Lauren Dunphy, age eighteen. Number three is Tamara Gray, age sixteen. And the fourth girl is Emily Strauss, age eighteen, who was just reported missing by her parents a day ago," I report. "None of their bodies have been found yet."

"How do we know they're all related cases?" Lucas asks.

"We don't just yet. But they're all a similar age, and all four have gone missing in the last six weeks," I tell them. "Annenberg is a safe place, and the local PD doesn't have experience with serials. They're lost and don't know where to start. They've asked for our help, and so Chief Ayad has decided to send us."

Clasping my hands behind my back, I pace the small dais at the front of the room, giving them a moment to absorb the information I've just given them.

"All right, you said the other three girls haven't been found yet," Astra pipes up. "How do we know they're not runaways?"

"We don't know for sure they're not," I admit. "But based on how close in time these girls have disappeared, Chief Ayad wants to exercise caution. If we get out there and find there is no connection, we focus on the murder of Juliette Templeton. If there is a connection, Annenberg has a problem."

"All four in the last six weeks, huh?" Mo asks. "Not much of a cooling-off period."

"Nope. Juliette was six weeks ago, Lauren went missing three weeks ago, Tamara Gray one week ago, and Emily Strauss a day ago," I say.

"So, if these girls have all been taken and aren't just off with their boyfriends or following a band around the country, our guy is speeding up," Lucas offers. "That could indicate that he's devolving. Going on a spree. That might make him easier to catch."

"Is that still a thing?" Astra asks. "The whole, following a band around the country, I mean. Do people still do that?"

"You know what I mean," Lucas says, his voice tight.

Lucas has made some real progress since joining the team. He's not the completely cold automaton devoid of any warmth or humor he was when he first walked in here. Not completely anyway. We've still got a long way to go before he's going to fit in as seamlessly as Nina has. He may never completely fit. But he's smart, has good instincts, is dedicated to the job—and more important than anything—is not Ayad's spy as I initially believed. I've come around on Lucas. He's a decent guy and an asset to the team.

"Tough room," Astra says with a grin. "You're right, though, it could indicate that he's devolving. It could also mean that he's confident that he's not going to be caught."

"But we don't know if these cases are even related," Mo adds. "I mean, most serials tend to be preferential. Juliette and Emily are both white, Lauren is obviously mixed-race, and Tamara is black. We don't often see a serial cross racial lines like that."

"That's true. But this guy's preference might not be racial. It could be economic," I say. "They all come from affluent families. That might be the linkage."

"Economic preferential serials are super rare," Astra notes.

"But not unprecedented," I reply. "Back in the 70s, Harmon Blalock killed fifteen people from different ethnicities, solely because they were wealthy. It's rare but not unheard of."

"Fair enough," Astra replies.

"What do we know about the town?" Lucas asks.

"Rick?" I ask.

"Annenberg, North Dakota, is never going to be considered a tourist destination, but it is a pretty affluent community," he says. "Population is just over thirty-two thousand, making it the seventh-largest city in the state. It's about seventy-five miles south of the Canadian border and has produced six players who've gone on to play in the NFL and thirteen to the NHL."

"Thank you, Rick," I say.

"Anytime," he replies and gives Nina a smug grin.

She rolls her eyes at him but chuckles. They seem to have a bit of a friendly rivalry growing between them. He's fantastic at what he does, but I'd hate to burst Rick's bubble by telling him she can probably run circles around him. And she doesn't seem inclined to show him up, which I'm grateful for. Men can be so sensitive sometimes.

"Nina, I need you to start doing a deep dive on the girls," I say. "I want to know where their paths crossed, who they ran with, activities—anything. I know it's a small town, so there is probably going to be a lot of overlap between them all, which is good. We're looking for a point of connection that links all four of them."

"I'm on it," she nods.

The doors to the bullpen open, and Stone walks in. He gives me a nod and gestures to my office as he walks toward it. I turn back to my team.

"All right, we're wheels up in two hours," I tell them. "Nina, Rick, run home and put together a go-bag. You're coming with us."

"We are?" they ask in unison.

"You are," I reply. "I want you guys on site with us. It's just more efficient than having to get somewhere I can videoconference you when I need something."

The truth is I don't want to have Ayad lurking behind them, shadowing their every move—and vetoing the things he doesn't like. It adds another layer of inefficient bureaucracy that I just don't want to deal with.

"Get yourselves ready to roll," I say. "I'll be with you in a few."

I turn and head into my office where Stone is already seated and waiting for me. I walk around my desk and drop down into my seat, looking at him closely. He watches me in silence for a moment then sits forward.

"I know you were in the garage the other night," he starts. "I know you were watching me with Senator Hedlund. Why?"

"I just wasn't aware you knew her."

"Not that it's your business or should matter to you in any way, but we're friends from college," he tells me.

I know I can't tell him anything. If he is part of the Thirteen, I don't want to tip him off that I suspect either he or Hedlund. That might shorten my life span considerably. At the same time, though, I can't not say something. He's clearly here on a fishing expedition, perhaps trying to figure out what I know or suspect. It's quite the standoff. And the only way to throw him off the trail is to give him something that could pass for the truth.

"I just—you know my history with Senator Hedlund," I say. "It just caught me off guard that you know her. I wasn't aware that you were friends."

"Why were you hiding from us?" he presses.

"As I said, you know my history with the Senator," I repeat. "I ducked behind the pillar because I didn't want to have a face to face with her, since I have absolutely nothing pleasant to say to her. So, I was just waiting for you two to leave so I could get to my car and go home."

"That's a little immature, don't you think?"

"Considering everything I wanted to say to her, I think it was prudent. I think you know me well enough now to know I say what is on my mind. And in that situation, I didn't think that would be… appropriate."

He looks into my eyes for a moment, seeming to be trying to see into me. I simply stare back at him. What I said is the truth, and he'll see that reflected in my eyes. It's not all I'm thinking, of course, but I'm in control of myself and won't give him more than that. Won't give him reason to be suspicious. A small grin curls the corner of his mouth upward.

"Fair enough," he says, seeming to accept my explanation. "Next time, be sure to turn your ringer off."

"Will do."

"So, I saw you had a case," he says. "Where are you off to?"

"North Dakota," I reply. "We've got a possible serial. One dismembered girl has been found so far; three more are missing."

"Pleasant."

"I'm hoping the cases aren't connected and that the other three girls just went off for a weekend away with their boyfriends and didn't tell their folks," I say.

"What does your gut instinct tell you?"

I frown. "That we're going to find three more dismembered corpses."

"Brace yourself then. It could get ugly real fast."

"Got a feeling it's going to be."

"Good hunting then, Blake. Stay safe."

"I will. Thank you."

I watch as Stone gets up and heads out of my office and let out a breath of relief. I'm pretty sure I passed the test. It's a good reminder, though, that I'm going to need to stay on my toes. With Hedlund behind the curtain pulling the strings, I need to stay sharp and be ready for anything. After all, Stone was right about one thing... it could get ugly real fast.

CHAPTER FIVE

Harrell Airfield, Hanger 5A; Annenberg, ND

PULL MY JACKET AROUND ME TIGHTER THEN WRAP MY SCARF around my neck. I'd expected it to be cold but not this cold. Everybody else seemed to be doing their best to bundle up and conserve their body heat, so at least I know it's not just me.

"This place is fun already," Astra grumbles, her breath coming out in steamy plumes.

"Right?" Nina asks with a giggle.

The hangar on the private airfield is open and gusts of frigid wind are blowing through. A pair of black Yukons, brought up from the field office in Minot, are sitting off to the side of the hangar. We've already loaded up our gear, and all I want to do is jump in and crank up the heat. Seattle gets cold, but this is cold on a whole different level. North Dakota doesn't mess around.

"All right, Rick and Nina, I want you both to get us checked in to the hotel. Grab a conference room we can use as our base of—"

"Yeah, I already checked it out, and the hotel doesn't have a conference room," Nina says. "In fact, none of the hotels in town are big enough for conference rooms. They're little more than places for people who are either passing through town or whose wives have kicked them out of the house for the night."

"Wonderful," Astra mutters.

"Yeah, I'd rather not work out of the sheriff's station if we can help it," I say.

"We may not have a choice," Lucas says.

"We'll find something," I reply and turn back to Nina and Rick. "Go ahead and get us checked in to the hotel anyway. After that, start digging in to the girls as I asked. Find the nexus between all four of them."

"Got it," Rick nods. "We're on it."

"Lucas and Mo, after you drop the kids off at the hotel, I want you two to go down to the Annenberg Sheriff's Station. Let them know we're in town, gather up whatever they have in terms of case files on the four missing girls," I tell them. "Also, ask them about empty buildings we can use as a base of operations. We want it secure, with electricity, internet, running water, definitely heat, and clean. Though we'll be flexible about the clean part."

"We will?" Astra asks.

I flash her a grin. "It's not going to kill you to pick up a mop if needs be."

She scoffs. "That's what we have Low-Man-On-The-Totem-Pole-Lucas for."

He starts to object, but I shrug and cut him off. "She's not wrong. You have to pay your dues, kid. Them's the rules."

He grins at that. "Yeah, yeah, yeah."

"Where are you two going?" Mo asks.

"I want to see Juliette's recovery site," I say. "It's probably not going to tell us a whole lot, but I'd like to see what it has to say for itself. We'll regroup at the hotel at six and grab some dinner. Figure out what the next steps are going to be. Any questions?"

Everybody exchanges glances, and I'm pretty sure they all just want to get into the cars and turn on the heat as much as I do.

"All right. Let's get moving then," I say. "We'll catch you guys back at the hotel."

We pull to a stop in the parking lot and sit there for a minute, letting the heat from the vents wash over us. The sky overhead is thick with a patchwork of light and dark gray clouds, and piles of snow are still scattered around the park in front of us.

"Well, the crime scene's not coming to us," I say. "Might as well get this over with."

Astra turns to me. "I thought the report said the weather was nice out here."

"It was," I tell her. "A couple of days ago."

She grumbles under her breath. "At least the weather back home is consistently drab, dreary, and wet," she says. "Why can't we ever catch a case somewhere nice like Southern California or Miami?"

"Well, maybe some psychopath will do us a solid and go on a murder spree in a warmer climate at some point soon."

"It'd be nice."

Laughing to myself, I pull on my knit cap and gloves then get out of the car and start down the trail. Astra is wrapping her scarf around the bottom half of her face, leaving just her eyes exposed as she falls into step beside me. The yellow tape stretched between the trees isn't hard to see, so we follow that and have to pick our way down an embankment to the forest floor where we find what we are looking for.

A six-by-six square hole was dug into the ground and cordoned off by yellow tape attached to sticks at the four corners. Amazingly enough, nobody's torn it down. Astra and I step over to the edge of the pit that looks to be about four feet deep, and a large pile of loose dirt sits off to the side. There's a heaviness in the air around us. It's like the trees that surround the makeshift grave have soaked in the pain and misery of what happened here and are imbuing the area with that darkness.

"What do you think?" Astra asks.

Before I can answer, the rustling of leaves and heavy footsteps sound on the embankment above us. I look up to see a man in dark brown trousers, a light brown uniform shirt, and a brown ball cap bearing the insignia of the sheriff's office, coming down. He's not a large man—five-nine or five-ten at the most—but he's got a stocky build. With wide shoulders, a broad chest, and arms about as thick as my thigh, the man obviously spends a lot of time in the gym. He's also young. I'd say he's in his late thirties, maybe early forties, which is pretty young to be the town sheriff. At least in my experience.

Colorful tattoos peek out from beneath the short sleeves of his uniform shirt, and his hair is cropped close to his skull. When he gets to the forest floor, he steps over to us and gives us a tip of his cap, his dark eyes probing both of us as he takes our measure. He's got a good poker face, so I can't tell if he's disappointed with what he sees or not.

"How in the world can you be out here in short sleeves?" Astra asks.

"You grow up here, you get used to it," he shrugs. "Besides, it's forty-three degrees. It's downright balmy."

"If you say so," Astra says, pulling her scarf back up over her face.

"Anyway, afternoon. You must be the FBI folk," he says. "I'm Sheriff Tucker Paulson."

"Word must travel fast around here," I reply and shake his hand.

"Like a wildfire," he says as he turns and shakes Astra's hand. "It's a good thing and a bad thing, I suppose. Anyway, I kind of figured you'd come here first."

"And what made you think that?" I ask.

He shrugs his broad shoulders. "It's what I'd do. I'd want to see the crime scene before it got anymore trampled than it already is."

Astra and I exchange glances. The man seems pretty sharp, and he's got good instincts. It's obvious that he's not just some country bumpkin.

"Agents Blake Wilder and Astra Russo," I introduce us. "Good to meet you, Sheriff."

"Nice to meet you too," he replies. "I'm grateful for the assist here. Annenberg just don't have many murders, and certainly nothing like what we found in that hole."

His expression darkens and his face grows tight. I can see the girl's death is hitting him hard. But he's able to rein it all in and cover it with a mask of stoicism.

"Did you know Juliette Templeton, Sheriff?" I ask.

"Yeah," he nods, his voice tight. "I'm good friends with her dad. He and I used to play ball together at McCumber High."

I recall from Rick and Nina's briefing on the flight out that Annenberg has two high schools—McCumber which covers the east and south sides of the city and Frazier, whose district is the north and west. It got me wondering about the family connections. It's a train of thought that's going to be twisted and convoluted though. In a city the size of Annenberg, families are going to know each other, and there is going to be a lot of overlap. It's, unfortunately, just the nature of small towns.

"Did you know the families of the other girls, Sheriff?" Astra asks.

"I know the Dunphy family pretty well—good people all," he tells us. "I don't know the Grays or the Dunphys all that well though."

"Do you know if the four families all knew each other? Socially, professionally, or in any other way?" I ask.

"Well, the Strausses and the Templetons are close—Matt played ball with us at McCumber too," he tells us. "The others, though, I think they're Frazier families. I'm pretty sure the families don't socialize or anything."

"The rivalry between the two schools run that deep?" Astra asks.

He chuckles. "No, nothin' like that. I mean, sure, there's a natural rivalry between the sports teams and all. But it's not like our community is divided like that," he tells us. "It's just different families exist in different orbits. Just because we're not that big of a town doesn't mean everybody knows each other, Agents."

"Fair enough," I nod. "What can you tell us about the two girls you do know? Juliette and Emily. What were they like?"

"Both of 'em are sweeter than honey. Nice girls. Smart too," he says as his voice thickens with emotion. "Both of 'em had real bright futures. They were active in the church and did a lot of good work in the community. I don't think there's a single person who'd say a bad word against either of 'em."

"How are the families holding up?" Astra says.

"About how you'd expect. Jeff and Cheryl—the Templetons— are devastated," he replies. "Shawn and Daisy Strauss are still clinging to hope. They think just because Emily hasn't been found yet, she might still be alive."

"And she might be," I say. "We don't know if these cases are connected yet. For all we know at this point, Emily ran off with a boyfriend."

"Did Tamara and Lauren run off too?" he asks, arching an eyebrow. "Seems like a mighty big coincidence. And I've never been a big fan of coincidences."

I slip my hands into my pockets. Sheriff Paulson seems like a decent enough man. He's also a straight shooter who doesn't like things to be sugarcoated. That's something I respect. So, I make a mental note to always give it to him straight.

"Truthfully, my personal opinion is that the cases are linked and both Tamara and Lauren are already dead," I tell him. "Just because we don't know how long he keeps the girls yet, I still have some slight bit of hope that Emily is still alive."

He rubs his jaw and nods as he processes my information. "All right, so how do you come to all that?"

"Juliette was the first one taken, and her body was just found," I explain. "Emily is the fourth girl taken, and I don't believe that he's keeping more than one at a time. That means Tamara and Lauren are still out there, waiting to be found. And if I had to guess, I'm going to say their bodies are somewhere here in this park—likely not far from where we are now. Just a suggestion, but you probably want to get a cadaver dog up here to have a poke around."

"Huh. I'll do that," he nods. "But I'm curious, how'd you get to all that? What makes you think the other girls are here?"

"Offenders like this man—serial offenders—are often creatures of habit," I tell him. "And they'll often use a single dumping ground so they can come back and visit their victims."

"Visit?" he asks.

"Some serial predators have been known to come back just to be near their victims—relive the kill in their minds," Astra chimes in. "Others like to come back and have relations with the bodies of their victims—"

"Relations?" he gasps. "Are you tellin' me this guy is comin' back here to have sex with the bodies of these girls?"

"Well, considering the fact that Juliette was found entirely dismembered, I don't think that's the case here," I say, trying to calm him down. "But it wouldn't surprise me to know he's come back to sit next to this spot just to relive the night he took her life. Or that he gets a thrill out of watching other people walk past her, never knowing that she was there."

"Jesus," he mutters.

Paulson takes his hat off and runs a hand through his crew cut. He looks disturbed by what we told him. Not that I blame him—it's a lot to take in. Especially if you're not pretty thoroughly desensitized to it. And in a place that's as pure and wholesome as Annenberg seems to be, I doubt he's had much of a chance to grow desensitized to the evil that people often do to one another.

"There's still a lot we don't know. We're just getting started here, Sheriff," I tell him. "As I said before, we don't know for sure all four girls are connected. Not with one hundred percent certainty."

"Right. Yeah," he nods. "Of course. Well, how can I help?"

"We've got two agents heading to your station actually," I tell him. "We need to find a place to set up shop."

He gives me a sheepish grin. "Afraid our station's too small for your operation. We're practically bumping into one another as it is," he tells me. "It's my fault really. I insisted the county give me the funds for half a dozen more deputies."

"How many deputies do you have now in total?" Astra asks.

"Twenty-four. Not including myself," he says. "It's not enough for a town of thirty thousand plus, but we get by. Not a lot of crime in Annenberg. At least, not until recently."

"Well, we're going to need an office of sorts. A place with electricity, running water, space for six of us—"

"I know just the place," he says. "I can take you over first thing in the morning."

"Sounds good to me," I say.

"All right, well, if there's nothin' you need from me right now, I should get," he says. "I just wanted to come by and introduce myself."

"We appreciate it, Sheriff Paulson," I say.

"It's nice to meet you," Astra adds.

"Yeah, you too," he replies. "Just swing on by the station in the morning and I can take you over to the office you can use while you're in town."

"Thank you, Sheriff."

"Please, just call me Tucker," he insists.

"Then call me Blake," I say.

"And you can call me Astra."

He gives us a nod then turns and climbs back up the embankment, leaving us there to stare at the empty hole before us. The light behind the clouds is starting to dim, and night will be falling soon. We're going to lose the light, and it's going to get cold quick.

"We should probably get to the hotel," I say.

"That's a great idea."

As we climb the embankment, heading for the car, I look over my shoulder and take in the dark, empty hole one more time and shudder. I can't say why for sure, but I just have the feeling this one's going to be bad. Really bad.

CHAPTER SIX

The Smokehouse; Annenberg, ND

"THE FOOD HERE IS AMAZING," ASTRA SAYS. "WHY can't we have steaks and barbecue like this back home?"

"It's all right," Nina says. "I still think we do it better back in Colorado."

"Of course, you'd say that," Rick chimes in. "But you think they do sushi better in Colorado, too, which leads to plenty of questions about your taste."

"If you want to talk about questionable taste, we should probably have a chat with your girlfriend," Nina fires back.

That gets the whole table laughing. I like the way Nina is fitting in with us. She's blended in pretty seamlessly and can stand in and trade barbs with all of us. We still need to work on loosening Lucas up a bit though.

Rick scrunches up his face with a mock groan of pain and places one hand on his back. "Yet again, I've been stabbed in the back. And I trusted you!"

That only gets everybody laughing more. We're thankfully seated at a large table in a back room of the steakhouse, out of sight of the public. Even for a weeknight, the place is pretty packed. It's got a lively atmosphere, and the food is amazing. I don't even think the chophouse back in Seattle I sometimes go to with Pax is as good as this place. It just goes to show, that just because something is more expensive doesn't mean it's better.

The whole evening has been something of a team-building exercise. We've all gotten to know each other better, have shared some personal stories—we've even shared our most ignominious moments on the job. It's been nice to have some levity as we embark on a case because I have a feeling it's going to be grim. But even more than that, it's nice to feel like a team for a change.

The only thing I'm not enjoying about the evening is the people passing by our room taking a minute to stick their heads in and gawk at us. Sheriff Paulson was right about word of our presence spreading like wildfire. And now that the people in town know we're here, they feel compelled to stare at us like we're animals in the zoo. I don't like being stared at.

"So, not to bring the room down or anything, but did you guys get anything out at the crime scene?" Lucas asks.

"And tonight's wet blanket award goes to Lucas Okamura. Kudos," Astra says. "Way to bring everybody down, man."

He chuckles. "Sorry. I just figured we should get a head start on things so we can hit the ground running tomorrow."

"You're the kid who always did his homework right when he got home from school, huh?" Astra presses. "You never waited until the last minute for anything."

"I didn't like the stress of trying to cram everything in at the last minute," he protests.

Everybody else showers him with boos and balled-up napkins, but Lucas takes it in stride and laughs along with them.

"He's not wrong, guys," I tell them as the laughter fades. "We probably should talk about what we have and what our next steps are."

"Can't we just drink way too much tonight and forget that it's like twelve degrees outside?" Astra asks.

"Need I remind you, babe, you're on the other side of thirty now. Any more of those martinis and you'll be out of commission all morning."

Astra's eyes light up in a simultaneous flare of laughter and anger. She swats me away. "Hey! Uncalled for!"

"I'm just saying," I grin. "But for real, no overindulging. I need everybody to be sharp," I say.

"I guess we're already ruling Rick out then?" Nina teases.

That touches off another wave of laughter, but it's short-lived and soon, they all turn to me with expectant expressions on their faces.

"To answer your question, Lucas, we didn't find much out at the gravesite," I say. "There wasn't much to see. But the site tells me Juliette's killer is likely a local."

"What makes you say that?" Lucas asks.

"The terrain is tricky, and it was in an out-of-the-way spot," Astra says. "I'd bet only a local is going to know about that park. If it were somebody just looking for a dump site, there are a dozen places between here and that park that would have been easier to get to. At least."

Lucas looks to me to see if I agree with Astra's assessment. He's going to learn soon enough that Astra is a very talented profiler and knows almost as much about profiling as I do. Her interest was never in behavioral sciences though. She's much more action-oriented and prefers kicking in doors to dissecting somebody's mind. Given her model-like looks, it's always been an interesting juxtaposition and something nobody would ever expect.

"She's right," I tell Lucas. "When you're profiling a killer, those are all things you need to be aware of. Things you always need to factor into your thinking."

"Doesn't the BAU do all the profiling?" he asks.

"Hardly. When we're out in the field, we're on our own as far as profiling goes," I tell him. "We can't wait on the BAU to work something up for us. We have to profile on the fly."

"If I were you, I'd read some of the BAU training materials," Astra adds. "I can't stress enough how helpful it is."

"Got it," he says. "Okay, so our guy is local."

"But why did he dismember the girl?" Mo asks.

I shake my head. "Your guess is as good as mine. First impression, I'm thinking maybe it's a forensic countermeasure. We don't have enough information just yet. We'll know more once we see the body."

"But there are some guys out there who just get off on cutting women to pieces. Literally," Astra notes.

"That's pleasant," Nina groans.

"Sorry you transferred into our team?" Mo asks with a grin.

"Hell no," Nina replies. "There's a lot more excitement here than where they were going to send me. No, I'm thankful I landed here."

"That makes one of us," Rick cracks with a grin.

Now it's Nina's turn to pretend like she got stabbed in the back, which sets the two of them laughing again. I'm glad that the two of them have already seemed to bond so well instead of holding pissing matches about who's better.

"Okay, so we assume our killer is a local," Lucas presses to get us back on track. "Are we any closer to thinking the cases are linked?"

"Not yet," I tell him. "But tomorrow, I want you and Mo to go interview the families of the three other missing girls. I know it's not going to be comfortable, but I want to know everything there is to know about the girls. I want to know if they knew each other, their habits, any mutual friend groups, their hobbies, anything and everything you can think of."

"Copy that," Mo nods.

"We can do that," Lucas adds.

He sits back in his chair, seemingly pleased that I'm giving him an actual job this time out. Our last time out, a complicated case involving the CIA and kill teams, I did my best to sideline him. My entire world had been turned upside down, my command stripped, and the unit I'd worked so hard to build was turned over to somebody else. My team was reassigned to Stone's unit and put under the command of Chief Ayad—a change in the command structure I didn't handle all that well.

Both Nina and Lucas were thrust upon me without my review or consent. I was just expected to absorb them onto my team without having had a chance to vet them myself. Naturally, I wasn't thrilled with it, and wasn't sure about Lucas's true allegiances, so I minimized his role in the investigation as much as I could—something he wasn't too thrilled about himself. He called me out on it, and after a conversation with Astra, I had to relent.

It turned out well. As the case wound on, Lucas proved himself to me and proved his worth to this team. He and I have had a meeting of the minds of sorts and have come together. We've gotten along a lot better since the case in Colorado, and there's a camaraderie building among the team. We're not quite friends yet, but there's a respect and a rapport there between us. It's a good feeling.

"What are you two doing in the morning?" Mo asks.

"Well, the first thing we're going to do is run by and talk to Sheriff Paulson," I say. "He tells me they don't have room for us at his station—"

"They don't," Lucas says. "The place is a cracker box."

Mo nods. "They're crammed in there like sardines."

"All the better," I say. "The sheriff says he has a place we can land though. We'll run by and take a look at it. Rick and Nina, if it passes muster, I want you two to get us set up in there. I want us to be up and running by midday."

"Can do," says Rick.

"After that, Astra and I are going by the morgue to check out Juliette's body," I finish.

"Oh, that sounds fun," Mo says.

Astra laughs. "We'd ask you to come along, but the last time you saw a dead body, you threw up all over the place."

Nina, Rick, and even Lucas all laugh as Mo's face flushes. It makes Astra burst into laughter with everybody else.

"Please. That only happened once," Mo defends herself, which gets everybody howling. "And it was a long time ago. I've seen dead bodies since then, you know."

Nobody hears the last bit, though, as they continue laughing. Mo smiles and shakes her head, letting them have their fun at her expense. She's always had thick skin. The truth of the matter is that the first time we took her into the field on a murder case, she did get sick at the crime scene. Since then, she's taken steps to toughen herself up in that regard, even visiting the body farm out at the University of Tennessee. And ever since then, she's been solid. Astra just enjoys winding her up about it from time to time.

"All right, let's go ahead and head back to the hotel and get some sleep," I say. "I want to get an early start on the day."

As we shuffle out of the restaurant, our bellies full of good food, everybody's still laughing and joking with one another like we're just another group of office workers out for happy hour. And those feelings of camaraderie continue to grow, which I enjoy. It almost makes it easier to ignore the fact that all conversation has stopped, and all eyes have turned to us as we make our way through the dining room. Almost.

God, I just love small towns.

CHAPTER SEVEN

Anderson Realty Building; Annenberg, ND

"**G**OOD MORNING, SHERIFF," I SAY.

"Mornin'," he replies with a tip of his cap. "You ready to see what we've got for you?"

"Absolutely."

"Terrific."

He unlocks the door of a freestanding office building that sits a few blocks away from the Sheriff's station and a street off the main drag through town. The windows have all been papered over and there are "For Lease" signs taped to the glass. The top of the gray stucco on the exterior of the building bears the outline of the former tenants—Anderson Realty.

Paulson holds the door open for us, allowing Astra and I to walk in ahead of him. The rectangular-shaped office is roughly twenty feet wide and sixty feet long, and there's a doorway that leads to a small office off to the right. The air is a little stale and musty. It's obvious the place hasn't been used in a while, but it's functional. It'll do.

"Ain't much to look at, but we got the electricity turned on and there's still runnin' water here. There are two bathrooms right there in the back," Sheriff Paulson says, gesturing to the rear of the office. "The Andersons moved their office across town about three months ago. The place has been empty ever since. As I said, it ain't much but it should suit you."

I walk around the small office and nod. "Yeah, this should be perfect," I tell him. "Thank you, Sheriff Paulson. I appreciate you opening this office for us."

"It's no problem. Place has been sittin' vacant for months now," he replies. "Figure you folks can put it to good use."

"Yeah, this is going to work well," I say then turn to Astra. "What do you think?"

She nods. "I agree. It's just what we need."

"All right then," Paulson says. "If you all need anything else, you be sure to let me know. Be happy to help."

"Thank you, Sheriff," I say.

"Oh, say, I've got a cadaver dog unit comin' up from Minot today like you suggested," he tells us. "We're goin' to start lookin' for more bodies in the area."

"That's good, Sheriff. Keep us in the loop if you find anything," I say.

"Trust me, you'll be my first call," he nods. "I'm just hopin' they don't find nothin.'"

"That makes two of us," I reply.

"All right, well, I should go."

"Good luck, Sheriff," I say.

He tips his cap to us then heads out. I'm encouraged that he's taking this seriously and is also open to taking our suggestions. That speaks pretty well of him. Paulson is somebody who obviously loves the town and the people he's charged with protecting.

"I'm really glad this isn't turning out to be some turf war pissing match," Astra says.

"Tell me about it. Paulson seems like a good man."

"He does. Wants to keep his people safe."

"Seems that way."

I wander around the office, taking it all in. It's not bad. There are half a dozen desks, the canary yellow paint on the walls is still in good shape, and it's remarkably clean and dust-free for having been vacant for three months. The gray industrial carpet on the floor isn't anything to write home about but there's a kitchenette in the back. The refrigerator looks like it hasn't been updated since the 90s but it's still functional, and there are his and hers bathrooms in the hallway behind it. Paulson's right, it's not much to look at, but for our purposes, it's perfect.

The door opens and Rick walks in followed by Nina. They're hauling their gear in from the car and set it all down on the desks they've staked out as their own. Rick takes a minute to look around and nods.

"Home sweet home, huh?" he asks.

"Indeed it is," I reply.

"We're going to need some things to make this place functional," Astra says. "Coffee pot, coffee, filters, creamer, sugar... you know, the usual stuff. I think there was a Target a couple of streets over. Nina, make sure Rick runs over there. He can use the walk."

"I'll have you know, I'm down ten pounds," he says and gives her a sly grin. "The girlfriend is making sure I get plenty of cardio these days."

"Huh. I didn't know that begging and groveling for sex burned that many calories," Astra muses, making Rick's face flush and Nina laugh out loud.

Before things can devolve any further, I step into the fray. "We're also going to need more practical supplies—we need all of our laptops set up in here, video conference monitor—"

"This ain't our first rodeo, boss," Nina says with a grin. "We'll have the electronics set up by midday like you asked."

"I appreciate that, Nina."

"Hey, I'm helping her get this joint wired too," Rick says.

"And a gold star for you too, pumpkin," Astra teases.

Everybody shares a smile and a laugh as I take another lap around the office, trying to think of anything else we're going to need to get our command post up and running.

"What about security?" Astra asks. "I mean, it's a small town and I'm sure the killer's going to know we're here. What's going to stop him from popping in and having a look at the status of the investigation?"

I pause and frown, silently slapping myself upside the head. It's something I hadn't considered. I should have. If the killer is a local, as I've already profiled, nothing is stopping him from waiting until we've gone home for the day to have a look-see at what we've collected on him. Setting up and breaking down the command post every day would be tedious, laborious, and wholly inefficient, which only leaves one viable option.

"Guess I'm going to have to convince the hotel to give me a rollaway and I'll sleep here," I say with a shrug.

"That's ridiculous," Astra replies.

"It's not going to be any different than sleeping in a hotel room." I point to the doorway to my left. "I can set up the rollaway in the office."

"Maybe we can get Sheriff Paulson to have one of his new deputies hang out here at night," Astra offers.

"And what if the killer is one of his new deputies?" I ask. "No, we can't trust anybody but our team. Sleeping here makes the most sense."

Astra chews on her bottom lip, thinking my words over and trying to find a different solution. She knows I'm right though.

"It's not going to be much different than sleeping in a hotel room," I tell her. "I've got electricity, the heater probably works… it'll be fine. And I'll just run back to the hotel in the morning to grab a shower. It's not a big deal."

"All right, we'll rotate then," she says. "We'll all take a turn staying here and keeping an eye on things."

Rick raises his hand. "I'd like to remind everybody that I don't have a gun," he says. "I don't even like guns."

Astra rolls her eyes and chuckles to herself. "Let me amend my statement," she replies. "Everybody who has a gun and isn't afraid of their own shadow will take a turn staying here and keeping an eye on things."

"I can live with that," Rick says.

"We'll figure out the logistics," I say with a laugh. "Do me a favor and put together a list of things we're going to need to get this place functional. I need to make a call."

"You got it," Astra replies.

As they get to work compiling the list, I step outside and into a bright morning. The sky above is a startling shade of blue and filled with scattered fat, fluffy clouds. It's still chilly but not as bitterly cold as it was yesterday and the air smells crisp, clean, and fresh. Seattle does a decent enough job keeping the air quality nice, but this is something entirely different. This is natural and pure. I can see why people enjoy living out here.

I take a moment to look up and down the street. Being that this isn't the city's main thoroughfare, foot traffic is low. I see a few people coming and going from the dry cleaners down the street and others stopping in at a bakery that's set about half a block away. Even from here, I can smell the sweet aroma of the treats they're serving and feel my stomach rumble.

Inhaling deeply and savoring the smell, I pull my phone out of my pocket, dial the number, and hold it to my ear. It rings twice before she answers.

"Hey," April says.

"Hey," I reply. "How's she doing?"

"No change," she replies with a heaviness in her voice. "She still hasn't woken up."

"Well, the doctor said it could take a little bit," I remind her.

"Yeah, I remember."

There's a pause on the line, and even through the phone, I can feel the tension between us. It feels to me like there's something she wants to say.

"What is it?" I finally ask.

"It's just... these guys here in the front room. Do you know them?"

"Personally, no. But I know the guy they work for," I tell her. "And I trust him. If he says we can trust his guys then—"

"I don't trust them, though. I don't know them."

"Have they given you any reason to not trust them?"

"Well… no," she admits. "But I don't like a house full of people I don't know."

"Fish is a friend of mine. And he would never put us in danger," I tell her. "He would give his life for me. And for Kit."

She falls silent again and I can feel her bristling on the other end of the line. I get what she's saying. I don't particularly enjoy putting my life in the hands of people I don't know, let alone trust. So, I get it. I understand her hesitance and wariness about having Fish's guys in the house. It's not going to change the situation though.

"Blake, I would really feel more comfortable if you let me move Kit somewhere different," April presses.

"She's in the safest place she can possibly be. She stays in the condo," I reply.

"Blake, come on—"

"She's my sister, April. And although I appreciate all you've done for her, this is my call to make. Not yours," I say. "Please, call me if something changes."

I disconnect the call and then drop the phone in the pocket of my coat, bristling with irritation. April has taken care of Kit but she's overstepping. Kit is my sister. Not hers. She's lucky I'm even letting her into the condo.

"Everything okay?" Astra asks as she steps out of the office.

"Yeah. Fine," I nod. "Let's hit that bakery then the coroner's office."

"You had me at bakery."

Trying to get my irritation and frustration under control, I turn and stride toward the parking lot where our Yukon is parked, forcing Astra to hurry to catch up with me. She can tell I'm upset about something but is good enough to not press. She knows I'll tell her about it later. I just need a little time to process it all before I'm ready.

And losing myself in the work will only speed that process along.

CHAPTER EIGHT

Annenberg Coroner's Office; Annenberg, ND

THOUGH THE CORONER'S OFFICE IS OFFICIALLY PART OF the sheriff's department, the building is on the other side of town. It's a drab, gray, one-story building that's virtually windowless and sits nestled in among warehouses and metal fabrication and extrusion companies, and a car collision center. To look at it, you'd never know its true purpose. The only thing marking it as a coroner's office is the lettering and city seal on the front doors.

"How creepily anonymous," Astra remarks as if reading my mind.

"Maybe it's by design," I offer. "No need to advertise what they're doing here, I guess."

"Yeah, I guess."

I pull one of the doors open and let Astra walk in ahead of me. I follow her in, letting the door silently swing closed behind us, and step into a lobby that's so quiet, the silence feels like it has a weight to it. The floor is hard and has linoleum that's aged and dingy, and the walls are all red brick. A metal embossment of the city seal hangs on the wall to our right, and a series of paintings depicting the prairie and cowboy life adorns the wall on our left.

Four hard, plastic chairs sit against each wall, and directly in front of us is a reception desk. It's chest-high, and sitting behind the desk is a middle-aged woman with a short, blonde bob and a pair of glasses low on her nose, clicking away at her keyboard. She casts a glance at us and her lips curl down into a disapproving frown. I get the idea that's kind of her default setting.

"What can I do for you, girls?" she asks.

Astra and I exchange a glance. Girls? That's about the most disrespectful and condescending greeting I've gotten in a while. We both whip out our badges for her to see. She doesn't look impressed. If anything, I'd say her expression got even sourer than before.

"Agents Wilder and Russo," I say. "We're here to speak with the coroner."

"About what?"

"We're investigating the murder of Juliette Templeton at the request of Sheriff Paulson," I reply, hoping dropping Paulson's name will grease the wheels a bit.

She doesn't reply and picks up her phone, angrily stabbing a couple of buttons on the keypad. The woman stares daggers through me as she presses the phone to her ear.

"Mr. White, I've got a couple of Feds out here who want to speak with you about the Templeton girl," she says, with a heavy hint of disdain in her voice.

I glance over at Astra who looks like she's doing her best to keep from laughing. The woman's attitude is surprising, to say the least—at least until I remember we're smack dab in the heart of militia country. Anti-government and nationalist groups are as abundant out here as heads of cattle are. There is no love lost for the federal government out this way. It's terrible, and my bosses would skin me if I ever said as much, but I can't say the attitude this woman is copping is entirely unwarranted.

Given my occupation, I know I shouldn't have the opinion I do, let alone express it. But government overreach is a real thing. And episodes like the recent massacre out at Haven—the raid that killed Senator Hedlund's daughter Selene—have done nothing to foster any sort of trust. Nor has it done anything but reinforce the belief that "Big Brother" isn't going to run roughshod over their rights when it's convenient. I don't agree with what some of these militia groups do or how they conduct themselves. Violence isn't the answer, and it never solves anything. But I understand their mindset.

"Of course, sir," she says and hangs up the phone. "Go through that door and follow the blue line down the hallway. He'll meet you at the end of it in the refrigerator room."

"Thanks," I nod.

She doesn't respond and turns back to her computer. Astra opens her mouth and looks like she's about to say something—no doubt something snarky and cutting—so I give her a subtle shake of the head. She gives me a look of disappointment but turns and follows me through the door the woman had pointed us to.

"Well, she seems nice," Astra says when the door closes behind us.

"Yeah, she seems like a real peach."

The walls around us are all painted a uniform gray, giving the hallway a dull and dreary feel. There's nothing to soften it up, and it all just looks antiseptic. It's depressing. We follow the blue line down to a pair of swinging operating suite doors and push through them. The room is smaller than the autopsy suites we're used to, but it's got all the same stainless steel equipment—table, refrigerators, sinks. The walls here have gone from uniform gray to uniform powder blue. I'm not sure if they think that's soothing or what, but whatever. Not my circus, not my clowns.

We're greeted by a tall man—at least six-four—and lanky. The man is the living embodiment of the word beanpole. He's got short black hair, a long equine face with a pointed chin, green eyes, large ears, and he wears a thick pair of glasses on the end of a patrician nose. Everything about the man is ungainly. His arms seem too long for his body—as do his legs. His torso looks abnormally small, adding to the appearance of a man who's wholly out of proportion.

He's got a youthful look to him—he looks like a kid, to be honest. So, maybe he's still growing into his body or something. White is dressed in green surgical scrubs and a cap, looking for all the world like a kid playing dress-up. It's all I can do to keep from laughing.

"Mornin', Agents," he greets us. "I'm Henry White."

"Nice to meet you, Dr. White. I'm Blake and this is Astra—"

"Oh, no, I'm not a doctor. Henry will be fine, thank you."

Astra and I trade a look before I turn back to him. "You're not a medical doctor?"

"No, ma'am. I was elected to this post by the good people of Annenberg."

I groan inwardly. I'm familiar with the fact that some smaller cities and towns elect people to be their coroners, but I've never actually run into one who's not a medical doctor before. That creates a lot of problems. Namely, that Mr. White here won't have conducted an autopsy. His job is to record the time of death, do an external examination, see if he can figure out what killed the person on his table, and jot down a few conclusions. He's not like the medical examiners on TV who can do a deep analysis into the victim's remains—or even like my good friend Beks over at the King County coroner's office. I'd bet the bulk of his job is to file the appropriate paperwork and shuffle the bodies on to the funeral homes for burial or cremation.

It's not a big deal, I suppose. Given the lack of experience in murder cases most small-town ME's have, I was probably going to send Juliette Templeton's body on to the field office in Minot for a secondary autopsy anyway. But I was hoping to have at least some medical information to go on. Granted, given the fact that she was completely dismembered, it was going to be tough for even an experienced ME to come up with a lot, but something would have been better than the giant nothingburger we're about to be served.

"All right, that's fine," I say. "May we view the remains?"

"Of course," he replies. "I just have to say, in the twelve weeks I've been in office, I've never seen something so ghastly before. We don't have a lot of traffic passing through here, as I bet you can imagine. And most of the people I've dealt with died of natural causes. Kind of boring. But I've had one gunshot victim. Oh, and I had a stabbing too. But I've never seen anything this gruesome before. And certainly, nothing that's attracted the attention of the FBI. It's all super cool and really exciting, to be honest."

Astra and I both look at him like he's just grown a second head. I couldn't possibly be more put off by somebody than I am right now, and judging by the look on Astra's face, she's feeling the same way.

"Mr. White, we're talking about the death of an eighteen-year-old girl," I say.

"An eighteen-year-old girl whose family is shattered by her death," Astra adds. "How about a little tact and compassion?"

White's face turns as red as his hair, and he clears his throat. "Of course. I apologize," he says. "That was unprofessional of me."

An expression of contrition on his face, White turns and opens the drawer in the middle of the bank of refrigerated drawers. Astra and I step around the stainless steel table in the center of the room and walk over to where White has Juliette's remains laid out. He pulls back the sheet and shows us the pile of bones in the center of the drawer and all I can do is stare at them. He didn't even bother putting the skeleton together.

But that's not what has me this close to blowing a gasket. The bones sitting in a pile in that drawer are gleaming white without a trace of tissue, soil, or detritus to be seen. Feeling my blood boiling, I look up at White.

"Did you clean the remains?" I ask.

He nods. "I did. I needed to clean them up before sending them to the funeral home."

I slap my forehead to keep myself from slapping him. Astra grabs my other hand down below the drawer where White can't see and gives it a squeeze as if to tell me to calm down. She's right. White's not a doctor, nor is he a forensic scientist, so expecting him to instinctively know he needs to preserve evidence is foolish. It's frustrating as hell, but it's not his fault.

I run a hand through my hair. "Mr. White, by cleaning the bones, you've destroyed any trace evidence that might have been useful in, you know, finding the murderer."

He pales and his mouth falls open. "I—I didn't know. Oh my God. I didn't know."

"I know," I say.

As I turn away and try to gather myself, Astra pulls a pair of latex gloves out of the box on a nearby shelf and pulls them on. I lean against the refrigeration cabinet and watch as she starts picking through the bones. There doesn't seem to be much point to it, but I glove up and join her at the drawer. White floats to the side of the suite where he stands unobtrusively, a mortified expression on his face. He looks like he's about to cry, which is only fair since the fact that he destroyed possible evidence makes me feel like crying too. Or punching something, which makes the fact that he's standing across the room a good thing.

Neither of us are doctors, but Astra and I do our best to reassemble the skeleton. I know there are some bones out of place but by the time we're done, I think it's reasonably close to being accurate. We give each other a look and a shrug and start to inspect the bones. I reach over to a shelf and grab a couple of magnifying glasses and hand her one. I lean down and look closely, quickly seeing the chips and nicks in the left femur.

"Are you seeing nicks in the right femur?" I ask.

Astra runs her magnifying glass over it and nods. "Yeah, I see some along the side here. What do you make of it?"

"Not sure yet," I reply. "Could be damage from him dismembering her. Or it could be that he was hacking at her in a frenzy. I don't think it was with an axe though. The nicks don't seem deep enough."

"Her pictures suggested she was a sturdy girl," Astra says. "She played soccer and had lots of muscle on her legs. Could have been an axe, but with all that muscle, it didn't get very deep into the bone."

"That's possible. But I'm also seeing the nicks on other parts of the body that weren't as muscular as her legs," I note.

She moves to the arms. "Yeah, you're right. There's some here in the ulna too."

"Not enough to tell us what sort of weapon was used," I say. "But maybe the medical examiner at the field office in Minot can narrow it down for us."

We study the bones closer, noting the cuts and nicks in the bones. This girl was worked over. As callous as it sounds, I hope Juliette was dead when it happened. I can't imagine the agony she would have been in if she was alive when she was being cut to pieces. There's one thing that stands out to me as I survey the bones though.

"Hey, look at the joints," I say.

Astra moves her magnifying glass down to the knees and leans forward, looking at them closely. After a minute she looks back up at me and shakes her head.

"Okay, I give up. What am I looking at?" she asks.

"I'm no medical expert, but the joints all look perfectly clean to me. There's no fractures or cracks in the bones," I tell her. "It looks like she was perfectly disarticulated."

She grimaces and looks at the joints again, nodding this time. "Yeah, I see that now. You're right. I don't see the same sort of scoring on the joints. What do you think it means?"

"I think it means our killer might have some working knowledge of anatomy and/or medical skill," I say.

"Or he watched a tutorial on YouTube," she says.

"I think somebody doing a DIY disarticulation he found on YouTube would still leave some cracking or scoring," I counter. "An internet doctor isn't going to be this clean."

"It's possible," she admits.

"As I said, I'm no expert. I'll leave it for the ME at the field office to determine for sure," I say.

"Wh—what does that mean?"

I turn and see White standing in the corner looking paler than a sheet as he listens to us discuss Juliette's remains. I'd almost forgotten he was there.

"It means our killer might be especially nasty and sadistic," I say.

"It also means we're going to need to wrap her up to go," Astra adds.

"T—to go?" he sputters.

"We're sending her remains down to the field office in Minot for forensic examination," I explain. "Not that we're going to be able to get much. But don't do anything with these bones, Mr. White. We'll have somebody come up to retrieve them for examination."

He looks away and doesn't say anything else, and I feel a stab of guilt for making him feel bad again. A small stab anyway. Preserving evidence in a murder case seems pretty common sense to me. Watching *Law & Order* would tell you as much. My phone rings, so I strip a glove and pull my phone out of my pocket and connect the call.

"Wilder," I say.

I listen for a moment then disconnect the call and turn to Astra.

"We have to go," I tell her.

CHAPTER NINE

Avendale Park; Annenberg, ND

"YOU WERE RIGHT," PAULSON SIGHS. "I WISH TO GOD you weren't, but you were."

We're standing in that depression in the park where we found Juliette Templeton. Two more areas have been cordoned off, and people in dark blue coveralls are carefully digging rectangular holes.

"I called in the state ME's office to handle the exhumation," Paulson tells us. "We're still running the cadaver dog around the park just in case, but she only alerted on these two spots."

"Lauren Dunphy and Tamara Gray," Astra says.

"Won't know for sure until we have them out of the ground," he replies glumly. "But, yeah, that's what we're thinkin'."

One of his deputies calls out to him so Paulson excuses himself. Astra and I walk over to the first grave being unearthed and look at the pieces of the girl's body being laid out. Judging by the darker skin tone, it's Tamara Gray. Like Juliette, she's been cut into pieces. But unlike Juliette, we're able to get a better look at the condition of her remains. She's only been missing a week, so the body hasn't fully decomposed, and it's not hard to see this girl went through hell.

"Jesus," Astra whispers. "I hope she was dead before he started cutting on her."

"You and me both."

The pieces of Tamara's body look like they've gone through a meat grinder. Patches of skin and chunks of the muscle and tissue beneath have been removed altogether, leaving the pieces of her body ragged and torn. It's sadistic beyond measure.

"I've never seen something so horrible," Astra murmurs.

I've seen some terrible things over the course of my career, but I have to agree with her. The torture inflicted upon this poor girl is about the worst I've ever seen. Pulling a pair of black nitrile gloves out of my coat pocket, I snap them on and then squat down next to the pieces of the body. The tech looks at me and shakes his head. He looks green around the gills and like he'd rather be anywhere but here right now.

Seeing the extent of the damage to Tamara's body makes it pretty easy to see where all the nicks and gashes in Juliette Templeton's bones came from. Our killer looks like he was in a frenzy and was just hacking and slashing her to hell. But I notice the one thing that argues against this being a disorganized and frantic attack.

"Look here," I say, pointing to the knee bones. "The disarticulation is clean. Just like with Juliette."

Astra squats down and looks at the legs, her lips curling down into a frown. She nods slowly and starts to look over some of the other joints, her frown deepening as she sees they too are clean.

"So, maybe there is something to this medical student angle," she says.

"Maybe. It's not easy to cleanly disarticulate a joint unless you know what you're doing," I reply. "At least it's a place to start."

I stand and look down as the tech puts Tamara's right foot with her leg bones, a grimace on his face. I'm guessing that like us, this is probably one of the worst things he's ever seen too. Astra and I walk over to the other dig site and watch as the techs pull pieces of Lauren Dunphy out of the ground. She's in a little worse shape than Tamara thanks to decomp. I can see, though, that she suffered the same way. Large sections of skin are missing, as are big chunks of the tissue and muscle beneath. It's like our killer took a large melon baller to these girls and scooped out their meat. It's horrifying.

As I look at the pieces of the two bodies, it strikes me that they're in far better condition than I would have suspected they'd be. They're ghastly as hell, of course. There's no other way to describe the dismembered corpses of two young girls. But they almost look like they were well preserved. Lauren's body is a little worse off than Tamara's, but for having been dead for, presumably, a couple of weeks, she's not nearly as decomposed as I would have thought.

"You've got that furrow between your eyes," Astra says. "What's going through that big brain of yours?"

I fold my arms over my chest and look down at the bodies lying spread out on the blue tarps, trying to put some order to my thoughts. After a moment, I turn to Astra.

"Our working theory is that our killer abducts one girl and keeps her until he's ready for another. Only then does he kill her," I start.

"Right. That's what we're theorizing so far."

"Lauren Dunphy was taken roughly three weeks ago, and Tamara Gray was snatched approximately a week or so ago," I say.

Astra nods. "Yeah, that sounds right."

"That means Lauren was killed almost two weeks ago, right?"

"Give or take a few days, sure."

"Do those body parts look like they've been in the ground for two weeks to you?" I ask.

Astra turns and looks at them, and I can see her processing it all in her mind. In truth, Lauren's body is only marginally more deteriorated than Tamara's. I mean, it's obvious Lauren's been in the ground longer. But the pieces of her they've pulled out of that hole so far don't look like they've gone through two weeks of decomp yet. Tamara's only been in the ground a few days—in theory, of course—but she still looks fresh as a daisy. Those parts might have been put into the ground yesterday. But with the police presence around the park, I doubt that's a possibility.

"Now that you mention it, no. They look like they've somehow been preserved," she finally admits.

"Which leads me to my first question—how is it they look as well-preserved as they do?"

"I think I can answer that for you."

We both turn to see Paulson stepping over to us. He's got his ball cap pulled low and is wearing a grim expression on his face. Looking pale and with dark half-moons beneath his eyes, the man looks like he's aged a decade in the last couple of days.

"Sorry, didn't mean to eavesdrop," he says with a nervous chuckle. "I was just listenin' to you two and tryin' to learn somethin.'"

"It's all right," I tell him. "Nothing for you to apologize for. We're all on the same team here and need to pool our resources to catch this man."

"Appreciate that," he says. "You're sure the killer is a man?"

Astra nods. "The likelihood that our offender is a woman is incredibly low. Not only are female serial killers incredibly rare, but the strength it would take to lug a dead body from the parking lot and down the embankment to here makes it seem more likely that it was a man. That doesn't rule out a woman being the killer, but it's incredibly unlikely."

"Fair enough," he nods.

"Got a theory, Sheriff," I ask, "about why the bodies are so well-preserved?"

He nods. "We've recently had a bit of a cold snap these last couple of weeks. I mean real cold," he explains. "Nighttime temps get down into the low twenties to high teens. That kind of cold will help prevent decomp."

He's right. It won't completely stave it off, but that sort of cold will slow down decomp quite a bit. That could very well account for the lack of decay we're seeing.

"We had an unseasonable warm front roll through the week you reckon Juliette was put in the ground," he goes on. "I'm no expert, but that might explain why her decomp was more advanced than these girls."

"We're not experts either, Sheriff," I say. "That's why we're sending the remains of these two, along with Juliette's bones, down to the ME at the field office in Minot. They're the experts and will be able to tell us a lot more than what the three of us can come up with."

"Not that we'll get much from the bones. Better to tick off all the boxes though, right?" Astra says with a wry chuckle.

"Why's that?" Paulson asks.

"Mr. White down at your coroner's office cleaned the bones, so we've got no tissue or samples to work with," she replies.

Paulson's eyes widen and his mouth falls open. He remains speechless for a minute as if he's trying to make sense of Astra's words.

"You're tellin' me, White didn't preserve the remains of a murder victim?" he finally asks. "That has to be a joke, right?"

"I'm afraid not, Sheriff," I say.

"In his defense, he's not a forensics guy or criminologist," Astra says.

"A moron would know to preserve the remains of a murder victim," he growls. "I've always thought that kid was a half-wit. Now I see I've been givin' him way too much credit."

I have to fight off the laugh that's sitting in my throat. It wouldn't be appropriate. Paulson is genuinely upset, and he's got every right to be. I'm upset too.

"If that idiot did anything to hurt our chances of findin' the man who did this to these girls…"

His voice trails off and he turns away for a moment, taking a moment to compose himself. Though his voice is thick with emotion and his face is red as he fights it off, Paulson is holding himself together well. He's able to remain objective, develop solid theories, and offer keen insights. He is conducting himself with a lot more professionalism than many other people I've encountered in his position normally do. My respect for the man is growing.

"We're going to catch him, Sheriff," I say reassuringly. "With Tamara and Lauren's remains, we'll have enough to start building a case from."

"I hope so."

"I know so. We just need to be smart and patient," I tell him.

He pulls his cap down lower and gives me a stiff nod. "I should get back to my deputies," he says. "Just let me know if you need anything."

He stalks away, and I can tell he's upset. Not just about White's gaffe. This whole situation is upsetting him. The weight of the devastation of the families he knows well is pressing down on him. I can't imagine the pressure a man like Paulson must be under, with all the families in this town looking to him to keep them safe. To find the monster among them. It has to be unbearable. And yet, he's finding a way to handle it all with grace and dignity.

"So, I guess there's no question that these cases are all linked now," Astra says.

I turn to her and shake my head. "Nope. No question at all."

I cast my gaze at the various body parts lying on the blue tarps beside the holes. Hands, feet, legs, and arms are all spread out like a jigsaw puzzle that was created in the depths of hell. And as I watch them lift Tamara Gray's decapitated head from the hole and see her wide, lifeless eyes, a cold certainty steals over me.

"This one is going to be bad before it's over. Really bad," I say. "I can feel it."

CHAPTER
TEN

Anderson Realty Building; Annenberg, ND

"FOR ONCE, I'M GLAD YOU ASSIGNED ME TO DO something other than going to the crime scene with you," Lucas says sardonically.

"That makes two of us," Mo chimes in.

"Is it super tacky to say I wouldn't mind seeing some of the crime scenes?" Nina asks. "I mean, does that make me some sort of freak or something?"

"Yes," Rick says. "Yes, it does."

The front door opens, and Astra walks into the office. She silently hands out everybody's order from the Starbucks a couple of blocks away. She offered to grab the coffee while I got everybody up to speed on what we found at the park. Astra usually likes to be part of the briefings, which tells me how rattled she is about what we saw out there yesterday. In all the years we've worked together, I've never seen her quite as shaken as she is right now. She's not herself. There are no jokes, no playful teasing, none of her usual personality. She's quiet, and that's just not her.

After distributing the coffee, Astra sits down at the workstation she'd chosen and leans back in her seat. She takes the lid off her cup and stares down into it as if she's going to find an answer somewhere in the dark brew. Cases dealing with kids are bad enough on their own. But a case dealing with kids like this, where they're treated so horribly, is even worse. I get it. I understand why she's struggling right now. She'll snap out of it and get her head back in the game soon enough. I just need to give her some time.

"So, what are we thinking?" Mo asks. "Why is he cutting these girls into pieces?"

"I'm still leaning toward forensic countermeasures," I say. "He thinks he can throw us off by destroying as much evidence as he can. But he doesn't realize he's not destroying evidence by dismembering the bodies."

"No, he's potentially giving us a lot of trace evidence on the bodies, plus data points for the profile," Mo says.

"Exactly," I reply. "What did you guys get from the families?"

"Not much. We only got to talk to the Templetons and the Dunphys," Lucas says. "This was obviously before Lauren was found in the park."

"All right. What did they say?"

"They didn't know much, to be honest," Mo says. "Juliette was taken on her way home from work—"

"Like Emily Strauss," I say.

"Right—exactly," Mo confirms. "And Lauren was taken from her house when her parents were out of town for the weekend."

"What about Tamara?" I ask.

Lucas shuffles through the papers in a file—it's the case file Sheriff Paulson's guys have put together. Even from where I'm sitting, I can see it's depressingly thin. Lucas grabs a sheet of paper—probably the incident report—and quickly scans it then looks up at me.

"Tamara was also taken from home when her parents were out," he reads out.

"So, two from home when they were alone, and two on the way home from work," I muse. "It sounds like our guy is stalking them. Knows their habits. Knows when they're going to be home alone and vulnerable. Yeah, he watches them for a little while before he takes them."

"That's creepy," Mo says.

"It's about what you'd expect from somebody who dismembers his victims," I shrug. "Did the Templetons or Dunphys say whether their girls had mentioned being watched? Seen anybody hanging around or following them maybe?"

Mo shakes her head. "No, neither family mentioned anything like that."

"The girls may not have said anything to them," Lucas points out. "It's possible they didn't feel comfortable telling their parents if they felt they were being watched. They were teenagers, after all."

"It's possible. Definitely," I say. "We're too early into this to rule anything out just yet. We need to keep all avenues of investigation open."

"Have you ever seen anything like this before?" Lucas asks. "Something this awful and brutal?"

I shake my head. "Honestly, no. Nothing quite like this."

"The savagery is off the charts," Mo adds.

"We might be dealing with a sexual sadist," I say.

"Do we know that he's sexually assaulted these girls?" Lucas asks.

"Sexual sadism isn't necessarily about the sex act. Sexual sadists get off on inflicting pain on others. Torture and hearing somebody screaming and having that power and control is what curls their toes," Astra chimes in. "It's a relatively uncommon disorder, but they're out there. Think of David Parker Ray—"

"The Toy Box Killer," Mo says.

"Correct," Astra nods. "There's also Dean Corll, aka the Candy Man. Andrei Chikatilo, the Rostov Ripper. Or Dennis Rader—"

"BTK," Lucas says.

"That's right," I reply. "They're out there, but as Astra said, it's an uncommon disorder. It does seem like our killer here might be that flavor of psychopath."

I glance over at Astra, who gives me a small smile and subtle nod. I'm glad to see she's come around and has gotten her head back into the game and is engaged. I knew she would. It was just a matter of time. As rattled as this case has her, Astra takes the job personally—even more so when kids are involved. She wasn't going to stay on the bench long. She just needed a minute to take a breath before she was ready to start hunting this monster.

"Okay, so, how does a sexual sadist profile out?" Mo asks.

I get to my feet and start pacing down the middle of the room between the two rows of desks on either side. Clasping my hands behind my back, I call up all the information I've gleaned about sexual sadists over the years and try to put it in some sort of order.

"They're narcissistic. They truly believe they are *it* and are not afraid to show that," I start. "Typically, white men in their thirties to forties. Highly intelligent. Many have some college in their background. But a lot of them found the college experience unchallenging and dropped out. Others never went. They feel it's beneath their intellect."

"They'll have a steady job," Astra adds. "And they can blend in with normal people. Most of those normal people, though, will find our sadist arrogant and off-putting. If we interview people after we catch him, many will say there was just something about him, some vibe he put off they found unsettling."

"Our guy is going to have a place that's secluded. A place that's private," I continue. "It's likely going to be a cabin in a remote area. Or perhaps a house with a soundproofed basement—"

"And how do you know that?" Lucas asks.

"He's going to need someplace that he can bring these girls and not fear anybody overhearing their screams. Their screams are what he needs more than anything," I reply. "And when he's cutting on them the way he does, they will be screaming. Loudly. So, he's not going to be able to live in an apartment. His place needs to be private."

"That's grim," he notes.

"Everything about this is grim," Mo chimes in.

"Well, buckle your seat belts because it's probably going to get worse from here," Astra tells them. "This is just the starting gate. Wait until we get in deeper."

"She's not wrong," Mo offers.

"Oh good, something to look forward to," Lucas mutters.

"I don't believe for a second that Juliette Templeton was his first victim," I say. "It was all too clean and too well choreographed."

"So, how do we figure out who his first victim was?" Lucas asks.

"We go through old, open, unsolved murders," I say.

"We're going to need to get the open-unsolved case files from the surrounding communities," Astra says. "He may not have hunted in Annenberg early on."

"That's a good thought," I nod. "Lucas, I want you and Mo to go to the surrounding towns and pick up open murder cases. Only the ones that haven't been solved. These small towns are usually fairly safe, so I don't imagine there will be many."

"Copy that," Mo nods.

The door opens and Rick and Nina come in carrying boxes of equipment. We spend a few minutes carrying things in from the car and helping them get set up.

"Okay, we're ready to roll," Rick says.

"What do you need us to dig up for you?" Nina adds.

"I need you guys to do a search of residents in Annenberg who've got some sort of medical training," I start. "Maybe people who've gone to college to be an RN, or even people who've gone to med school and dropped out—especially those who've dropped out."

"You also might want to do a deep dive on actual medical professionals in town," Astra adds. "Dig up any dirty little secrets they might have."

"My favorite kind of secrets to dig up," Nina says.

"We'll go in there like truffle pigs and root 'em all out, boss," Rick adds.

"Excellent," I say. "We all have our assignments. Let's get to it then."

CHAPTER ELEVEN

Annenberg Sheriff's Station; Annenberg, ND

T HE SHERIFF'S MAIN STATION, LIKE THE CORONER'S OFFICE, is a squat, one-story building. That's where the similarities end though. The sheriff's station is made of red brick and is beautifully landscaped out front. There are plenty of signs telling you what the building is—not that the parking lot full of police vehicles couldn't tell you that.

Astra and I head up the walk which is lined by colorful flowers on either side. The front doors are glass and open automatically with a soft hiss. We step into a lobby with freshly cleaned tile floors that are gleaming brightly. The wall to our right is filled with framed photos of deputies who've fallen in the line of duty, just opposite framed photos of the Sheriff and his command structure on the wall to the left. Directly ahead of us is the reception desk. On the wall behind it in embossed lettering, it says, "Annenberg Sheriff's Department," which is flanked by an American flag on a stand to the right and the North Dakota state flag on the left.

Behind the desk is a man who's completely bald, but he makes up for it with a dark and bushy beard that seems well-groomed. He's got intense green eyes and is built like an offensive lineman. At six-two or so, he's broad through the chest and wide across the shoulders, and has biceps that strain the sleeves of his shirt to the breaking point, a square jaw, and not much of a neck to speak of. The man looks like he bench-presses Cadillacs for fun. He's intimidating, for sure, and his name tag says Hinson.

"Help you?" he asks, his voice surprisingly soft and high-pitched.

"Yeah, we're here to see Sheriff Paulson," I say as we flash him our badges. "Agents Wilder and Russo."

"Yeah, Sheriff Paulson isn't here right now. He's in a meeting with the mayor. Said you'd be by though," he replies. "Said to give you run of the place."

Paulson is really on the ball and seems to anticipate what I need before I even realize I need it. The man's instincts are razor sharp.

"Great," I nod. "Then we're going to need access to your files. Specifically, we're looking for all your open-unsolved homicides going back say… fifteen years."

"That's quite a length of time," Deputy Hinson notes.

It is. But if the profile is right and our unsub is, say, mid-thirties, then that range would allow for his first murder to have been committed in his late teens or early twenties. That sounds about right to me. That should give us a good base to start from.

"You have a lot of open homicides in Annenberg, Deputy?" I ask.

He chuckles. "I suppose not," he says. "I'll have Deputy Koda give you a hand."

"Thank you," I say.

He picks up his phone and dials an extension. "Koda," he says in the mouthpiece. "Get up here. Got a job for you."

He disconnects the call and sets the phone down in its cradle then turns to us.

"Koda will be right up," he says.

"Thanks for your help, Deputy Hinson."

"No sweat," he replies. "So, you two think you'll catch who's doin' this to these girls?"

"That's the plan," Astra says.

"Got any suspects yet?"

I laugh softly. "Not yet. We've only just gotten onto the case," I tell him. "But we'll find out who's doing this and bring him in."

"Confident," he remarks.

"We've been doing this a while. We know what to look for," Astra responds.

"That so?" he replies. "So? What are you lookin' for?"

"A very bad man," I say with a grin. "Agent Russo is right though. We're very good at what we do and know what to look for. And guys like this always make a mistake somewhere along the line."

He stares at us for a long moment, a small grin curling one corner of his mouth upward. The way he's looking at us almost feels like a challenge to me. A dare.

"Then how come it took you guys so long to catch a guy like Dahmer. Or Bundy?" he presses. "Hell, you ain't never caught the Zodiac."

"Those were different times," Astra says. "A different Bureau. And very different agents in charge of those cases."

"So, y'all think you could have caught them sooner, huh?"

Hinson's tone has gone from amicable and helpful to almost accusatory and hostile in the span of sixty seconds. He's looking at us with thinly veiled contempt in his eyes, and I'm not sure what it was that precipitated the switch in his demeanor. My only thought is that he's one of those with little love for the federal government. There are more than a few of those around here. If he's looking to get a rise out of us, though, he's most definitely barking up the wrong tree. I cast a subtle glance at Astra just to make sure she's on the same page and is keeping herself in check.

"I don't know about what happened in the past, Deputy Hinson," I say. "But I'm confident we're going to catch the man who's been killing young girls in your town."

I emphasize the last sentence just to drive home the point that we're here basically doing his job for him. He can rag on us all he wants, but three girls have been brutally murdered on his watch and a fourth has been taken—and unless we find her soon, we're going to be pulling her parts out of the ground too. I want to make sure Hinson knows and understands that. For all his bluster, he hasn't been able to catch a killer in a town of just thirty-some-odd-thousand.

He seems to get the message and looks down as his expression darkens. Just then, a young woman approaches us from the bullpen area. She's small—no more than five-three and petite. She's got warm, russet skin that's smooth and flawless, rich black hair that's pulled back into a bun, and wide eyes that sparkle like chips of obsidian.

"Agents, this is Deputy Cara Koda," Hinson says. "She'll help you out and get you whatever it is you need."

And just like that, we're dismissed. Hinson turns away and starts banging at the keyboard, his attention riveted to the computer screen.

"Hey," Deputy Koda smiles. "Follow me."

With all eyes on us, we follow her through the bullpen and then down a long hallway to a metal door, not saying a word the entire way. She taps a code into the keypad mounted to the wall beside the door. A moment later, a sharp beep sounds followed by a loud clunk as the locks disengage. Koda opens the door and motions for us to follow her.

We descend a flight of stairs and step into a large concrete room underneath the station. The room is filled with tall metal racks of shelves that contain banker's boxes that, judging by how yellowed some of them are, have been down here for a while. On the opposite wall, an area is sectioned off with a metal floor-to-ceiling fence with another electronic gate. I'm assuming that's where they store the evidence they collect.

"We're still digitizing a lot of our records," she explains. "But we keep all of our open-unsolved cases segregated."

Astra and I exchange a look of relief. Neither one of us was looking forward to combing through all those boxes, so I, for one, am glad they had the foresight to segregate the open-unsolved cases. Still not saying much more than she has to, Koda grabs a box marked with the year 2000 and carries it over to a table, and drops it. The box hits the table with a hard thud, sending puffs of dust into the air.

"Doesn't look like anybody gets down here much," I note.

"We come down when we have to," she replies.

She grabs another box off the shelf, this one was unmarked. She tossed it onto the table beside the first one.

"The first box has the city case files," she explains. "The second one has files from around the county like you asked for."

"Terrific. Thank you," I say.

Koda stands off to the side of the room, seeming like she's trying to keep as much physical distance between us as she can. She isn't making eye contact with us, and her posture is stiff, her shoulders tense. I get the feeling that she doesn't like us, but I don't sense the same sort of hostility that was wafting off Hinson. There's something else.

"Is everything all right, Deputy Koda?" I ask.

"Yes, ma'am. Everything's fine."

Astra takes the lid off the box and starts thumbing through the files inside. I turn to her.

"We'll pull the files of all the girls anywhere between the ages of sixteen and twenty," I say. "That seems to be our guy's sweet spot."

"Copy that," she replies.

I turn back to Koda, who still isn't looking our way, and frown. She's got a sour expression on her face and a general air of irritation coalescing about her. Astra and I exchange a glance, neither of us seeming to know or understand why we're getting the cold shoulder.

"Have we done something to offend you, Deputy Koda?" I ask.

"No," she says.

I give her a moment, waiting for her to continue. But she doesn't.

"So, are you naturally just this cold and aloof?" I ask. "Or is this something we should be taking personally?"

"It's not you. Not... directly anyway," she admits.

"You're upset about something," I press. "What is it?"

Koda opens her mouth as if she's about to say something, but no words come out, so she closes it again. That sour expression on her face only deepens though.

"You might as well spit it out," Astra chimes in. "Otherwise, she'll just keep digging at you and digging at you until you get so sick of hearing her voice that you tell her just to get her to shut up. I speak from experience."

The first hint of a smile touches Koda's lips, but quickly vanishes, and that expression tinged with anger returns. She looks away for a moment as if gathering herself then finally turns back to us. The strained and dark look on her face tells me that whatever it is she's got to say is deeply personal to her.

"Deputy Koda?" I press.

"It's just that... when it's girls from poor, indigenous families going missing, nobody raises much of a fuss. Nobody says anything really," she replies. "But when a few rich girls from prominent families go missing, local PD pulls out all the stops to find them. We even get the damn FBI out here."

She pauses and takes a breath as the emotions cycle across her face. Koda finally exhales and looks up at us.

"I'm sorry. I don't mean to go off on you guys. I know you're just here doing your jobs," she says. "It's just frustrating when indigenous girls who've gone missing or been killed don't get the same sort of attention as rich white girls."

Astra and I share a glance. It's not the first time we've heard these kinds of complaints about nobody taking the abduction and even murder of indigenous girls seriously. We've both heard more than a few stories about local departments sweeping them under the rug. It's unfortunately a problem that isn't getting any better with time, and something that, in this day and age, I find entirely disheartening.

"I hear you, Deputy Koda. And I'm sorry," I say. "We don't have any choice in where we go or what cases we work. They point, and we go."

"Yeah, I know," she says, her voice colored with frustration. "I get it."

I feel for Koda and understand her frustration. The disparity in the attention given to indigenous girls versus non-indigenous girls is appalling. And though I obviously can't relate to it, I can certainly empathize. It's not right. But we, unfortunately, don't get to play politics or dictate policy out here in the field. We're here to do our job. Nothing more.

"So, are you telling me that you suspect the man responsible for these three deaths has taken and killed indigenous girls as well?" I ask, trying to steer the conversation back on track.

"Yeah, I do," she replies.

"All right, do you have anything that backs that up?" Astra asks.

Koda walks over to the shelves with the open-unsolved cases and pulls another box down. She brings it over to the table and drops it beside the first one, then looks at us with a gleam of challenge in her eyes.

"These are the case files of indigenous girls who've gone missing over the same period you're looking at," she says. "But they've all been classified as closed-no resolution."

"Why were they closed?" I frown.

"You'd have to ask the powers that be," she shrugs.

"Did Sheriff Paulson close these?" Astra asks.

"He signs off on everything that's closed. So, yeah. He knows. And he's let it happen as much as anybody else has," she says bitterly.

I open the box and start sifting through the files inside. There are a lot of them. More than the open-unsolved cases we've been looking through. Almost twice as many, I'd say. It's unlikely that most of these are connected to our case, but some of them may be. The problem is that all the files in this box have a red flag on them—closed-no resolution.

"Look, Deputy Koda, I can't promise any of these cases are connected," I say. "But I do promise that we are going to look through these files, and if any of them are connected, I can assure you that we will be looking into them. You have my word."

"That's more than anybody else has promised," she grumbles. "I guess that's something."

"And I give you my word we will keep rattling cages and try to get more Bureau resources devoted to these cases," Astra adds, tapping her finger on the box of the indigenous girls' case files. "I promise we'll get somebody to look into these."

Koda gives us a small smile that says, *"I'll believe it when I see it."* And rightly so. Given the history, I can't say I blame her. Koda has every right to be upset about the fact that little to nothing is being done about cases involving indigenous girls.

"I give you my word, Deputy Koda," I say. "We're going to do everything we can."

"We'll see."

CHAPTER TWELVE

Strauss Family Residence; Annenberg, ND

"WE KNOW THIS IS DIFFICULT," I SAY. "THANK YOU for seeing us."

Astra and I are sitting on the loveseat, and the Strausses are perched on the sofa across from us. Their home is nicely upper middle class, and when we first came in, I caught sight of their maid bustling toward the back of the house with a laundry basket in her arms. They're fairly well off, and it makes me think back to what Koda said about all the stops being pulled out for the wealthy families while those already struggling are pretty much left to fend for themselves. It sends a sharp stab of guilt through me.

"Of course," Mrs. Strauss says. "We'll do anything we can. We just want our little girl to come home to us."

She covers her face with her hand as her husband wraps his arm around her shoulders and pulls her to him. He's trying to remain composed and stoic, but it's not hard to see the emotion creeping at the edges of his face. His face is drawn and pinched, his cheeks are flushed, and his eyes glimmer with the tears he's fighting to keep from falling. He's trying hard to be strong for his wife, but I can see the whole thing is tearing him up inside. It's heartbreaking to see.

Mrs. Strauss wipes her eyes with a tissue and sniffs loudly. She's only five-four or so, with dirty blonde hair, brown eyes, and pale skin. She's a sturdy woman who's wide through the hips and bust. Mr. Strauss is almost the polar opposite of his wife. Six-two with blond hair so stark it's almost white. His eyes are the color of jade, and his skin is so pale that he almost seems like he's suffering from albinism.

The maid, in her shapeless, gray dress and white waist apron, steps into the sitting room and sets a tray with full coffee service down on the table between us. Judging by the dusting of gray in her dark hair, I'd say she's probably somewhere in her forties. She's a bit older than I thought when I caught a glimpse of her. She's got warm, tawny skin and eyes that are black and mysterious.

When I'd first glimpsed her bustling toward the back of the house, I'd thought she was Hispanic. But looking at the woman up close and being able to study her features, I realize that I was wrong. I don't think she's Hispanic; she's probably indigenous. Which, of course, reminds me of Deputy Koda and everything she said again.

"Thank you, Chianne," Mrs. Strauss says.

"Of course, ma'am," the woman replies softly then turns and leaves.

Mrs. Strauss pours four cups of coffee and then dresses her own. Not wanting to be rude, I grab one of the saucers, throw a splash of creamer and a couple of sugars in, and sit back. Astra follows my lead, but Mr. Strauss doesn't partake. We all sit quietly for a moment as we sip our coffee. It's all very genteel. In the social circles this family seems to run in, appearances and proper social protocols matter.

"Do you think this is about ransom?" Mrs. Strauss asks, a faint strand of hope coloring her voice. "We haven't gotten a call yet, but do you think it could be somebody looking for money?"

She had to have heard about the other three girls who were taken by now, so deep down, she likely knows this isn't about money. But as a mother with a missing girl, I'm sure she's clinging to whatever shred of hope is available to her. She's probably grasping at whatever idea she can to keep her from spiraling down that dark hole of despair. I can't blame her, nor do I want to burst her bubble. I don't want to be the one who strips her hope away.

Mr. Strauss pulls her to him a bit tighter. "If this was about money, we would have heard from the kidnappers by now, hon," he says. "This isn't about money. It's about something else."

His voice is resigned, almost as if this is something he's explained to her before, which makes the fact that she continues clinging to the idea even sadder. But selfish as it is, I'm glad Mr. Strauss is the one who said it so I don't have to address it myself.

"Wh—what can it be about if it's not money?" Mrs. Strauss asks. "Agents?"

"I'm afraid we can't say at this point, Mrs. Strauss. There are still too many variables in play right now," I say gently.

"But what have you found so far?"

"We, unfortunately, can't go into specifics of the investigation," Astra says. "I'm very sorry. But we are doing everything we can to find your daughter. I promise you."

Mrs. Strauss sniffs again. "Do you—"

"Enough, Daisy," her husband says kindly but firmly. "Let the agents do their jobs and ask their questions. They're doing everything they can."

Mrs. Strauss looks down at her hands which are clasped together in her lap as she wrings them together furiously. Emily's parents are so different in personality, physical appearance, and temperament that it seems to prove the old saying, "opposites attract," true. Even in this very brief meeting, I've been able to observe their personalities. Mrs. Strauss is the dreamer and the optimist. Mr. Strauss is the realist. He's the one who has his feet on the ground and sees things as they are, not as he hopes they'll be. He's a stoic and seems the type to handle difficult situations while keeping an even keel. But even now, I can see cracks in his armor and his emotions bubbling below the surface.

He angrily wipes away the tear that's tracking down his cheek and sniffs loudly. He's a pragmatic man who isn't into self-delusion and knows, in light of the other girls being found dead already, the likelihood he'll ever see his little girl again is slim. He's clutching those last strands of hope as tight as he can, but Mr. Strauss looks like he knows the odds aren't great and is just trying to cope with this new reality.

"Go ahead, Agents," Mr. Strauss says. "Ask your questions."

"All right. Do you know if Emily was having difficulties with anybody?" I ask. "Had she mentioned anybody following her? Watching her? Anything like that?"

Mr. Strauss shakes his head. "No, she never mentioned having trouble with anybody," he says. "She certainly never mentioned anybody stalking her."

"Does Emily have a boyfriend?" Astra asks. "Is she seeing anybody that you know of?"

"No, she's a shy girl. She's not very outgoing where boys are concerned," Mrs. Strauss replies. "She gets that from me, I'm afraid."

"And you're certain she wouldn't have kept that from you?" I ask.

"Of course not," she says. "Emily is very open with us. She tells us everything."

If I had a dollar for every time I heard that and it turned out to not be true, I'd have more money than Jeff Bezos at this point. It seems pointless to ask the question and expect a realistic answer anymore, so I typically use it to gauge the reaction of the parents. Some are realistic enough to know their kids hold things back while others believe the fantasy that their kids tell them everything. Even stoic Mr. Strauss believes the fantasy, which I find somewhat surprising given his pragmatism.

"How long has she worked at the coffee house?" I ask.

"Oh, about a year or so now," Mr. Strauss tells us.

"And she never mentioned any customers who may have been paying a little too much attention to her or anything out of the ordinary like that?" Astra questions.

Mrs. Strauss shakes her head. "No, never. She has her regulars and seems to get along with them all. She never has anything negative to say about anybody. That's just who she is."

I glance at the mantle over the fireplace and look at the array of family photos in beautiful silver frames all lined up for the first time. The pride these two take in their daughters is easy to see. It makes me wonder if my own folks hadn't been murdered and my sister abducted, if our mantle would have looked like this one.

I give my head a shake and push those thoughts away. Not only are they pointless, they're counterproductive. They're also self-centered. Selfish. This is about the Strausses and their missing daughter. Nothing more.

"Emily has a sister?" I ask.

"Is that important?" Mrs. Strauss answers my question with one of her own.

"I—I don't think so. Not at this point. We're just gathering all the information we can right now," I tell her.

"Erin is a sophomore up at Cornell. She's going to be a lawyer and has her sights set on eventually becoming a federal judge," Mr. Strauss tells us with an obvious note of pride in his voice.

"Emily is off to NYU after she graduates. She's already been accepted," Mrs. Strauss adds. "She's going to be a doctor."

"Your girls sound truly exceptional," I reply, not knowing what else to say.

"They are," Mrs. Strauss says with a shaky smile.

Mr. Strauss clears his throat, and his face tightens as he looks at me with a solemn expression. I'm pretty sure I already know what his next question is going to be, and I'm praying that I'm wrong, or that he'll decide he doesn't want to know the answer after all.

"Those girls who were found in the park," he says softly. "A— are they connected to our Emily? Is there some connection ..."

His voice trails off and his composure finally cracks. Tears spill down Mr. Strauss's face, and he quickly tries to wipe them away. He draws in a long, shaky breath, trying to rein it all back in and regain his footing. I hate being right sometimes. Despite this stoicism, he's clinging to the same hope his wife is, and I don't want to be the one who dashes that hope for them. I also don't want to give them false hope either. It's a delicate line to walk.

"It's too early to say, Mr. Strauss," I say evenly.

"But what does your gut tell you, Agent Wilder?"

I know what he wants me to say. He wants me to give him and his wife something they can latch on to. But I learned long ago that you don't make promises and you don't offer hope that can be crushed when things don't turn out how you said they would. It's a lesson I learned the hard way. It's always better to manage expectations. Especially when you're dealing with loved ones who are desperately searching for some reason for optimism.

"It would be pointless for me to speculate at this point, Mr. Strauss," I tell him. "But I promise that we keep you apprised of anything we find."

He looks down, and though I can see he hates that we won't give him straight answers, he seems rational enough to understand why. Mr. Strauss takes his wife's hand and pulls her close, doing his best to comfort her.

"Mr. and Mrs. Strauss," Astra says, "may we look around Emily's room, please?"

"Yes, of course," he nods. "Turn right at the top of the stairs and it's the second door down from there."

"Thank you. We won't disturb anything," I reply.

Astra and I get up and head up to Emily's room. It's not unlike the rooms of almost every other teenage girl we've run across in our time. The walls are all a light shade of pink, there's a large queen-sized bed with pink and white bedding against one wall, a dressing table, and a mirror against another. Across the room from us is a desk beneath the windows, giving her a beautiful view of open land and a lake beyond as she studies.

The walls are adorned not with popular bands and celebrities but with moody black and white photographs and framed inspirational quotes. Over by the walk-in closet, though, there are posters of Maya Angelou and Marie Curie, both emblazoned with iconic quotes. A quick perusal of the books on her shelves shows me Emily is a very well-read, well-rounded girl. Her room is clean and tidy, everything on her desk and shelves organized and neat. She's not a typical teenager.

I tap the laptop sitting on her desk. I'm surprised Sheriff Paulson hasn't impounded it already. It seemed a basic first step in an investigation. I have to remind myself that we're dealing with a town that isn't used to murders like this. Situations like this are almost unheard of in a place like Annenberg. It would be easy to be cynical and cast blame for bungled investigations on the incompetence of local law enforcement, but the Sheriff is simply in over his head, so it's best to cut him some slack. He's been very helpful and accommodating, and I'm grateful for that. I'll take an enthusiastic, professional small-town sheriff who may not have the best resources in the world a thousand times over one who'd prefer to smugly shut out the Feds of an investigation.

"We should see if Rick and Nina can get anything off this," I say, tapping on the laptop. "I know her parents think she tells them everything but—"

"No kid tells their parents everything," she finishes for me.

"Exactly."

I unplug the laptop and set it aside then rifle through her desk drawers. Astra pokes through the closet and Emily's dresser. We've both been doing this long enough that neither of us expects a smoking gun to pop up and crack the case for us. We're experienced enough to know it's usually the small, innocuous clues that look insignificant but turn out to be massively important and help turn a case. That's the mistake a lot of people make. It's usually not the big reveal that makes a case anywhere outside of television or the movies. It's an accumulation of smaller things and persistence that break a case open.

Unfortunately for us, we're not finding much of that variety either. Emily does seem to be a straight arrow without many secrets. The girl doesn't even have a diary—unless it's on her computer. There are a lot of online journaling programs people use. They're usually more secure than paper diaries, which is why they use them. Snooping parents are less likely to find them. Hopefully, if there's something there, Rick and Nina can find it. But as of now, we have nothing more than we did when we first stepped through the Strauss's door an hour ago.

"All right, there's nothing to see here. Let's get back to the command post," I say.

"I'm right behind you."

We head downstairs and find Mr. and Mrs. Strauss standing together near the landing in the foyer. Their faces are red and puffy and they're clinging together like they're adrift in a storm-wracked ocean and they're one another's life preservers.

"We need to take Emily's laptop to have it examined," I tell them. "I promise you we'll get it back to you ASAP."

"Why do you have to take it?" Mrs. Strass asks.

"There may be something of evidentiary value—"

"What could possibly be on it?" she cuts me off.

"We don't know yet. Possibly nothing," I reply. "But on the other hand, there could be a key to the case on it. It's just due diligence, Mrs. Strauss. We have to look under every rock we can."

"It's all right," Mr. Strauss says. "Just return it when you're through with it."

"I will. I promise."

He looks at me with a hard, flinty gaze. "Find our little girl," he implores us. "No matter what. Find her and bring her home to us."

It's dangerously close to that line of making a promise I try to avoid crossing, but the resignation in his voice tells me he's bracing himself for the possibility—maybe even the likelihood— that Emily is dead. Or soon will be. He's simply asking me to make sure she comes home. Even if it's only for burial.

"We're going to do our best, Mr. Strauss. I promise you that," I say.

Astra and I head out of the house, and as I'm closing the door behind me, I hear Mr. Strauss's resolve crack as a sob is torn from his throat. It's primal and raw. And it's beyond heartbreaking to hear.

CHAPTER THIRTEEN

Anderson Realty Building; Annenberg, ND

"**S**O, WHAT ARE WE LOOKING FOR?" LUCAS ASKS.

"Connections. Links," I tell him.

He looks at the piles of case files and casts a skeptical eye at me. "There are a lot of files here. Between the two boxes you've brought over, we've got a ton."

"This is the job, Agent Okamura," I say. "At least, part of it anyway."

"Most cases are made on paper. There are always connections or case-breaking clues to be found in the paper. At the very least, we're going to find things that can't be found anywhere else. The files are important," Astra tells him.

"Fair enough," Lucas replies. "So, I guess I need to circle back to my original question. What are we looking for?"

I look down at the tablet in my hand, scanning the faces of the four girls who've been taken. Or at least, the four non-indigenous girls who've been taken. On the surface, they're as different as can be. Two white, one mixed-race, one black. Two of them have siblings and two are only children. Three had jobs, one didn't. Other than the fact that they all come from affluent and prominent families, they have nothing in common.

I pace back and forth through the office, staring at the pictures on the table. It takes me a minute, but I finally find something—a commonality. It's flimsy, I know, but it's the only thing I see that our victims share in common. It's a thread worth pursuing.

Rick and Nina set up a pair of large monitors on one of the desks. It's a poor replacement for the four video screens mounted on the wall in the bullpen back home, but we've got to work with what we've got.

"Rick, do me a favor and pull up the photos of the four victims on the big screens, please," I ask.

"Comin' right up, boss."

A moment later, the screens flare to life, each monitor showing two photos. They're the school photos, but that's not what I want.

"Change the pictures," I say. "Give us the full body candid photos."

Rick taps at his keyboard, and the pictures change to each monitor showing two candid, full body shots of the girls. I give everybody a minute to take them in.

"Who sees the common link the girls share?" I ask.

Astra takes another beat before the lightbulb flickers on over her head. "None of them are exactly petite. Both seem to be on the heavier side."

"Exactly right," I nod.

"That seems like a pretty loose connection," Lucas says.

"It might be. But it's a connection nonetheless," I say. "It's the one thing we can see that links all four girls together—their body types."

Lucas grimaces, and I can see he's not buying it. But he doesn't need to. I know that coming over from counterterrorism, he's not used to having to profile killers. It's a completely different mental skill set. Profiling a serial killer isn't in the same ballpark as profiling terrorists. It's not even the same sport. Not really.

"All right, so how do we use this?" Mo asks.

"We need to go through those files. All of them," I say as I point at the boxes sitting on the table. "We need to find girls who fit the victimology profile—"

"And what is the victimology profile?" Lucas asks.

"We're looking for girls between, say, fifteen and twenty," I reply. "Throw out the economic status and focus solely on body type right now. We want girls in that age range who are a little thicker."

"Well, we've got to start somewhere, I suppose," Lucas says skeptically. "But I'm not sure we should be hanging our hat on the weight and body type of these girls. It just doesn't make sense to me."

"Lucas, one thing you're going to find is that this is right in Blake's wheelhouse," Astra tells him. "When it comes to profiling killers, she knows more than anybody I've ever met."

"She's right," Mo adds. "I'm constantly astounded by Blake's knowledge and her ability to profile a killer. I know this is working different mental muscles than you're used to, but keep an open mind. I think you're going to learn a lot."

"But still. We don't know that any of the girls in these files are even dead," Lucas points out. "These are all just missing persons cases, right?"

"That's true. But like you said, we need to start somewhere," I say. "We're going to take these files, follow up on the girls, and see if we can definitively link them to the four cases here."

"It's kind of a standard investigative technique," Astra quips.

I understand that Lucas isn't used to this sort of thing yet. I'm confident he'll get there, but it's going to take some time. Unfortunately, I think the Bureau did him a real disservice by not having him take any profiling classes before sending him to me. I get why he's so skeptical. But my team backing me like they are makes me feel good.

"Fair enough," he says. "So, where do we start?"

"Lucas, I want you to dig through the box of nonindigenous girls and pull the files of anybody who matches the victimology profile," I say. "Mo, I want you to do the same with the box of indigenous girls."

"Got it," Mo nods. "What are you going to do?"

"Astra and I are going to talk to a few people," I say. "Specifically, I want to talk to anybody working at that coffee shop the night Emily Strauss went missing."

"What about us?" Rick asks. "Got a job for us?"

"Oh yeah, I almost forgot you two were here," I say with a grin.

"Funny," he replies.

"I want you and Nina to start doing backgrounds on the girls Mo and Lucas identify," I say. "I want anything and everything you can find in the public sphere. We don't want to have to apply for a warrant and alert Ayad until it's necessary."

"Copy that," Nina says. "And if we find out they're dead?"

"Same thing. Find what you can in the public sphere, and we'll go to Ayad when we have all our ducks in a row," I tell her. "We may need him to twist some arms to get us those case files. And he won't help us if we don't have all our I's dotted and t's crossed."

"Sounds good," she says.

"All right," I say. "We've got our assignments. Let's get to it."

As the team dives into their assignments, Astra and I head out. I'm not overly optimistic about finding much of anything useful. So far, this guy has been meticulous about covering his tracks. No evidence and no witnesses. But nobody's perfect, and everybody slips up eventually. All I can hope for at this point is that our boy already has and somebody knows something.

"So, you were working with Emily the night she went missing?" I ask gently.

The girl sniffs and wipes her eyes with the back of her hand and nods. "Yeah. She left at closing, but I had to stay and count the drawer and all."

Our trail led us to Caffeine Corner, Emily's place of employment and the last place she was seen before she vanished. Sitting across from us is Kira Rice, Emily's best friend and the shift supervisor the night Emily went missing. She's a seventeen-year-old petite redhead with fair skin and green eyes that are shimmering with tears. She's got a tissue clutched firmly in her hand that's crumpled and damp and an expression of agony etched into her features. She looks lost, and my heart goes out to her.

"Did you happen to notice if anybody was hanging around the shop you didn't recognize?" Astra asks. "Or did Emily mention anything perhaps?"

Kira shakes her head. "No, everything was super normal that night. It wasn't real busy or anything, and nothing out of the ordinary happened."

"So, just walk me through it," I say. "You two worked your normal shift, and nothing out of the ordinary happened."

"Right."

"And then Emily left, leaving you here alone," I go on. "Was it usual for her to leave before you?"

Kira nods. "Oh yeah. Dale—he's the owner—he doesn't like paying overtime and wants the non-leads to get out as soon as their shift is over," she tells us. "Leads have to stay late to count the drawer as I said. But Dale wants the non-leads out of here by 9:15 at the latest. Any later than that and he has to pay OT."

"The parking lot is in the rear of the shop," Astra points out. "Did you happen to notice if anybody was hanging around back there in the days leading up to the night she went missing?"

"No, I didn't notice anybody back there. And nobody else mentioned anything about somebody being back there either."

"I don't suppose there's a camera in the back lot, is there?" Astra asks.

"There is, but Sheriff Paulson already got the footage from Dale. There wasn't anything on the tape. It was just Emily getting into her car and driving off," she replies.

"How do you know that?" I ask.

"Oh. Right," she says. "My sister is dating one of Sheriff Paulson's deputies. He told her, and she told me."

Astra cuts a glance at me. "Sheriff Paulson had better tighten up the flow of information coming out of his office ASAP."

I nod. "Agreed."

The girl pales and looks mortified. "I'm sorry. I didn't mean for anybody to get into trouble. I just—"

"Nobody's in trouble," I say gently. "But when we're investigating a crime, it's important that information doesn't get leaked out like that. You didn't do anything wrong though. So, don't worry. We'll figure it out."

Kira pauses and lowers her head as she dabs her eyes with her tissue. Her face is red and splotchy, and her lips are quivering. In the heat of an investigation, it's sometimes hard to remember that some of the people we talk to are just kids. Though almost an adult, legally speaking, Kira is just that—a kid. A kid whose best friend has gone missing. And it's not hard to see she's having a really tough time with Emily's disappearance.

"I know this is hard for you, Kira," I say softly. "And I'm sorry we have to ask you these questions. We're just trying to find her, and unfortunately, you're the last person who saw her that night."

"Okay," she says without looking up.

"Kira, do you know if Emily was seeing anybody?" Astra asks. "Like maybe seeing him in secret or something? Her parents didn't think she was, but we were your age once, and we didn't always tell our folks everything."

Kira shakes her head. "No, she does tell her parents everything. She's annoyingly honest with them sometimes," she says with a laugh that immediately fades away, an expression of guilt crossing her face. "And no, she isn't seeing anybody. She's shy around boys. She's never even kissed a boy. Besides, she's focused on school."

"Her parents said she was NYU-bound," I say. "To be a doctor, right?"

"Pediatrician. She loves kids," Kira tells us. "She volunteers in the children's ward down at the hospital. Does a lot of work with kids."

"She sounded like a wonderful girl," Astra says.

Kira looks over at Astra. "Why do you keep referring to her in the past tense?" she asks. "You're both doing it. Do you know if—" I hold up my hand to cut her off before she gets rolling down a line of questions we can't answer for her. She's a sharp girl. Normally, I'm very conscientious about not using the past tense when talking about a victim when we don't know if they're dead or not. The use of tense, while a small thing to most, can tell you a lot about a person's thoughts on the matter of a missing person. It's a small piece of the bigger puzzle, but something as simple as verb tense has helped me break cases before.

For instance, Mr. Strauss earlier was referring to Emily in the past tense. That tells me he's anticipating that his daughter is already dead. Mrs. Strauss referred to Emily in the present, indicating she believes her daughter is alive. It's sometimes nothing. It's sometimes merely hope or resignation. But once in a while, it provides a keen insight into somebody's mind. It can create false hope or subject somebody to a powerful wave of grief, and I'm silently kicking myself for being so damn careless. I should have known better.

"We don't know anything at this point, Kira," I say, trying to put the toothpaste back into the tube. "Right now, we're still gathering information—"

"Was she one of the girls who were found in the park?" Kira presses.

Astra shakes her head. "No, she was not one of the girls in the park. I give you my word on that."

"But you think she's dead. Don't you?" Kira counters, unwilling to let it go.

"Kira, we don't know anything yet. Completely honest," I tell her. "Right now, Emily is just missing. For all we know, she took off with a boy she met—"

"She didn't, though. I told you, she's not like that. She wouldn't just take off with some boy," she argues. "She doesn't have a boyfriend."

The girl is starting to get worked up and angry, but I know it isn't us she's angry with. She's angry and hurt that her best friend is missing. I get it. I understand her frustration, worry, fear, and anger better than most. I've been there.

I reach across the table and take Kira's hand, giving it a light squeeze. She looks at me and I can see the agony in her eyes.

"We're doing everything we can to bring her home," I say gently. "Right now, the best thing you can do is keep a good thought for her and wrack your brain and try to come up with anything that might help us do that."

She looks down at our hands, and as the tears spill down her cheeks, I can see some of the wind going out of her sails. Kira sniffs again and nods as she raises her gaze to mine.

"I don't think there's anything I can think of that will help," she mutters, her voice colored with her frustration. "But I'll try."

"That's all we ask. Thank you."

I give her my card, and Astra and I leave the coffee house without anything significant to trumpet. We do, however, have confirmation of the fact that Emily was a socially awkward girl who didn't have a boyfriend. Teenage girls might hide things from their parents, but they wouldn't hide them from their best friends, so I think we can take those two things to the bank.

It's not much. They're just small bits of information that, on the surface, don't seem like big deals. But we're in the business of accumulating all the data points we can and trying to create a picture with them—a picture that will lead us to our suspect and hopefully save a life. Right now, I'm not feeling so bullish on the latter part of that, but I'm trying to keep be hopeful that we can find Emily Strauss before anything happens to her.

I just have a sinking feeling deep down in my gut that this is going to get a lot worse before it gets better.

CHAPTER FOURTEEN

Anderson Realty Building; Annenberg, ND

"ALL RIGHT, PEOPLE, TALK TO ME," I CALL OUT AS Astra and I return to the office. "What have you managed to dig up so far?"

Astra sets the tray of sandwiches down on a table and then starts to hand them out to everybody. I follow that up with bags of chips and bottles of soda.

"Thanks for lunch, boss," Rick says.

"Thank Astra. I was content to let you all starve," I reply with a grin.

I give them all a few minutes to dig into their lunches and take the opportunity to tuck into mine. It was a busy morning, and I didn't have anything to eat, which my rumbling stomach reminded me about on our way back to the command post.

"All right," I say around a mouthful of roasted chicken sandwich. "What did you guys find while we were gone?"

Mo takes a quick drink then wipes her mouth and taps the stack of folders sitting on her desk. Her expression is grim.

"I've got missing indigenous girls who fit the physical profile going back more than twenty years, Blake," she starts. "More than forty of them in surrounding counties."

"We've only been able to background about six of them so far," Nina says.

"All six are still alive, according to their social media profiles," Rick adds. "They just moved away from Annenberg without telling anybody."

It's frustrating, but that's part of the job. I let out a sigh. "All right, well, we knew we were going to get some of those," I admit. "That doesn't change the mission. There are still a lot of girls we need to account for."

I lean back in my seat and finish chewing the bit of sandwich in my mouth, my mind spinning. That's a lot of girls. More than I'd been anticipating—and over a far longer period of time to boot. I know that not all forty of the files Mo pulled are going to be connected to our guy. But I have a gut feeling some of them will. More than a few. And the idea that our guy has been operating for more than two decades and nobody has gotten even a whiff of him in all that time is mind-boggling. It's frightening because I don't know whether it's because of a lack of concern or utter incompetence.

"We'll need to verify these girls have some connection to our cases before we do anything," Astra gives words to my thoughts.

"Agreed," I reply. "Mo, any details or leads in the reports worth pursuing?"

Mo shakes her head. "No. And to be honest, the files on these girls are thin," she admits. "Really thin. It doesn't look like there was much practical investigating done. Everything is pretty pro forma. I mean, all the right boxes have been checked, but details are scarce. It's like nobody was even trying to find them."

"That's what has Deputy Koda so upset," I nod. "And I can't blame her for it. The disparity between the way indigenous and nonindigenous victims are treated is real."

"It certainly looks that way," Mo says. "These case files are all marked closed-no resolution. They've all been written off. The few that have any follow-up to them at all have them put down as runaways. A couple of them are suspected of running off with boyfriends according to the notes."

It's a depressing thought, but it's better I don't get myself too worked up just yet—not until we know how many of the forty or so she pulled belong to our current case.

"How about you, Lucas?" I ask.

"Well, your friend Deputy Koda brought in another box of case files of missing nonindigenous girls from surrounding counties—"

"Surrounding counties? How did she—"

"Don't know, didn't ask, don't care," Lucas cuts me off. "That's above my pay grade."

That makes me crack a smile. The boy's getting savvy after all. "All right, fair enough."

"Anyway, I've got two dozen that fit the physical profile," he goes on. "The earliest one is from 1999. So, it fits the same general time frame as Mo's cases."

I whistle low as I take in the potential enormity of what we're dealing with. More than twenty years' worth of bodies that could be attributable to one person is not what I'd been expecting when we walked in here. I have no doubt we're going to thin that stack considerably. I'm reminded of a case I worked with my good friend Paxton Arrington a few years ago in catching Alvin Perry, a horrific monster who'd claimed over forty lives over the course of decades.

My gut is telling me our guy is bad, but I just don't think he's going to turn out to be quite as prolific. However, I'm almost positive we're going to have a lot more than the four we're looking at right now. I just don't know how many more yet, and I'm eager to find out since it might help bring a little peace to the families.

"All right. So, we've got more than seventy case files to dig through and no guarantees we're going to find a connection. We don't even know if these girls are still missing," Lucas says. "This should be fun."

"It's the job, kid," I shrug. "Nobody ever said it was all glamour all the time."

"A little glamour some of the time might be nice," Lucas replies with a grin.

"Then you're in the wrong squad," I reply. "We are not the glam squad."

"You should go to Organized Crime if you want face time on the news," Mo quips. "OC loves getting their faces on camera."

"That's right," I say. "We work behind the scenes and try to avoid the cameras. We're not in this for the glory. We're in it to do some good and tackle all the challenges thrown our way."

"You've always loved a good challenge," Astra says.

"True enough. That's why I love this work," I say and look pointedly at the stacks of files. "And I'd say this time we've got our work cut out for us."

"Then I guess we've got to get to it," Lucas smiles.

"Let's do it," I say. "Everybody, grab a handful of files—you too, Rick and Nina. We should each have eleven or twelve? That about right?"

"Close enough," Astra says.

"Great, what are we looking for?" Lucas asks.

"The first thing we need to find out is whether these girls are alive. Check for social media footprints, check for anything in the public sphere—check for birth records under their names. Maybe they moved away to have a child," I tell them. "Check for utility bills, cable bills, car registrations, library cards—literally anything in the public sphere that can be tied to the girls and prove they're still alive and are out there somewhere."

Heads nod around the room as I explain the strategy. Everybody seems to be on the same page and ready to go, which is a good thing. Spreading out the workload is going to make this operation a lot more efficient, and with any luck, we'll be through all the case files by the end of the day. I feel like the clock is ticking and time is running out for Emily Strauss. The offender's window between abductions and kills seems to be getting shorter—which, for all we know, means he might already be scouting out his next victim.

It's troubling to me, though, that if this guy has been moving in the background for the last two decades, cutting a bloody swath through the communities and nobody's picked up on it, that he'd suddenly do something shocking—and public—which is guaranteed to put eyes on him. What was the motivation for the change? It wasn't because the Bureau was in town and looking into matters. The change in his MO occurred before we ever got to Annenberg. Something changed though. Something that's potentially making the man change his entire pattern of behavior. And that's a little concerning.

But first things first. We need to separate the wheat from the chaff and get a clear picture of what it is we're looking at right now. All my conjecture isn't doing anything but adding more unnecessary noise to it all. We need facts. Which means we need to get to work.

"Any questions?" I ask.

I look around the room, but nobody seems to have any questions.

"All right, folks," I say. "Let's hit it."

We spend most of the rest of the day poring over the files in front of us. We're running the names through every database we can think of, trying to match them up with social media profiles or anything else that's out there. My first two files are both indigenous girls and are busts—meaning the girls are alive and well. They're both just living well away from Annenberg.

It seems like there are a lot of people who can't wait to get out of here. Maybe it's because I essentially grew up in Seattle that I think a place like this town is kind of idyllic. Perhaps it was because I was born in the small town of Cockeysville and still have some residual and possibly overinflated feelings of what a small town is like that I'm fond of them. It's not that I don't love Seattle. I do. But there is something about small towns I enjoy.

It could also be that I'm romanticizing the small-town life. I was young when I left Maryland for Seattle, so I may be simply looking through rose-colored glasses regarding life in a small town.

Clearly, not everybody agrees with me since there is such a mass exodus of young people from the area—something bolstered by having found the girl in my stack of files, Janelle Hollins, living her best life in Florida with her very attractive husband and their three children.

"Wow," Astra says and leans back in her chair.

"Yeah," I reply as a sense of dread descends over me.

As we've come up with possible victims, we've been hanging their photos on the whiteboard Sheriff Paulson loaned us. We've put them in chronological order with their names and the dates they went missing below the photo, and when we've gone through the last of the files, we've put together a mosaic of faces that stretches back twenty-two years. Our first victim, an indigenous girl from the nearby Turtle Mountain reservation named Amber Blackrock, went missing in February 2000, and there hasn't been a peep from her since. Not one posting on social media, no utility bills or car registered in her name, no credit cards or library card in her name in more than two decades.

In all, we have twenty-six possible additional victims of the man responsible for the murders of Juliette Templeton, Tamara Gray, Lauren Dunphy, and the presumptive abduction of Emily Strauss. Thirty girls in twenty-two years—four in the past couple of months alone. He might not be the most prolific killer in history, but he's still an absolute monster. He's been busy, and the worst part is, he's not done yet.

As I take in the faces of the girls, it feels like they're staring back at me. It feels like they're imploring me to help them, and I feel a stitch of pain in my heart. The thought of the pain and misery the families of these girls must be enduring is overwhelming. Thankfully, before I can be consumed by the wave of emotion that's cresting within me, my cellphone rings, pulling me back to the present. I slip it out of my pocket, connect the call, and press it to my ear.

"Wilder."

As I listen to the voice on the other end of the line, I feel that sense of dread inside of me growing even thicker.

"We'll be right there," I say and disconnect the call. The expression of disgust and despair that crosses my face is enough to catch everyone's attention.

"You all right, boss?" Rick asks.

"You look a little pale all of a sudden," Nina agrees.

"Yeah, I'm fine," I reply.

"What's going on?" Lucas asks.

I take a swallow of my soda and set the bottle down. "You guys can knock off for the night. Go get some dinner, go back to the hotel, and unwind for a bit. When you go, make sure you lock this place up tight," I say as I get to my feet. "Astra, with me."

"Where to?"

"That was Paulson," I reply with a sigh. "Different park this time."

"Oh, no."

CHAPTER FIFTEEN

Spellman Running Park; Annenberg, ND

THE SUN IS NOTHING BUT A GLOWING THUMBNAIL ON THE horizon as it slips behind the distant mountains in the west. And to the east, the purple and blue hues of the night are rolling across the sky like the evening tide as we pull into a parking lot that is buzzing with activity. Half a dozen sheriff's cruisers sit in the lot with their lights spinning, a fire truck and ambulance sit off to the side, and there is an army of uniformed people milling about.

"I hope Paulson had the good sense to cordon off the crime scene," Astra mutters.

"I'm sure he did. He's got good instincts," I say. "But let's go and see for ourselves just in case."

We climb out of the SUV, badge a deputy walking by, and ask him where the scene is. He points to a copse of trees about a hundred yards off the main footpath through the park. I thank him and we turn and head for the trees. I pull my jacket around myself a little tighter. With the sun going down, it's starting to get cold. We step through the trees to find a ring of yellow crime scene tape strung around the trees.

"Guess he cordoned off the scene after all," I comment.

"Will small wonders never cease?"

I flash her a glum smile as we step beneath the tape and into the clearing that's ringed by tall pine trees. The air is saturated with their scent, and I can't help but be reminded of those little trees you hang from your rearview mirror. Well, that and the antiseptic Pine-Sol odor that seems to be a standard in almost any medical examiner's office. People seem to think a heavy pine scent masks a wide variety of foul odors, but in my experience, it only seems to amplify them. That's why I always equate the smell of pine with death.

Paulson is standing off to the side with one of his deputies who's setting up a stand-up Klieg light at the edge of the scene. He notices us walking toward him and meets us halfway. In the center of the clearing is a pile of leaves, dirt, and branches, which would seem ordinary enough for a setting like this if not for the pale hand sticking out from beneath all the debris.

"Is it Emily Strauss?" I ask.

"We're not sure yet. I wanted lighting and cameras for proper documentation before we got started. I also wanted to make sure you were here as well," he replies. "But if I were a bettin' man, I'd say it's probably her. That looks like a young girl's hand."

"I agree. Look at the nail polish. That's definitely a young girl's color palette," I reply. "And thanks for waiting."

"Of course."

Paulson's eyes shift to the nails, and he nods. Though the nails are chipped and cracked, there is still enough to see the sparkling purple color they'd once been. The sparkle is undoubtedly glitter, which suggests to me that it's a young girl beneath all the rubble.

In my experience, there just aren't a lot of older women wearing glitter on their nails.

"Who found her?" Astra asks.

He grimaces. "A couple of young kids. They were runnin' around back here while their mother was jogging," he tells us. "This park is used primarily by runners."

Paulson's deputies get their generator cranked up, and the Kliegs come on with a loud snap, casting a harsh flood of light on the debris pile in the center. Astra and I glove up, then move to the center of the clearing and start picking off the leaves and branches. With his man filming, Paulson gloves up and joins us.

It's not long before we have the pile cleared and are brushing away the leaves and other debris. I squat down and gingerly brush the leaves away from her face, and we confirm that it is Emily Strauss.

"Aw, damn," Paulson mutters.

He puts his hands on his hips and turns away, overcome with emotion. My first thought is for Emily's parents. In my mind's eye, I can still see the hopeful Mrs. Strauss and her stoic husband. They were both teetering on the edge before, and I fear this is going to push them over. This is going to break them, and the damage will probably be irreparable. My heart breaks for them.

Astra and I get back to work, uncovering the rest of her remains. Just like the others, she's been dismembered, her body completely disarticulated at the joints. It's a grim thought, but we caught a break by those kids finding Emily. She's still fresh and hasn't had time to decompose, which will allow us to get a good look at the damage done to her body. Even now, I can see there are large pieces of her that are missing around the torso and legs.

"Jesus," Paulson mutters. "Why would somebody do this? Why would they cut her up like this?"

I shake my head. "It could be a forensic countermeasure. It could be this guy just gets off on torturing his victims. It's difficult to say at this point."

Paulson looks over at me, his face pinched and tight. "How can you two be so removed from all this? It's like it doesn't even touch you."

"We've been doing this a long time, Sheriff, and we've seen some terrible things," Astra tells him. "We've seen some of the most terrible things humans do to each other."

"Honestly, it never really gets easier. But you get used to it. You learn to compartmentalize," I add. "We wouldn't be able to do our jobs if we let ourselves be paralyzed by our emotions. So, we lock them away and focus on the case—on catching the offenders and getting justice for the victims."

"And after that, we go home and drink until we forget," Astra chimes in.

We all share a laugh, but it's uneasy—Paulson isn't sure if she's kidding. She's not, of course. But I don't want to confirm that for him.

"We also have the added layer of removal because this isn't our community. We don't know these people, so it's easier for us to remain objective," I tell him.

"Don't beat yourself up, Sheriff. Let yourself feel what you feel," Astra says. "My only advice is to be sure you can lock it away when you need to focus. When you need to kick your brain into logic mode. If not, step away and take a few minutes. Just remember that these people—this entire community—are looking to you for answers and leadership."

"Yeah, don't I know it," he murmured sardonically.

"Heavy is the head that wears the crown, Sheriff."

He gives me a wry smile. "Apparently so."

"Sheriff?"

We turn and see one of his deputies waving him over. Paulson turns back to me.

"Excuse me."

He gets to his feet and walks off, and I turn back to Astra, who is examining Emily's head closely. Her brows are furrowed, and she's concentrating on something.

"What is it?" I ask.

"Can you give me a light?"

"Sure."

I pull a flashlight out of my pocket and turn it on as Astra is forcing Emily's jaws apart with a wet cracking sound that's thoroughly disturbing.

"What do you have?" I ask.

"There's something in her mouth."

Astra pats her pockets and then looks around. When her eyes fall on one of the crime scene techs standing at the periphery of the light, Astra waves.

"Hey, bring your kit," she calls. "I need a pair of forceps."

The tech comes over and sets her kit down, doing her level best to avoid looking at what's left of Emily's body. The tech is mid-twenties, I'd guess, with black hair cut short, dark eyes, and cool, pale skin. She's wearing a pair of protective goggles over her eyes, blue coveralls, and rubber boots. With her back practically to Emily's body, she opens her kit and hands Astra a pair of forceps.

"Thank you," Astra says.

The girl nods but doesn't say anything. She's starting to look a little green around the gills, which reminds me of the first crime scene we took Mo to. I don't want to embarrass her, but I also don't want her contaminating my crime scene.

"If you need to take a breath, just step away. No shame in it," I say.

"I'm fine," she replies, her shaky voice sounding anything but fine.

"Haven't been to many crime scenes, huh?" I ask.

"Not like this."

I glance over and see that Astra's already got the forceps in Emily's mouth. She's clenching her jaw and frowning as she concentrates.

"Got it," she says.

Astra withdraws the forceps and with them, what looks like a folded-up piece of paper. Setting the forceps aside, she unfolds the paper, her frown deepening. She looks up at me and then hands over the note. I take it from her and read the words scrawled across the paper.

"All for one, one for all," I read out, and then frown. "The Three Musketeers? How is that relevant?"

"Your guess is as good as mine," Astra says.

"McCumber High School," the tech utters.

"What's that?" I ask.

"McCumber High School," she repeats. "Their mascot is the Musketeer. The McCumber Musketeers. The school's motto is that... all for one, one for all."

Astra and I exchange a glance, not knowing for sure how the high school fits into the case, but it does somehow. I turn back to the tech, and she gives me a shrug.

"I was McCumber class of '14," she explains.

"All right. That's good information. Thank you," I say. "Do you have a plastic evidence bag handy?"

"Sure do," she says and produces one from her kit.

I drop the note into the bag and seal it, then jot down the necessary information to document the chain of custody. That done, I stand up.

"Okay, we'll get out of your hair and let you do your work," I say. "Thanks for all your help..."

"Kim," she replies. "Kim Olave."

"Well, thank you for your help, Kim Olave."

"Of course. Glad I was able to help."

Astra and I walk off to find Paulson and to let Kim Olave do all the proper documentation of Emily's body. I glance back and see that she's still looking shaky. But she also looks determined to do her job, which I silently applaud her for. It's not always easy to push through stuff that makes you uncomfortable and do your job.

We find Paulson standing off to the side talking on the phone. We give him a little space to finish his conversation. He sees us and puts a finger up, telling us to give him a minute. I look down again at the note in the bag I'm holding. *All for one, one for all.* The connection to the high school is obvious. It's up to us, though, to figure out what that connection is.

"So?" he asks as he slips his phone back into his pocket. "What do you think?"

I hand him the bag, and he quickly scans the note, his face darkening. Paulson's jaw is clenched, and it's taking all his effort to keep from balling up the note in his hand. He hands it back to me and shakes his head.

"McCumber," he muses. "What's all this got to do with the school?"

"That's what we need to find out," I tell him. "Can you think of anybody who harbors a grudge against the school?"

Paulson shakes his head. "Not off the top of my head, no. The school's a pretty tight-knit community. Hell, the entire town is for that matter."

The minute the question had come out of my mouth, though, I knew it wasn't right. It didn't fit. It isn't a grudge against the school. The four girls didn't even all go to McCumber. Two of them went to the other high school—Frazier. So, that makes no sense.

"Why do you think he didn't bury Emily's body like he did with the others?" Paulson asks. "I mean, you'd think he'd want to hide what he's done."

"It could be that he's devolving. He might be feeling the pressure and is starting to spin out," Astra offers. "He's going off script and is getting a little careless."

"And what happens when he spins out?" Paulson asks.

"It's a good question," she replies. "Something's changed with this guy."

Paulson gives me a look then turns back to Astra. "What's changed?"

"Don't know yet. But if I had to guess, I'd say it's probably something big. Like something life-altering big," she replies.

"Why do you think that?"

"Because we believe this man has been preying on girls in surrounding communities going back twenty years," she says. "But he didn't start hunting in Annenberg until he took Juliette Templeton."

Paulson's eyes widen, and he looks from Astra to me, and back again, an expression of shock etched into his features.

"You can't be serious," he says.

"It's a theory at this point," I tell him. "There's still a lot up in the air and facts we have to nail down. But it's possible."

Paulson takes his hat off and runs his hand through his hair. "Jesus."

"As I said, don't get too freaked out just yet. There's still a lot that needs to be confirmed, Sheriff Paulson."

"I'll try. But it's … a lot," he says.

"It is. And it can feel overwhelming," Astra says. "But don't let your people see you feeling overwhelmed."

"I'll do my best," he nods.

"I'd like you to have Emily's remains sent to Minot with the others," I tell him.

"I figured you would," he says. "I already have my people making the arrangements."

"That's terrific. Thank you, Sheriff."

"Of course. Anything I can do to help you catch this monster."

A moment of silence descends over us as we watch the tech working with Emily's remains. She's putting them all into a body bag and still looks shaky, but she's holding it together well enough.

"I can't believe this is happening in my town," he says. "And has been happening for the last two decades. How could we have not known?"

"Don't blame yourself, Sheriff," Astra tells him. "These kinds of killers are adept at blending in and avoiding detection."

"Yeah, well, he doesn't seem to be hiding anymore."

"He's not. He's definitely sending a message," I say.

"What's the message?" Paulson asks.

"That he's not done. Not by a long stretch."

CHAPTER SIXTEEN

The House of Sugar; Annenberg, ND

WITH LEONARD COHEN'S DEEP, SMOOTH VOICE coming out of his car's speakers, the man glanced at his watch and smiled. It was just about eight o'clock. The sky was blanketed with clouds, blotting out the light of the moon and making the world around him even darker. It was like a sign. The back door to the bakery opened and a teenage boy and girl came bustling out laughing and joking with each other. Scott Parham and Nadia Wilkes.

"Quittin' time," he said.

Scotty was the captain and star pitcher of the McCumber baseball team. Athletic. Smart. The kid had dreams of going to the Show, but the man didn't think he'd ever make it past Triple-A. At best. His slider was average, and his fastball didn't have the pop the majors required. He was a star in Annenberg, but would be batting practice meat anywhere else. Parham was the classic case of a big ol' fish in a teeny, tiny pond.

Nadia, on the other hand, was going places. She was tall, lean, and had a beautiful figure. She was a classic Hollywood beauty. But more than that, the girl was smart as a whip. Top of her class at Frazier High with an interest in science. If there was somebody who was going to find a cure for cancer or a way to repair broken bodies better and more efficiently, the man was putting his money on her. It's too bad she wasn't around when he was her age.

The man watched as Scott pulled Nadia into a tight embrace and kissed her with the sort of passion only teenagers can seem to muster. That was surprising. He'd always had a good pulse on the town of Annenberg. Always listened when people talked—people had always liked sharing things with him. He was always up on the latest bit of gossip making the rounds. Or so he'd thought. That Scotty Parham and Nadia Wilkes were an item was news to him.

After their romantic interlude, he watched as they both got into their cars and drove away, heading in opposite directions. When they were gone, the man shut the car off and then got out. The buildings around him were dark. The other businesses were already closed for the day, but Rachel, the owner of the House of Sugar, liked to get everything prepped for the next day early, so her employees were there until eight. All except for Brooke.

Brooke Haverson was an eighteen-year-old high school student at Frazier who came from one of Annenberg's wealthy and influential families. She was a middling student, a pretty good softball player, and an extremely popular girl at school. She didn't have the athletic prowess or the grades to get into an elite school the way Emily or Erin Strauss could, but she was set to go to a local state school and enroll in the veterinary program. That was her plan.

Unfortunately for Brooke, she'd caught the man's eye. He'd been keeping close tabs on her for a while now, learning her every move and habit. He learned what she liked, didn't like, who her friends were, who she didn't like. He'd ferreted out all her dirty little secrets. He knew Brooke inside and out. He thought he knew her better than she even knew herself.

The man walked across the parking lot softly singing the Leonard Cohen song that had been playing in his car before he got out.

"I smile when I'm angry. I cheat and I lie. I do what I have to do to get by. But I know what is wrong, and I know what is right, and I'd die for the truth, in my secret life…"

When he finished the line, he giggled to himself. Cohen's words struck a chord within him. He had a secret life. People saw him one way and believed they knew him. But they only knew what he allowed them to see. Once upon a time, he'd been like Brooke. Like all these girls. He came from a wealthy, influential family. He was a beloved figure in Annenberg, and he was worshipped by man. He'd had a future all laid out for himself— just like these girls.

But life seldom worked out the way you planned. Just ask Juliette, Tamara, Emily, and Lauren. Ask all the others. Life will always find ways to throw curveballs at you and knock you off whatever perch you're on. And when you're at your lowest, when your life has conspired to push you all the way down to rock bottom, you'll find out who your real friends are. You'll find out who cares about you.

When the man found himself at rock bottom, when the life he'd planned out had been ripped away from him, he learned that he had no real friends. He learned that nobody truly cared about him. Those people in his life he'd counted on all drifted away. In his greatest time of need, the man found himself alone. Utterly and completely alone. They'd cast him aside. They all had. They'd thrown him out like yesterday's trash and forgotten about him.

But they were going to remember. He was going to make them all remember him. And when he was done, they would never forget his name. Ever.

"The people of Annenberg are going to remember me forever," he muttered to himself.

He stood at the back door to the bakery beneath the camera that he'd disabled a week ago. The man reached out and pressed the doorbell button and stepped back. A couple of moments later, the door opened, and Brooke stood there smiling at him.

"Hey," she said, her voice tinged with surprise. "If you're looking for Rachel, she's not here, but I can—"

Brooke never got to finish the sentence because the man drove his fist straight into her face. It connected with a sound like a baseball hitting an old leather mitt. Brooke's head snapped back, and she crumpled to the floor in a heap, out cold before she ever hit the cold tile.

The man walked down the stairs and stepped into the basement and smiled. Brooke was awake. He'd cleaned the blood that had spilled from her nose after he'd punched her and got her looking fresh-faced again. But her cheeks were red, and she wore an expression of terror as tears raced down her face.

Brooke let out a mighty scream that made him smile and shake his head at the futility of the effort. The basement was windowless, and the walls were all soundproofed. She could scream all she wanted, and nobody was going to hear her. The man was nothing if not careful. It was why he'd been doing what he did for so long.

"Please," she begged. "Please, don't do this. You—you don't have to do this."

"Just calm down. Calm down and everything will be all right."

She sniffed loudly, and though she was trying to control herself, her body was shaking wildly. Brooke was stripped naked, her hands and feet bound to the corners of the upright steel frame he'd built a long time ago.

"Please," she said with another sniff. "Don't do this."

The man stepped forward and reached out. Brooke tried to flinch away from him, but her bonds held her fast. He gently caressed her face and then tucked a lock of hair behind her ear. He looked her up and down, taking in her curves and the sturdy set of her body. She was a healthy girl with some meat on her bones. He liked that about her. He thought it was one of her best qualities. Physically speaking, anyway.

The man slid his hands from Brooke's shoulders down to her knees then back up again, firmly squeezing the fleshier pieces of her body. He enjoyed the tenderness of her body beneath his hands and pressed his fingers even deeper into her flesh. Brooke's cheeks were wet with tears, and she was trembling violently.

"Please don't. Please—"

He gave her a gentle smile as he removed his hands. The man turned and walked back to his worktable and unrolled the black leather case revealing his set of knives. It was a new set he'd purchased online a couple of weeks ago. He was looking forward to trying them out. He selected the butcher knife and ran the tip of his finger along the slightly rounded tip. The edge of it gleamed sharply in the fluorescent lights overhead.

The man glanced over at Brooke. Her eyes were comically wide and laser-focused on the blade in his hand. Her mouth hung wide open, and a stuttering gasp passed through her lips. Brooke shook her head as if to deny what was about to happen.

"No…. no—no—no," she said, her voice quavering. "I'll—I'll do anything. Please don't—"

"You're perfect, you know," he said.

"Please—"

"They're never going to forget my name after this," he said.

"What? Who? Who's not—"

"People think they can just throw me away like trash—I'm going to make sure they never forget who I am. After all this is over, I'm going to be immortalized. This town, a hundred years from now, will always remember me," he said, his voice low and calm.

The man looked at her with hunger in his eyes. He turned away from the table with the knife in his hand, and as he approached Brooke, she struggled and thrashed at her bonds, but they held her fast. As the light glinted off the edge of the blade, flashing across her skin, she let out a sharp, blood-curdling shriek.

CHAPTER SEVENTEEN

Anderson Realty Building; Annenberg, ND

"MY GOD," PAULSON GASPS, A HORRIFIED expression on his face.

He's standing in front of the whiteboard looking at the photos of all the victims we believe are attributable to our guy. Rick, Nina, Lucas, and Mo spent a good portion of the evening after we left running down the names on all the files we pulled. They still haven't found anything on them. As far as the world is concerned, the twenty-six faces staring back at us have simply vanished into thin air.

Sheriff Paulson came by early this morning to see what we've put together so far. After we dropped our theory on him at the Strauss crime scene last night, he seemed pretty shaken up, so Astra and I thought it best that we give him a visual of where we are. Lucas, Rick, Nina, and Mo are still back at the hotel, taking a little extra time after pretty much pulling an all-nighter. Fruitlessly as it turns out, unfortunately.

"Thirty girls over twenty-two years," Paulson says. "I—I can't believe that."

"Right now, the only ones confirmed are the four from town—Juliette, Lauren, Tamara, and Emily," I tell him. "The other twenty-six are from surrounding counties. Eighteen indigenous girls, eight of other ethnicities."

"But we should stress that not all of these girls may be victims of our guy," Astra points out. "It's also possible they all are. We won't know until we find out if these girls are alive or not."

I nod. "Exactly. That's what we were telling you at the Strauss scene last night," I say. "There are still a lot of unknowns at this point, but we can say definitively that the four girls in town are linked."

"Because of the condition of their bodies?" he asks.

I nod. "It's a signature. It's his signature," I say. "That's why we need to get additional intel on these twenty-six. We need to find out—"

"If they're dead, and if so, how they died. Specifically, we need to know the condition of the bodies," Paulson finishes.

"Exactly right," I reply.

"How is it nobody put this together before?" Paulson asks.

"Because nobody was looking," I reply. "You might want to speak with your Deputy Koda about the disparity in how crimes against indigenous versus non-indigenous people are handled—"

"Come on, now," Paulson argues. "You can't hold me responsible for how other counties handle their caseloads."

"I'm not. But that sort of disparity is in your department as well, Sheriff. Of the eighteen missing indigenous girls, fourteen of them are within your jurisdiction," I counter. "They're outside town proper, but are still within your jurisdiction. And yet, their files are all flagged closed-no resolution. It was Deputy Koda who alerted us to these."

A grim but thoughtful look crosses his face. Paulson turns away for a moment, seeming to be ordering his thoughts. It's not difficult to see that he's troubled by what he's seeing and hearing. He finally turns to me, that same expression on his face.

"It would be easy for me to put this all on Sheriff Boden—he was my predecessor," he says. "But this is my fault too. I've let things slip through the cracks and haven't followed up on cases as diligently as I should have. I simply accepted the findings on cases—especially those outside town proper—and didn't dig when I should have."

"Well, the good news is that you can atone for those shortcomings, Sheriff Paulson. And you can help bring peace to some families who need it," Astra tells him. "You can help me by trying to close out some of these twenty-six other cases. We need to know how many are attributable to our guy."

"What makes you think they are?" he asks. "I mean, don't serial killers usually stick to one type? I see black, white, indigenous, Hispanic—"

"One type doesn't necessarily mean one ethnicity. These girls are all around the same age and all have the same body type. His preference in this case might not be racial. It might be a specific type," I explain.

He nods and turns back to the board, taking in all the pictures again. I can see that this is impacting Paulson pretty hard, and he's taking it personally, which I think is a good thing. He should take this personally, and he should be looking to atone for his shortcomings. Paulson should be seeking justice for these girls—all of them. And I'm glad to see that he's at least willing to take this criticism seriously. It's an important first step in not only closing these cases and bringing justice to these families but also in rectifying much broader patterns of injustice in this community.

"All right, so how can I help?" he asks.

"You can start by following up on all these open cases—the twenty-six we've ID'd as potentials," I tell him. "Use your contacts wherever you have them. Squeeze them hard and see if you can track them down. We need to know if they're alive. And if so, where they are."

"And if they're dead, we need all the data we can get on it," Astra adds.

"I can do that," Paulson says. "I will do that."

"Good. Use their social security numbers, driver's license numbers—anything you can think of to get information on them," I tell him.

"I'm on it. I give you my word," he says. "I know we've failed these girls—I know *I've* failed these girls—and I'm going to do everything I can to make things right."

"That's good to hear, Sheriff."

It's great that Paulson is determined to set things right. It means we can get him to do all the dirty work we'd have to get approval from Ayad to do. We don't have enough for warrants. Not even close. And Ayad would shut us down quicker than I can say my own name. But Paulson can dig into areas we can't without a warrant. So, if he wants to make good on his shortcomings and try to get justice for the girls who've gone missing on his watch, he'll do what he has to do and deal with any repercussions later.

He turns to Astra. "Last night, you said something changed with this guy and that's why he's killing girls in town," he says. "I've been thinking about it all night. What did you mean by that? What's changed?"

"What's changed with this guy specifically, I can't say," Astra explains. "I just meant that his hunting habits have changed."

"I don't understand."

"Most serials have a well-defined comfort zone. They don't often hunt where they live," I chime in. "That was why I wanted the files from the surrounding area. We wanted to verify his hunting ground and put together a geographic profile."

"A geographic profile?"

Astra nods. "It gives us a better understanding of his hunting map," she says. "His comfort zone will likely be in the center, and it may well be where he lives."

"That's interesting. I'm learnin' a lot from you folks," he replies. "But I pray to God I never have to use it again."

"We hope so too, Sheriff," I say.

His phone rings, and he excuses himself then steps away to take the call. His face pales almost immediately, telling me something happened.

"Yeah, thanks. We'll be right there," he says and disconnects the call, then looks over at us. "Another girl's been taken."

"It's okay, Rachel," Paulson says. "Just, tell us what happened."

Paulson is standing with his arm around the shoulder of the owner of the House of Sugar, Rachel Porter. She's tall, easily five-ten, with straight, mousy brown hair, brown eyes, and she is way skinnier than somebody who owns a bakery full of sugary treats should be. Porter is probably in her early forties, her eyes are red and puffy, her cheeks wet and splotchy, and her face is pinched and drawn.

She sniffs loudly and dabs at her eyes with the crumpled tissue in her hand. It's easy to see the affection between her and Paulson. They seem to have a level of comfort only people who've known each other for a long time can share. Paulson himself seems to be stricken and looks like he's holding back his own tears.

Porter looks at me and draws in a long, shuddering breath. "When I got here this morning to do the day's baking, I—I found the back door open," she said, her voice shaking. "Brooke's car was still here in the parking lot, and—like I said—the back door was open."

Porter buries her face in her hands and her body shakes with quiet sobs. Sheriff Paulson pulls her a little tighter, which makes Astra and I exchange a glance with each other. I catch Paulson's eye and gesture to the back door to let him know we're going to take a look and give him a minute with Rachel. He gives us a thankful nod and then pulls her into a tight embrace, letting her cry into his shoulder.

There are two patrol cars in the rear lot with their lights spinning. A ten-year-old silver Honda Accord is parked in the lot, which is presumably Brooke's. Astra and I walk over to the back door of the shop. I stop and look at the frame, running my hand along the smooth wood and cutting a glance at Astra.

"It's not splintered," I note. "Doesn't look like entry was forced."

"So, it looks like Brooke knew our guy. That means he could be a known member of the community," she offers.

"Could be," I reply and point to the exterior of the door. "Looks like he knocked on the door, got her to open it, then blitzed her."

There is a line of crimson droplets with thin rivulets running down the door. They're dry, which tells me it's been there a while.

"So, he punches her hard enough to draw blood then carries her off," Astra muses.

"Seems like it. I think it's the easiest explanation," I say.

Astra nods. "I agree," she says, then gestures to the camera above the door. "I hope that's working. It'll make our lives a hell of a lot easier."

"Right?"

Paulson walks Porter over to us, his arm still around her shoulders. She looks absolutely miserable. She looks so grief-stricken that you'd think it was her child who'd been taken. Porter dabs at her eyes with that tissue again and shakes her head.

"Brooke is such a sweet girl. Who'd want to hurt her?" she asks, her voice soft.

"We're not sure yet, Ms. Porter," Astra says. "But can you tell us if you have the footage for that camera? It'd be a big help."

"It was one of the first things I checked when I got here. Somebody disabled it," she says. "It looks like it stopped working about a week ago. I didn't think to check it before because this is a good area. Bad things just don't happen around Annenberg."

That's the second biggest lie people tell themselves, just behind parents believing their kids tell them everything. Bad things happen everywhere. Yeah, there are places like Annenberg that are statistically safer than other cities, but no place is ever one hundred percent safe.

"Ms. Porter, has Brooke mentioned anybody coming around a lot, maybe watching her or paying extra attention to her lately?" I ask.

She shakes her head. "No, nothing like that."

"It appears to us that she opened the back door willingly, which tells us that she might have known whoever took her—"

"What? No, that can't be," she gasps. "Who would have taken her?"

"That's what we're trying to find out, Ms. Porter," Astra says. "Did she have a habit of letting people in through the back at night?"

"No, absolutely not. She was always very conscientious about security," Porter says. "She never opened the door at night."

"Well, it seems like she did last night," I say. "Did she have a boyfriend?"

"Nobody serious," she replies. "Brooke didn't want to be saddled with one guy, you know? She dated around a bit."

"Okay, so is it possible one of the boys she was seeing stopped by?"

"I guess it's possible."

"All right, do you have names? Anybody she dated more seriously than anybody else?" Astra presses.

Porter screws up her face and seems to be thinking. I can tell she's reluctant to give us any names, not wanting to get anybody into trouble.

"Ms. Porter, we need names," I say.

"The boys she was seeing—they're good boys, Agents. I can't see either of them doing anything like this. I can't imagine either of them hurting her."

"And it's possible they didn't," Astra tells her. "But we need to talk to them anyway. We just need to ask some questions."

Paulson looks at her. "It's all right, Rachel. You can trust them," he says gently. "They're here to help."

She still hesitates, not wanting to set the small-town rumor mill going. I get it. With four—now five—girls missing, tensions in the town are high, and even the appearance of impropriety can be damning. Dragging two boys in for questioning, even if they're completely innocent, could still brand them as killers, facts be damned. So, I get it. But we still need those names.

Paulson turns to me. "Steven Roman and Matt Carson," he says. "Those are the boys she's been seeing."

Porter looks at him. "How do you know that?"

He shrugs. "It's my business to know what's going on around town. Besides, I'm friends with Roland," he says then turns to us. "That's Brooke's father."

"All right, that's a good place to start," I say.

As I watch Paulson trying to comfort Porter, I think about the dynamics of a small town, then add in everything we know about our guy so far. My gut tells me it's somebody she knows—somebody who's well-known in town perhaps. My gut also tells me it's neither Steven Roman nor Matt Carson. But still, we need to talk to them for the sake of doing our due diligence. Thinking about small-town dynamics, though, gives me an idea.

"Sheriff Paulson," I say. "Do you think you can get the word out that we're going to search for Brooke Haverson?"

He nods. "Yeah, of course. We can do that. I'll have my deputies start making calls," he says. "Where should we start the search?"

"I'm thinking we can get everybody together at the running park where we found Emily's body," I reply. "Have anybody willing to help meet there at, say, eight tomorrow morning?"

"Yeah, that sounds good," he nods. "That's a really good idea."

"Great," I reply. "Go ahead and get things working on your end, we'll start coordinating things on our end."

"Then we'll see you at Spellman tomorrow morning."

"We'll see you then, Sheriff."

CHAPTER EIGHTEEN

Anderson Realty Building; Annenberg, ND

PACE BACK AND FORTH IN FRONT OF OUR COMMAND POST with my phone pressed to my ear. The morning is crisp, and the azure sky overhead is cloudless. It's been a few days since I last spoke with April, and I wanted to check in on my sister. The line rings once and then twice before she answers the call.

"Blake," she says. "How are you?"

"I'm fine. I'm good," I reply. "How are you?"

"I'm fine too. Thank you," she says with that faint Bahamian accent coloring her voice.

I can feel the tension radiating across the phone line which leads to an awkward silence, which is silly. But given how we left things the last time we spoke, I guess it should be expected.

"How is Kit doing?" I ask.

"There's been no change. She still hasn't come around," she says, and I can hear the fear and grief in her voice.

I frown and feel my stomach churning. The fact that she's been in a coma this long has me worried. I expected that she would have come around by now.

"Has the doctor been by to see her?" I ask.

"He has," she confirms. "He checked her out from head to toe and says he can't find a medical reason for her coma. But he remains optimistic that she'll recover. Not that he gave me a reason for his optimism."

"Well, as long as her condition hasn't worsened, I'll keep feeling optimistic," I say.

Another long, awkward pause follows my words, but it feels like April has something to say and is trying to decide whether to say it or not.

"What is it?" I ask.

"I just… I wanted to apologize for what happened the last time we spoke," she says softly. "I overstepped. You're Kit's sister and have the final say over matters regarding her care. I sometimes get emotional and shoot my mouth off without thinking."

I laugh softly. "I sometimes suffer from the same foot-in-mouth disease."

She laughs with me. "You're a great sister to her, Blake."

"Thank you, April. I appreciate that. And you're a great friend to her," I reply. "I'm grateful you've been there for her all these years when I haven't been able to. I know you only want the best for her."

"I do. I want the best for her," she says. "And I'm thankful you have a friend who can provide her with the care and protection she's getting. It puts my mind at ease to know that there is an army here to guard her."

"If there's one thing Fish doesn't do, it's skimp or cut corners."

"No, he does not."

I see Astra pull to a stop in front of the shop and climb out of the SUV. She reaches in and grabs a tray loaded with coffee cups and a bag of pastries then gives me a grin as she steps into the command post.

"Listen, April, I need to run," I say.

"Do you know how much longer you'll be away?"

"I don't," I reply. "I hope it won't be too much longer though."

"I hope you're back soon."

"Me too," I say. "I'll give you an update when I have one."

"Great. I'll look forward to talking to you soon."

"Me too. Talk soon."

I disconnect the call and make my way back into the command post. My coffee and a cheese Danish are already sitting on my desk when I walk in, so I pick up the cup and take a drink. Everybody is talking quietly as they get their caffeine and sugar fix and start getting their head into the game, preparing for the day ahead.

"All right," I say, drawing their attention to me. "Are we ready to roll?"

"Tell me why we're doing this again?" Lucas asks.

"Because the one thing you can count on in small communities is that when one of their own is in trouble, they'll rally," I say. "And when you're hunting the sort of monster we're hunting, you can also guarantee that they'll try to inject themselves into our investigation."

"So, you think the killer will be out there in the field with us today?" Lucas asks.

"Oh, I guarantee it."

"That's twisted," he replies.

"It's very twisted," Astra nods. "These guys get off on watching the chaos they've caused. That, and the feeling of superiority they get from watching everybody dancing to the tune they called."

"So, what is the game plan out there today?" Mo asks. "How is this all going to work?"

"We're going to divide Spellman Park into four grids. Each of us will be leading a team to search our grids," I say.

"But we're not really expecting to find Brooke Haverson's body out there?" Lucas asks. "I mean, wasn't your initial take that our killer keeps the girls for a number of days—"

"Right. I think we can guarantee Brooke's body will not be out there," I confirm.

"Brooke's body is not the point," Astra jumps in. "All of our volunteers will be signing in. We're going to feed the names of the volunteers to Rick and Nina, who will be looking for criminal records."

"And also cross-referencing that against anybody with any sort of medical experience," I add. "The fact that the bodies are so cleanly disarticulated suggests that whoever our killer is has some sort of medical training."

"So, this whole episode is just a ruse," Lucas says.

"Well, look who's finally catching on," Astra responds with a grin.

Lucas smiles back, but it doesn't quite reach his eyes. He's asking these questions not because he's casting doubt on the process but because he's curious. I can tell he's genuinely trying to learn. This is a way of running an investigation he's not used to, and although he's playing it cool and low-key, I can see he's excited about learning new skills.

"What makes you think our guy is going to be there?" Mo asks. "He's never reached out to police or drawn attention to himself in any way."

"Because we've profiled this guy as being meticulous. Careful. Methodical," I say. "That's why we believe he's preyed on girls outside the community—a suspicion we are getting confirmation is correct. For more than twenty years, he's been hunting around Annenberg and has never come into the city. He's maintained that bubble—that comfort zone."

"And yet now he's hunting *inside* his comfort zone," Astra jumps in. "He's screaming for attention and is putting the entire town on notice. He's sending a message. So, yeah, he's going to be at the search if for no other reason than to make himself feel superior to everybody there because he knows where Brooke is."

"But tell me why he's hunting inside his comfort zone now? What's made him break a rule he's had in place—successfully, I might add—for two decades?" Lucas asks.

"That's the million-dollar question. We don't know what's changed," Astra replies. "But something clearly has."

"Could be some sort of trauma he suffered. Death in the family, somebody humiliated him—it could be any of a million different things," I add. "The thing is, it only needs to make sense to him."

"All right, and how does the school motto fit in to this?" Rick asks. "That seems to be the outlier here."

"Maybe not," Nina offers. "Maybe this trauma you're talking about that he suffered—maybe it has something to do with the school."

Astra and I look at each other. Nina has a solid point. Something about McCumber High School triggered him—and triggered him hard enough to violate his comfort zone. Something about the high school—and I feel comfortable enough saying this was his high school—hit him so hard that he needs to show the people in town just how powerful he is. He needs to lord his power over everybody in the city and show them just how much better he is than they are. I have a feeling that when we figure out what that inciting event was, we'll find out who our killer is.

And hey—maybe we will find Brooke's trail after all, or something on any of the other victims. I'm not holding my breath or anything, but we're running out of options at this point.

"All right, Rick, Nina, we're going to head out to the search site," I say. "Until we start feeding you names, I want you both to dive as deep on McCumber High as you can. I want you to pull up significant names, events—anything you guys can find."

"On it, boss," Nina says.

"Copy that," Rick chimes in.

I turn to Lucas and Mo. "All right. It's time to go to work," I tell them. "Let's get out there and see what we can dig up."

CHAPTER NINETEEN

Spellman Running Park; Annenberg, ND

I STAND WITH MY TEAM OFF TO THE SIDE AS WE WATCH THE line of volunteers checking in at the sign-in booth. Paulson set it up exactly as I'd asked.

"It's quite the turnout," Lucas remarks.

"That's the one thing I've always admired about smaller communities," Astra replies. "They always seem to turn out for each other."

"And I like that they're all here knowing there's a killer among them," Mo says. "It's almost like they're giving him double middle fingers and telling him they won't let him take their community from them. That he won't force them to cower in fear."

"I hadn't thought of it like that before, but I like that, Mo. I like that a lot," I say.

With more than a hundred people here, I can't argue with that. She's right. These people are planting their flag and will not be cowed by the monster who lives in their midst. It's heartening to see. Besides the volunteers who've shown up to search, a couple of pop-up tents have been set up by business owners in the community to provide refreshments for the searchers. The smell of barbecue coming from a smoker in one of those tents is as thick as the buzz of conversation in the air. In another tent, a woman is setting out tubs of cold water and soda, and even Rachel, Brooke's boss at the House of Sugar, is setting out pastries in a tent she's set up beside the other two.

Standing about twenty yards to our right is a cluster of teenage boys, all of them in the black and scarlet letterman's jackets from McCumber High. There is a fleur-de-lis patch on the sleeves and, below that, numbers that I assume correspond to their jersey numbers. On the back is a patch depicting the school's mascot—a man with a mustached face wearing a large-brimmed hat with a long feather in it who is gripping a blade in his teeth. It's reminiscent of the old Tampa Bay Buccaneers logo.

Standing alongside the football team are a group of girls in letterman jackets of their own—I assume the school's softball team, which Brooke was a part of—all of them looking grim and worried. A third group of girls stands with them as well, their lettermen's jackets with a patch on the back near the bottom that says "McCumber Cheer." As I look around the crowd, I notice there are a lot of kids mixed in. It's a very diverse crowd of students. I even see a fair number of blue and yellow jackets from Frazier High School mixed in as well.

"Looks like Brooke was popular with a very wide cross section of both McCumber and Frazier's student bodies," I observe. "I see the jocks as well as the academics—"

"There's even a crowd of burnouts and skaters over on the far side," Astra notes with a subtle gesture. "Nice to see the burners show up."

"I'm sure Rick would feel right at home with that group," Mo quips, drawing a quiet laugh from us.

With the food and drink flowing like the conversations among the various clusters of people, there's an almost carnival-like atmosphere hanging around the staging area. I watch as the man from the barbecue booth checks his smoker and then closes the lid. He slides into a faded and aged letterman's jacket and quickly brushes it down with his hands. It almost seems like a prized possession that he's taken good care of for a long time.

He's in his early forties and has the look of a former athlete that time has caught up with. The man is still fairly broad through the chest, but he's wearing a slight paunch around the middle these days. He's got lank brown hair that's dusted with gray and hangs down to his shoulders. His eyes are brown, his skin cool and pale, and he walks with a slight limp as he makes his way over to the group of McCumber's athletes.

The kids all seem to know who he is and listen to him as he holds court, lavishing tales about his glory days on the gridiron. I can see by their faces what they really think of him though. They're doing their best to be respectful, but I see a couple of them bow their heads close together and whisper to one another and laugh quietly, no doubt verbally eviscerating the man. But they look bored. They look like they've heard these stories before and are trying hard to not be rude to the man who's regaling them all with his stories of football greatness. I guess they still teach kids to be respectful of their elders in Annenberg, North Dakota.

"There is nothing sadder than a man who peaked in high school and can't let it go," Astra comments quietly to me.

That's the other thing I've found about small communities. They turn out for each other, yeah, but some of them can't ever seem to move on from their pasts. In the small communities we've worked cases in, there always seem to be at least a few guys—it's always guys—who think everybody is still as enthralled with that time they scored four touchdowns in a game twenty years ago as they are and are dying to hear the story. Again. Astra's right, it's kind of sad. No, scratch that, it's really sad.

"I'll bet you cash money he still goes to the after-game parties," Mo says.

"That's a fool's bet. I'm not throwing money down the toilet like that," Astra replies.

"Make fun of the guy all you want—and I'm not saying reliving those twenty-year-old glory days isn't sad," Lucas starts. "But the fact is, the guy turned up when he didn't have to. Not only that, he's spending his own time, money, and resources to feed everybody else who turned out as well. I think it's kind of cool. Not to mention a little wasteful, given that this is all a ruse."

Lucas isn't wrong. In fact, he's very right in what he said about everything. A quick glance at Astra tells me she's feeling just as guilty as I am about poking fun at the guy. As far as this being wasteful, though, that's where Lucas and I part company. It's not wasteful if we can get a lead on the killer.

"All right, I think we're ready to go," Sheriff Paulson says as he steps over to us. "Everybody's signed in, and we're all just waiting for our assignments now."

"Okay, let's get to it," I reply.

We walk over to the sign-in tent, and I take a casual glance at the sheet as Paulson picks up a bullhorn. He turns and keys it open with a sharp squelch. The crowd turns and starts to fill in, gathering in front of Paulson. The faces I see are grim and grief-stricken. Some of them are dark and angry. But all seem determined.

"First of all, I want to thank everybody for coming out today. I wish we could get the whole community together like this for a less grave reason," he starts. "But thank you for giving your time to come out and help us look for another missing girl. And I'd like to give a special thanks to Rachel Porter, Jay Scopes, and Sylvia Brenner for making sure everybody has food and drink out here today."

A polite round of applause ripples through the crowd as Rachel, Jay the barbecue man, and Sylvia all step forward and give everybody a nod. They step back, and the applause fades as all eyes turn back to Paulson.

"Okay, folks, you've all been assigned to a grid with one of my deputies leading the search team in that grid. I want you all to walk slowly and carefully," he says. "I want you to call out to a deputy if you find anything suspicious. Even if you think it's nothing, it's worth bringing attention to. Do not touch anything you find out there. They've got markers and will flag it for you. Leave it to my deputies or these folks here from the FBI to gather the evidence."

At the mention of the Bureau, I notice quite a few people casting surreptitious glances our way while others just outright gawk at us. I'm surprised some of the people look shocked to learn that we're out here helping with the case. I assumed everybody already knew, given that gossip in small towns usually spreads like wildfire. Maybe we're just not interesting enough to generate gossip anymore.

"Are there any questions before we get started?" Paulson calls through the bullhorn.

I see heads turning left and right, but nobody has any questions. Paulson looks at me and I give him a nod, so he turns back to the crowd.

"All right. Again, thank you all for coming out here today," he says. "Go ahead and report to your grid leader, and they'll deploy you."

To add legitimacy to this whole stunt, each of us deploys into a grid and helps the searchers look for clues. I suppose it's not outside the realm of possibility we'll find something relevant. But if we do, I'm pretty sure it's going to be relevant to the Emily Strauss case, not the Brooke Haverson abduction. And if that's the case, then this whole thing wouldn't be a waste of time after all.

Paulson and I trail behind the line of searchers who are beating at the grass with sticks as they look for clues. He's pensive and unusually quiet, so I look over at him. His eyes are narrowed and hard, and his jaw is clenched. He looks angry. No, he looks ready to rip somebody's head off their shoulders.

"You all right, Sheriff?" I ask.

He nods. "Yeah. I just … I've put the word out about those files you asked me about. Sent a slew of emails last night begging for help," he says. "I got a call this morning from a sheriff in a nearby township. Says he's got the remains of two of the missing girls…"

His voice trails off as he collects himself, but I have the feeling I know what he's going to say next. The pain on his face makes it obvious.

"They're from 2005 and 2006. Hikers found 'em in a shallow grave some animals had dug up" he says. "Both were in the same condition—total disarticulation. Seems pretty certain it's our guy, right?"

"I'd say it's very likely, yeah," I reply. "That's a pretty unique signature."

We walk on in stony silence for another minute. Paulson is taking this personally, which is both a good thing and a bad thing. Good because it means he'll be motivated to help us close this out. Bad because his emotions might cloud his judgment. I'm going to have to keep an eye on him to see which way he goes.

"The crimes should have been logged in to the NCIC and NDVRS," I say. "I'm going to have to follow up with the counties to see why the files weren't appended and closed out."

"Paperwork. Stupid paperwork," he grumbles. "If it wasn't for somebody not filing the paperwork and following up as they should have, this could have been stopped a long time ago. These girls are dead because somebody didn't do their damn job."

His voice is tight, and his hands are clenched into fists. He's not wrong though. The Bureau maintains national databases that log violent crimes—and criminals—that are accessible to all law enforcement agencies. It's a handy tool for law enforcement to use in cases just like this. For instance, if the bodies Paulson is talking about had been logged when they were found and the details of the crime listed, investigators could have pulled up the information, determined there was a serial at work, and either investigated it themselves or called in the Bureau for an assist. But because they weren't, this guy has been invisible for twenty years.

I get it. I know that things like this don't happen in towns like Annenberg every day. But to me, that argument is worthless because they should have more than enough time to log in the cases. Because they don't, because they're not taking the time to get it done, they're putting lives at risk. And in this case, they're allowing young girls—and a lot of them—to be killed and disposed of in one of the most gruesome ways I've ever encountered. And I've seen some things. So, I will be following up with these other counties when we're done in Annenberg.

It takes us more than half the day to walk the grid that had been laid out. And when we come to the end of the line, unsurprisingly, we're all empty-handed. By the time we make it back to the staging area, most of the searchers are already back, all of them looking downtrodden and dispirited at having found nothing.

The volunteers are all lining up at the different tents to grab something to eat and drink. I watch as they sit in small groups, speaking in low tones with one another, the sense of optimism that had infused the group that morning gone. It's as if not finding Brooke Haverson out there has made them all think they signed her death warrant.

"You should go grab a couple of these sliders," Lucas says as he steps over to where Astra and I are standing. "They are amazing."

The small brioche buns are stuffed with what I assume is either shredded beef or pork slathered in a tangy-smelling barbecue sauce and topped with coleslaw. It looks amazing. But I've had one of Rachel's sticky buns on my mind all day. Mo walks over, and as if she'd read my mind, hands both Astra and me a small paper plate with a sticky bun topped with chopped pecans and drenched in sweet, white frosting.

"Bless you, my child," I say.

"You must be psychic," Astra says with a grateful smile.

"Psychic? Nah," she replies. "I just remember that given a choice, both of you will choose the sweet over the savory every time."

"That's a shame," Lucas says. "You guys don't know what you're missing. This guy Scopes is a barbecue god."

"I'm going to have to agree with Lucas on this one," Mo says. "I'm not sure what seasonings he uses, but this sauce is incredible."

"Well, it's our loss then," I say.

I grin at her as I pick up my sticky bun and take a bite, my eyes rolling back into my head as a noise that's borderline obscene drifts from my mouth. It's every bit as amazing as I thought it was going to be. As Mo and Lucas enjoy their sliders, I look over at Jay Scopes, the man at the grill. He's busy portioning out the sliders and setting them onto red-and-white-checkered, small trays then handing them to the volunteers.

I notice he's taken his letterman's jacket off and has it set far to the side as if he's keeping it well out of range of the barbecue to avoid getting it dirty. The fact that he seems to put more pride into those high school glory days than he does in what seems to be a thriving business built on good food is kind of sad.

But as I think about the hold the past has on him, I realize that in some ways, he and I aren't so different. I think what we chose to do with our lives is vastly different. But there's no denying the grip the past has on both of us is strong and has shaped our lives. For Jay Scopes, he lets the past consume him to the point that he still tries to relive those glory days and impress everybody with his sports exploits years after the fact.

For me, the past drove me to do what I'm doing now—taking down bad guys. But on a more personal level, I know the past has also shaped my life in other ways. On deeper levels. It's kept me from forming meaningful relationships. Whether it's because of my issues regarding the murder of my parents, my lingering issues over the abduction of my sister—though those are thankfully dissipating—or the fact that a man I was intimately involved with, Mark Walton, turned out to be spying on me for the organization that is the source of most of my issues, my past continues to hold sway. Continues to shape me.

In that regard, I suppose I'm a lot like Jay Scopes or any of those guys who continue to live in the past and let it continue to influence their lives.

CHAPTER TWENTY

Anderson Realty Building; Annenberg, ND

"IT'S BEEN A LONG DAY, YOU SHOULD GO BACK TO THE hotel and get some sleep," I say.

"And leave you to enjoy all this luxury without me?" Astra cracks.

Sitting on the desk we'd pushed against the far wall, I look around the back room in the office that we repurposed into our makeshift bedroom. Lucas and Mo split the first few nights here as we share the responsibility of keeping an eye on our command post. Tonight is my turn in the barrel.

There's a cot Sheriff Paulson loaned us against the wall, with bedding and pillows from the hotel for comfort. Astra is currently perched on the edge of it and doesn't look entirely impressed with it, probably knowing that tomorrow night, it will be her turn to luxuriate in this four-star retreat.

"All things considered, it could be worse," I say, perhaps trying to convince myself. "We've certainly stayed in places that are shadier than this joint."

Astra laughs, knowing I'm right. There's a bathroom behind the office that has a sink and running water, so it's not completely primitive. At least I'll be able to wash my face and brush my teeth. I will have to go to the hotel and use one of the rooms to shower, but that's not so bad. I can live with that.

"So, how do you think things went today?" she asks.

I shrug. "About as well as can be expected, I guess. We put on a show," I say. "Tomorrow, I'll have Rick and Nina start doing the real work."

"Think he was there?"

"Guarantee it," I nod. "I don't think there's any way in hell our guy wouldn't put himself in the middle of all that. He wouldn't be able to resist thumbing his nose at everybody carrying a badge out there."

Astra leans back against the wall and takes a long sip of her coffee. I can see something spinning around in that big brain of hers and am curious to know what it is. As if she's picking up on me trying to read her mind, she looks over and grins. That mischievous smile soon fades, though, and her expression sobers.

"You know, I've been thinking a lot about the note we found in Emily Strauss's mouth," she says. "All for one and one for all."

"Yeah? What about it?'

"Well, it just bothers me. I mean, you saw how many guys out there today were wearing their old letterman's jackets and talking about their glory days like they were just last week," she says. "Some of those guys walked around like they're still relevant."

"Yeah, I noticed that."

I know where she's going with it because I had the same thought. There are a lot of guys in Annenberg who are still clinging to those halcyon "good ol' days" that were their high school years.

The sports stars were gods in town—friends, girls, the unabashed adoration of everybody. When you're on a peak that high, it's got to be hard to settle into a mundane, regular, sedate life of working a nine-to-five job in a cubicle. It's probably tough to not be celebrated or worshipped the way you were when you were young or to realize that despite how you were treated during your glory days, you're just not that special anymore.

For a lot of them, those high school days where they were revered and held up on pedestals represent the high point of their lives. At least for those who didn't get out of Annenberg. Some of them went on to live bigger lives in other parts of the world. Some of them are still celebrated for their achievements and continue to accomplish tremendous things. But for the ones who were left behind, this is all they have. They cling to that past, to those days where they were glorified because, for some of them, that's all there is.

"I'm positive it's one of those guys," she says. "One of those guys wearing their old letterman's jacket is our monster. I'm sure of it."

I am, too, but I'm curious to know if she and are arriving at the same destination by the same path or coming at it from different directions.

"What makes you sure of it?" I ask.

"It's simple. If these guys are still clinging to the past—trying to avoid living in a world that passed them by a long time ago—it jibes with what we're thinking about the message left in Emily's mouth," she says. "A guy who is so dissatisfied with the present world he's living in is going to feel like he's been forgotten. Like he's been left in the past. That note was his way of reminding us that he used to be a big shot around here. That he was somebody. That he still thinks he is but nobody else remembers him. And he's pissed about that."

"I agree—with every word of what you just said. But there's more to it than that," I say. "We need to figure out what triggered him. We need to figure out what made him start venting that rage on the girls in town. We now know he's been an active serial for at least twenty years. And he's gone undetected for that long. So, what happened that made him risk it all to make this point? Why now, after all these years?"

"You're right. If we find out the why, we'll find out the who," she replies.

"Exactly."

Astra yawns and stretches, and I can see how tired she is. We've been going a hundred miles an hour since we landed and haven't had much downtime. That's just the nature of the beast. Sleep is, unfortunately, a casualty of the job.

"Go get some sleep," I tell her. "We'll pick this up in the morning and see if we can start figuring out the why."

She nods. "That sounds good. You sure you don't want the hotel room tonight?"

"Positive. I can't wait to get into that cot. It just looks so inviting."

She laughs as she gets to her feet. "You're such a liar."

I walk her to the door and follow her out to the car.

"Be careful," she says. "Keep your gun close."

I wave her off. "Haven't you heard? Nothing bad ever happens in Annenberg."

She's laughing as she gets into the SUV and drives off. The night is dark and cold, so I hurry back inside and shut the door. I make sure to throw all the locks, then shut off the lights in the main office. Thankfully, the office has heat, so I make sure to turn that on and then start getting ready for bed. I feel about as tired as Astra felt. I'm so tired, in fact, I'm almost positive that cot is going to feel like a goose down mattress.

I grab my bag and head into the small bathroom. It's no bigger than a closet—a really small closet. Setting my bag down on the toilet, I fish out my small bathroom kit and open it up. After washing my face, I use one of the towels I stole from the hotel to dry off then brush my teeth. As I do, I look at myself in the mirror and grimace at the dark circles under my eyes. My complexion seems paler than usual, and I just look tired.

"I need a spa day when this is all over," I mutter to myself.

Once I'm done washing up and brushing my teeth, I put everything back into my bag and carry it back out to my makeshift bedroom and drop it on the table. That done, I set the alarm on my phone and set it down on the table beside the cot then climb in. I fluff my pillows and lie down on my side, then pull the blankets up and get comfortable—or as comfortable as I can on this hard cot. Truth be told, it's not as hard as some of the beds in the hotels we've stayed at over the years. Or maybe I'm just that tired.

Sleep starts to settle down over me, and I feel myself drifting down through the gauzy twilight into the darker folds of slumber. My body relaxes, and my breathing starts to slow and become more regular. Before I can fully slip below the surface, though, a sound pulls me back up to wakefulness. At first, I assume it's Astra coming back for something she forgot. But then I hear it again, and it sounds like it's coming from the back door.

Adrenaline flows through my veins like a rushing river, and I'm suddenly wide awake, my body tense, coiled, and ready to strike. I reach over to the small table beside the cot and grab my weapon as I get to my feet. The Glock in my hand, I creep out of the makeshift bedroom and into the main office. Standing still, I hold my breath and strain my ears, listening for the sound that pulled me out of sleep.

A moment later, I hear it again. It's a slight metallic jingle, and I know immediately what it is. Somebody's trying to jimmy the lock on the back door. Moving slowly and as quietly as I can, I make my way through the office to the rear of the building, stop about five feet from the back door, and raise my weapon. I lick my lips nervously, my stomach churning wildly, and then hear the click of the lock as it disengages.

The door slowly swings open, and I see the silhouette of a tall man. He's dressed in black and is wearing a hoodie with the hood pulled up. It's deep and casts dark shadows that obscure his face. But when he sees me, he freezes.

"FBI," I call out. "Don't you move."

But of course, he does move. With an almost supernatural quickness, the man turns and bolts. I give chase, running down the alley behind the office, shouting at the man to stop. He runs on, though, undeterred by me screaming at him to stop. The dark figure has a fifty-yard lead on me and cuts down another alley. I stop at the corner and hunker down before leaning out, not wanting to walk into an ambush. The alley is empty though.

Getting up, I turn into the alley, then throw myself to the ground as the figure rises up from behind a dumpster. I see the muzzle flashes a split second before I hear the thunderous report of the gun. I hit the ground hard enough to drive the breath from my lungs; the sound of bullets cracking off the bricks around me echoes in my ears. My chin bounces off the concrete hard enough to make my teeth clack together, sending a bright jolt of pain through me.

I hear the sound of another shot. It's as loud as a cannon, and I see sparks flash off the concrete near me as the bullet bounces off the ground. I wince as a shard of concrete opens a slice across my cheek, the sting of it making me grimace. My blood, warm and sticky, spills down my cheek, and I roll to the side, seeking shelter from the hail of bullets. The next thing I hear is the sound of footsteps pounding away. I jump up, my weapon raised, but see that the alleyway is empty.

My frustration boils over and I reach down, picking up a beer bottle that's sitting on the ground. I hurl it at the wall as hard as I can and listen as it shatters, the shards of glass spraying everywhere and hitting the ground with a high-pitched ringing.

"Dammit!" I shout, my voice echoing off the brick alley walls as loud as the shots.

I turn and head back the way I'd come, rage filling every cell in my body. By the time I make it back to our command post, red and blue flashing lights fill the street outside as Paulson and his deputies flood the realty building. Paulson takes me by the shoulders and looks me in the eye, his face etched with concern.

"Are you all right?" he asks.

"How did you know—"

"We got reports of shots being fired near here," he says. "I knew it was you. I knew you needed help. What happened?"

"Somebody came in through the back door. I'm almost a hundred percent positive it was him, Sheriff," I say. "It was our killer. I think he came to see what we had on him. How our investigation is progressing. And maybe to sabotage it if possible."

Paulson looks away, his face clouding over, troubled by what I just told him. "Are you sure it wasn't just kids looking—"

I shake my head. "No. I know it wasn't," I tell him. "It was a man. He was alone."

"That doesn't necessarily mean—"

"It was him, Sheriff. I know it in my gut."

A pair of paramedics rush in and sit me down in a chair. Gritting my teeth, I start to stand up, but Paulson puts his hand on my shoulder and keeps me seated.

"Let them look at those cuts," he says softly.

Muttering to myself, I let the paramedics do their thing. As they're cleaning my wounds, I look up at Paulson. He's frowning and looks upset.

"This isn't good, Agent Wilder. You've got a target on your back now."

"I disagree. This is exactly what I wanted," I reply.

"How's that?"

"We have his attention now."

CHAPTER TWENTY-ONE

Anderson Realty Building; Annenberg, ND

"WHY IN THE HELL DID YOU NOT CALL US LAST night?" Astra demands.

"Why? What could you have done?" I fire back. "It was over. Our killer was gone, and the medics were tending to my wounds. Paulson and his deputies were here. There was no reason to disturb you guys or keep you from getting some sleep."

"Blake, you should have called us," Mo says.

"They're right," Lucas adds. "We're a team—"

"I appreciate you guys. I do," I cut him off. "But I'm fine. There wasn't anything you guys could have done. I appreciate your willingness to stand by me and wanting to be here, but really, there's nothing you could have done. Now, can we forget about all this and get to work, folks?"

"No," Astra insists. "We're not done talking about this yet."

"We are."

"This is exactly why I didn't think it was a good idea setting up shop here in the first place," she says. "Or letting somebody stay here alone."

"And if I hadn't been here, everything in the office would be gone right now," I argue. "The killer would have everything we have. He would know where we are in the investigation, which would give him a leg up on us and make it easier for him to keep evading us. If I wasn't here, he'd be able to keep murdering girls with impunity."

I clench my jaw and feel the anger burning its way through my veins. I don't like the pushback I'm getting from my team, but I know my frustration and anger aren't entirely directed at them. It's mostly because of what happened last night. I can't say I'm not a little embarrassed about it. The fact that the guy got one over on me, made me look like an idiot, and got away from me on top of it all just burns my ass.

"I understand where you're coming from, Blake," Astra says. "And you're not wrong. Not entirely. I think—"

"We can't set up and break this place down every day. It's just not practical," I snap.

"I know that," she says. "But that's not what I'm talking about either."

"So, what's your point then?" Lucas asks.

"That we need two people to stay here. Or we find a space we can all stay at," she says. "A place we can use for work and sleep."

"Again, that's just not practical," I say.

"It's true," Mo pipes up. "I've looked for multi-use spaces, and Annenberg simply doesn't have them available."

"Fine," Astra admits. "Then we need two people to stay here at all times. We're going to take shifts. Lucas and Mo will stay here on even nights, Blake, you and I will stay on odd nights."

"I'm sorry, did I die and put you in charge?" I ask.

She turns to me, her jaw clenched, her eyes narrowed. "I almost lost my best friend last night," she growls. "I am not going to go through that. I'm not going to let you take that sort of stupid risk again because you're a stubborn fool."

There's real heat in her voice, and I can tell she means what she says. I can't say I'm not moved by the fierce protectiveness she's showing, but I don't want anybody to think I need a bodyguard. I don't. I can take care of myself.

"She's not wrong, Blake. Don't let your pride cause you to do something stupid or something that can gets you hurt," Lucas says.

"Gee, Lucas. I'm touched," I say. "You care."

"Yeah, a little bit," he replies. "But it's mostly that you and I are getting along now, and I don't want to have to get used to a new boss all over again."

That gets us all laughing and bursts the bubble of tension that had been settling down in the room. I wouldn't have expected a lightening in the tension to have come from Lucas, of all people. But it makes me feel good. It makes me think that he's finally starting to fit in with the team. He's got the skills. I've always thought he was a talented investigator and has the chops to be a good agent. He just needs to develop the social skills to fit in with the team's dynamic. And he finally seems to be coming around on that count.

"All right. Astra, you make a fair point—"

"I always do," she cuts me off.

"And from now until the end of this case, whenever that might be, we will have two people in this place at all times," I say. "Nina, call over to the hotel and have them send over another rollout bed please."

"You got it, boss," she says without looking up from her laptop.

"Rick, go to the hotel and steal more bedding from housekeeping when you have some time later on today."

"On it."

"Lucas, Mo, it's an odd night, so you two will be bunking here tonight."

"Yes ma'am," they both say in unison.

I turn to Astra. "Happy?"

She shrugs. "Yeah, I suppose so. That's better, I guess."

"You're impossible," I say with a laugh.

"Yeah, but that's what you love about me."

"It's one of your many charms, it's true," I say.

"I think it's her only charm," Rick says.

Astra shoots him the finger but laughs. Her point made, having gotten what she wants, Astra gives me a nod and sits down at her desk. I grab a cup of coffee and a donut from the box that seems to have just appeared out of nowhere and take a seat. I glance over at Nina who has her head down, her earbuds in, and is banging away at her laptop, bobbing her head to the rhythm in her ears. She looks like she's in the zone.

"Nina, you're awfully quiet over there," I call. "What are you working on?"

She hits another key and then turns to me. "I've been doing the backgrounds on the volunteer sign-in sheets," she says. "I thought it'd be great to get it all sorted and do a little work while you guys were arguing over sleeping arrangements."

"I appreciate you taking charge and getting it done like that," I say.

"That's what I do. I get things done."

"She just likes being bossy," Rick says. "Likes to show me up."

"That too," she chirps. "I just wish you wouldn't make it so easy to do that."

"All right, well, what do you have to show for your initiative so far?" I ask.

"I'm only a few names in so far, but surprisingly, I have somebody we might want to look at," she tells us.

"Talk to us," I say.

"Philip Morgan," Nina starts. "Fifty-three years old. Works at Simmons Mortuary. He was pre-med at North Dakota State but dropped out after a year."

"Criminal record?" Astra asks.

"Two DUI's, an indecent exposure, and one count of sexual assault at his college—he took a plea deal and managed to avoid jail time on that one," Nina reads off her computer screen.

"He seems like a nice guy," Astra remarks dryly.

"After he pleaded out on his sexual assault case, he was asked to leave campus," Nina continues. "He started working for the mortuary just after that and has been there ever since. Almost thirty years now."

Astra and I exchange a glance. I can see her train of thought is on the same track as mine.

"What high school did he go to?" I ask.

Nina taps on a few keys and frowns. "It looks like he went to McCumber."

"It fits with the theory we're developing," I say.

"What's the theory?" Lucas asks.

"That somebody in this community—a McCumber graduate—is behind these killings," Astra replies. "He's been killing for twenty years now. He's kept it to the fringes and out of town proper, but he's been preying on young girls for a very long time."

"But something happened recently that made him feel overlooked. Marginalized," I say. "That note in Emily's mouth— all for one, one for all—was his way of saying as much. He was reminding everybody that they're leaving him behind."

"All right, but how is he being overlooked and marginalized?" Lucas asks.

"That's a question we don't have the answer to just yet," Astra says.

"I can see how being forced to drop out of med school and working as a ditch digger might make a person feel overlooked," Mo offers.

"But what happened six weeks ago that made him snap and take Juliette Templeton?" Lucas wonders. "He's worked that job for thirty years and has kept his predilections outside of town proper. It must have been something massive that made him change his MO that radically."

"Something life-altering," I confirm. "Something so profound it made him change the way he operates and put his own personal freedom on the line. He wants the attention right now. He wants people to know he's here, and they've forgotten about him. And he's doing that by taking girls from some of Annenberg's most prominent families."

"So, what are we going to do?" Lucas asks.

"We are going to go talk to him," I say. "I want you and Mo to go run down Brooke's boyfriends and have a chat with them. Get them to give you alibis and then confirm them."

"Oh sure, you get to go talk to the potential serial killer and stick us with babysitting duty," Mo quips with a grin. "I see where we fit into this production."

"Just remember people, there are no small parts, only small people," Astra says. "Play your role to the hilt, my friends."

"Easy for you to say," Lucas says. "You don't have to go talk to a couple of snotty teenage boys."

"Which is why I figure you'll be able to relate to them better than any of us," I say.

That sets the room laughing again. Even Lucas laughs and gives me a nod, acknowledging the burn. The reason I'm having Astra and I take the mortuary guy is simple and comes down to one thing: experience. I know the only way to get them experience is to let them do it, but this situation is delicate and there are too many lives on the line right now.

Neither Mo nor Lucas knows exactly what to look for when questioning a potential serial killer. I'll get them the experience, and their lack of training is on me. I'll make it up and get them properly trained. But right now, I need to see about catching a killer who's responsible for six murders that we know of so far and has a seventh girl already. And I want to catch this guy before he kills Brooke Haverson. Which means, we can't afford to miss a thing.

"Nina, Rick, keep doing the backgrounds on the volunteers," I say.

"You got it, boss," Nina says.

"Copy that," Rick adds.

"Okay, we've got our assignments," I say. "Let's hit it."

CHAPTER TWENTY-TWO

Simmons Mortuary; Annenberg, ND

WE PULL INTO THE LOT OF A ONE-STORY BUILDING that's built in a Mediterranean design. It's dusty brown stucco with a red tile roof, lots of rounded archways, and beautiful, lush landscaping. There are flowering bushes in a riot of colors, massive oak trees, and expertly pruned shrubs. It's beautiful and soothing, which I imagine is the exact point when dealing with the clientele of this place.

We get out of the car and walk across the concrete parking lot. I hold the door open for Astra then follow her in, letting the door swing closed softly behind me. The silence in the lobby is deep and almost has a physical weight to it. The floors are dark hardwood and the furniture all looks to be hand-carved and antique.

We're standing on a replica Persian rug, and the air is redolent with the aroma of incense and flowers. There are several potted ferns and decorative sculptures set around the lobby and gorgeous landscape paintings on the walls. Soft string music plays quietly from speakers that are discreetly hidden around the lobby, and the atmosphere is calming.

"I had a shrink who had a lobby just like this once," Astra observes.

"Wow. You saw a fancy shrink then," I reply. "Mine had framed art from Target hanging on the walls."

She laughs softly. "You're such a liar. I've seen your shrink's office. Swanky as hell."

Dr. Reinhart's office isn't that swanky, but it's nice. She has prints from some of the old masters—she favors Rembrandt— on the walls and comfortable furniture. It's not nearly as swanky as this place, and it's not as swanky as Astra's shrink's office.

A door in the far wall opens, and a man in a dark three-piece suit steps through and approaches us. He clasps his hands in front of him and stops a few feet in front of us with a well-practiced expression of concern on his face.

"Good morning," he says, his voice as soothing and calm as the atmosphere inside the mortuary. "My name is Jefferson Simmons. I'm the director of this establishment. How may I assist you?"

We badge him, and he can't quite contain the surprise on his face. But he manages to rein it in and get himself under control again, putting that polished expression of concern back onto his face.

"Blake Wilder, Astra Russo," I introduce us. "We're with the FBI."

"And how may I assist you, Agents?"

"We're looking for one of your employees," I tell him. "A Philip Morgan?"

"And may I ask what you want with Philip?"

"Just to ask him a few questions."

"About?"

"I'm afraid that's between us and Philip," I reply.

The mortician eyes us warily, a frown on his lips. "Very well," he says. "Philip is on the eastern rear grounds. He should be trimming the grass."

"Thank you, Mr. Simmons."

"Please don't keep him too long," Simmons says. "He does have quite a lot of work to do, and he's easily distracted."

"We'll do our best."

Astra and I walk out the back door and head for the grounds. The grass is perfectly manicured, and the landscaping on the burial grounds is as lush and gorgeous as the front. A soft wind blows, stirring the boughs of the trees overhead.

"That guy wasn't too creepy or anything," she remarks.

"I hate to say anybody falls into a particular stereotype, but I'm one hundred percent certain I'd know what he did for a living if I ever ran into him on the street."

She nods. "No joke."

We find Philip where Simmons said we'd find him, but he's not trimming grass. He's leaning against a tree, his arms folded over his chest and a faraway look on his face. He seems so far away that he doesn't seem to even notice us walking up.

"Philip Morgan?" I ask.

He doesn't answer. He doesn't even seem to hear us. He just stands there, leaning against the tree, staring off into nothing. Astra steps forward and snaps her fingers in front of his face.

"Earth to Philip Morgan," she says. "You with us?"

He gives himself a little shake and then seems to come back to the present. He turns to us with a look of surprise on his face, as if he doesn't know how we got there.

"Yes?" he asks, his voice soft and smooth.

"Philip Morgan?" I ask.

"Yes. That's me. How may I help you?" he asks.

We flash him our badges, but his face remains perfectly composed and neutral. It's as if a couple of FBI agents showing up to talk to him is no more remarkable than somebody commenting on the weather. It's not a reaction I see every day. Usually, when we badge somebody, there's a glimmer of concern in their eyes, even if they aren't guilty of a thing. But Morgan is as blank as a sheet of paper.

"We just wanted to ask you a couple of questions," I say.

"All right. Sure," he nods. "But you're not here about old Mrs. Grady's complaint, are you? Because if you are, I can tell you she didn't see what she says she saw. I swear it. Even Mr. Simmons says I didn't do anything."

"What did she see, Mr. Morgan?" Astra asks.

"I was supposed to dress her sister for the funeral. So, of course, I had to undress her first," he asserts. "But that's all—"

I hold my hand up. "All right, we're not here for that."

"And I for one don't want to hear another word about it," Astra adds, the tone of disgust in her voice matching my own.

There's a long, awkward moment of silence between us as I try to clean my brain of the images Morgan put into it. I shudder and clear my throat. Astra looks both disturbed and amused at the same time. Though how she can be amused by any of this is a mystery to me.

"So, anyway," she starts. "This must be a real step down from med school, huh?"

His face darkens and for the first time I see a hit of emotion cross his features. He doesn't like to be reminded of that time in his life.

"I didn't do it. What I was accused of," he says. "I didn't do it."

"No? Then why'd you take a plea?" Astra presses. "Why'd you leave school?"

"Because they had already determined that I was guilty. If I didn't take the plea, I was going to end up in prison," he tells us. "I never would have survived in prison—"

"Innocent people don't usually take a plea. Innocent people usually fight to prove they're not guilty," Astra presses.

"You obviously don't know how justice works in North Dakota," he grouses.

"Tell us about the girls in town, Philip," I say.

He cocks his head and looks at me. "What girls?"

"Juliette Templeton, Tamara Gray, Emily Strauss, Laura Dunphy?"

"And Brooke Haverson," Astra finishes.

I watch him closely, looking for any microexpressions that might give him away. People can learn to control their faces, but it's tougher to control microexpressions. A twitch of the eye, a flicker of the lip, a tic in your cheek—these are all unconscious reflexes that can give a person away. But as I scrutinize him, Morgan's face remains perfectly passive. The only expression I see on his face is confusion. He genuinely looks like he doesn't know what we're talking about.

We hit him with the question about the girls simply to gauge his reaction. We have nothing connecting him to the abductions and the murders, so I want to see if he'll give us something. But his reaction remains perfectly blank. No reaction, no expression, no emotion whatsoever.

"Those are the girls who have been found dead, right?" he asks.

I confirm his statement with a nod. "Yeah, that's right. Four dead, one missing," I say. "And I just wanted to know if you knew anything about that?"

He shakes his head. "I know nothing about it."

"I see. Let me ask you a different question," Astra tries. "You ever feel like people in this town ignore you? Like they've discarded you?"

A grim smile touches his lips as sadness fills his eyes. "They've been ignoring me for thirty years, Agents," he says. "Ever since I took that plea deal, people have been crossing the street when they see me walking toward them."

"That has to make you mad, huh?" Astra asks.

"It used to. I'm not afraid to admit that it used to hurt. A lot. It doesn't anymore though," he shrugs. "This is my life, and I'm fine with it. I don't need anybody. Besides, I've got lots of friends online—people who won't judge me for my past. That's all I need."

"Uh-huh," I say. "And can you tell us where you were two nights ago when Brooke Haverson was abducted? Say between, eight and ten p.m.?"

"I was online. I'm online every night. I log on when I get home around six and stay on until really late—well after midnight usually," he says. "It's the only sort of social life I have anymore, thanks to... well, you know."

"And what sites were you on?" Astra asks.

"Twitter, Facebook, a couple of forums for gardening or photography," he says. "I also play a lot of chess."

"Did you know the girls?" I ask.

He shakes his head. "I didn't."

"So, if we go around town asking, nobody is going to ever say they saw you with any of them? Not walking with them? Not talking to them?"

He shakes his head. "If anybody tells you they did see that, they would be lying," he says. "The only time I leave the house is to come to work, go to the grocery store, or out for food. Take-out food, always take-out. I don't go out into public often as you can imagine."

"So, do you resent working here?" Astra asks.

"On the contrary, this is my best-case scenario," he shrugs. "The people around here don't bother me. And they don't judge me."

A wry grin twists my lips. He's not wrong. Nobody around here is going to judge him. People here will give him what he needs—solitude.

"And no, I didn't harm any of those girls. I never knew them," he says. "Any of them."

"We'll look into that," Astra says.

"Please do," he says. "I have absolutely nothing to hide."

A lot of suspects say they have nothing to hide. But most of them say it believing we'll just take their word for it and not look into things any deeper. Rare is the person who says it and means it. But as I scrutinize him closely, I believe Morgan means it. I believe he doesn't have anything to hide and that he's being straight with us.

As we stand there, I start to believe that this isn't our guy. But I've been wrong before.

"All right, well, thank you for your time," I say.

"Of course."

"Keep yourself available," Astra says.

He gives us a salute. "Yes ma'am."

We turn and walk away, neither of us speaking until we get back to the car. Once inside with the doors closed, I shudder then turn and look at Astra.

"Are you as creeped out by those two as I am?" I ask.

"Probably more so."

"A necrophile? I mean—"

"Stop. Let's not talk about it," I say. "In fact, let's forget we ever heard that."

"Deal."

I start the car and drive out, convinced Morgan isn't our guy. But just in case I'm wrong, I'm going to have Paulson assign a man to shadow him.

CHAPTER
TWENTY-THREE

Anderson Realty Building; Annenberg, ND

"S O, THE TWO GUYS SHE WAS SEEING—STEVE ROMAN and Matt Carson—both have solid alibis for the night Brooke was taken," Lucas says. "Airtight."

"Roman was on a church trip out in Bismarck and Carson was streaming his all-night gaming session," Mo says. "Though why people want to watch somebody else playing a video game is beyond me."

"It's big business these days," Rick tells her. "Some of the top streamers are making piles and piles of cash."

"Of course, you know that," Astra cracks.

"I didn't say I subscribed to their streams. I'm just saying some people are willing to pay to watch these guys like Ninja and Shroud playing. I don't. It seems like a waste of money. But these guys have literally millions of followers who tune in to watch them play," Rick shrugs.

"Methinks the lady doth protest too much," Nina piles on.

"Please. I've seen your browser history. I know what you subscribe to," Rick quips.

"Porn. Like any other red-blooded American woman," Nina replies. "There's no shame in my game."

Rick clearly didn't expect her to cop to it, probably thinking she was going to be too demure and ashamed to admit to enjoying adult entertainment. But Nina is staring back at him with a *"What else you got?"* look on her face that leaves Rick flummoxed and red-faced, but Mo, Astra, and Lucas are all bursting out in laughter. Nina's bold and unashamed. I like that about her.

"Is there any way Carson could have prerecorded his gaming session and simply played it, acting as though it were live, and slipped out to grab Brooke?" I ask.

"I mean, technically it's possible. And we accounted for that possibility when Lucas and Mo asked us to look into him," Nina says.

"But a prerecorded session would leave markers that would be easy to find," Rick adds. "And they weren't there when we went digging."

"Unless this kid is some crazy good computer hacker type— better than the two of us even—his live streaming was… well… live," Nina finishes.

Rick turned to her with a smile on his face. "Aww, better than us? You included me. Thanks for the compliment, partner."

Nina rolls her eyes. "Don't make this weird."

I take a sip of my coffee and nod, unsurprised by the news. I didn't think either of them was involved, especially with the news Paulson had laid on me about two more victims from '05 and '06 being found. Carson and Roman were still in diapers when those two were killed, but we had to check to be sure anyway. As I'm always saying, no stone left unturned.

"How'd it go with the guy at the mortuary?" Lucas asks.

"Pretty sure that's a dry hole too," I say.

"Oh, he's creepy as hell and has a fetish for having relations with the dead, but we're not here for that, so I suggest we stay well away from that can of worms," Astra says.

"Yeah, I'm comfortable saying that's well outside our purview here," I confirm. "I don't think Morgan is our guy—I just didn't get that hit off him. But I've asked Sheriff Paulson to have a guy watch him anyway."

"If nothing else, they can keep him from defiling any other corpses since that seems to be an issue," Astra says with a laugh.

Lucas pinches the bridge of his nose and looks pained. "Dear God. I will be so glad when we can wrap this up and put Annenberg, North Dakota firmly in the rearview mirror."

"What? A little necrophilia got you feeling a little squeamish?" Astra teases.

Lucas gives her a deadpan expression, drawing a laugh from everybody else.

"Where are we on the rest of the volunteers on the sign-in sheet?" I ask.

"We're probably about three-quarters of the way through," Nina says. "We should be able to finish them up by the end of the day."

"Have we found anything interesting?" I ask.

"We've got fifteen people worth looking into so far," Rick says. "All have criminal records, though nothing major. Charges are mostly petty stuff—bar fights, vandalism, trespassing."

"Though there are a few with sheets for domestic violence and sexual assault," Nina adds. "We also have one who was tagged for attempted murder, but that seems to have stemmed from a bar fight."

I stand up and pace the room, my eyes fixed on the whiteboard with all the photos of the girls fixed to it. Grabbing a red marker, I walk over and circle the names of the two victims Sheriff Paulson alerted me to. That leaves twenty-four still unaccounted for. That's a whole lot of names. A whole lot of missing girls.

"Any luck tracking down the other girls?" I ask. "I asked Paulson to contact you if he found anything else about the girls on our board."

"Right," Nina nods and gets to her feet. "I didn't have time to update it yet, but Deputy Koda did call us with some information." Nina walks over to me, her expression grim as she takes the marker from me and circles the names of seven additional girls. The squeaking of the marker on the whiteboard seems as loud as a gunshot in the silence of the room. And as she circles the last name, the mood in the room seems to grow heavier. Seeing the nine names circled in red in addition to the four confirmed girls from Annenberg—and now Brooke in addition to them—has cast a pall over the entire command post.

"Paulson assigned Koda to follow up, and she's been relentless in digging up information from these surrounding townships and all. She's really been kicking ass on this case. I like her a lot," Nina said.

I do too. I admire her determination and her passion. To be doing what she's doing by being a cop in a town like Annenberg, knowing the prevailing attitude toward indigenous people, takes strength. But then to agitate for a change in how cases involving indigenous people are handled takes a level of courage I'm not even sure I have. It's hard, if not impossible, to not like and respect Cara Koda.

"Anyway," Nina goes on. "Koda's been squeezing her contacts with the tribal police on the nearby reservations—that's where all seven of those names came from."

"And why we didn't know about it," Astra says. "The communication between tribal police and non-indigenous LEOs is worse than our communication with local LEOs."

I look at the faces of the girls we now know are dead as well as the others whose fate is still shrouded in mystery. A heavy weight is pulling my heart down into my stomach. I've known for a while that this story wasn't going to have a happy ending and that this was likely going to be bad. But it's getting worse than I thought, and I'm sickened and frustrated with my inability to crack this case and get some answers.

I've worked serials before, but not like this. This one's different somehow. I can feel it. Something dark and heavy sitting in the pit of my stomach is telling me there are layers to this I haven't even scratched the surface of yet. My team is looking to me for

ELLE GRAY

answers and for direction, and right now, I have neither. This guy is a ghost. He's stumping me at every turn, and it's infuriating me. We just can't seem to get ahead of this guy. Hell, we can't even seem to pull even with him at the moment.

I'm used to some cases being a slower burn than others. Some cases take a little while to build momentum. But even in those kinds of cases, I can usually find some lead, no matter how vague and nebulous, to start unpacking. There is usually something I can point to as a direction we should be running. But with this one, I've got nothing. I'm literally standing flat-footed with no idea what to do.

In times like these, when I'm struggling to find answers or dig up a clue, I've found the best thing I can do is go back to basics. Answers are usually simple. It's people—it's me—who complicate things with all kinds of wild theories and speculation. When I'm grasping at straws, I sometimes throw everything at the wall with the hope that something sticks. And that's a method that sometimes works. Right now, though, it's not working. I'm throwing everything I can, but there is absolutely nothing sticking to the wall. It's as blank right now as it was the day we arrived.

I set my cup of coffee down on my desk and walk to the board. Folding my arms over my chest, I force myself to stare into the face of every girl whose photo is looking back at me. Closing my eyes for a moment, I focus on my breathing as I try to clear my mind. When I'm ready, I open my eyes again. I turn to the second whiteboard that's next to the one with the photos and erase everything on it, leaving it as blank as I'm trying to make my mind.

"All right," I say. "We have thirteen confirmed dead. All perfectly disarticulated, and in the recovered bodies that were still more or less intact, there were large sections of skin, tissue, and muscle had been excised. Cut down to the bone," I say. "Why?"

"Forensic countermeasure," Astra offers.

"Then why not take the tips of the fingers? Why did he bury the heads with the bodies?" I ask. "If he's worried about forensics, why would he allow us to ID his victims?"

"Because it's a small town and they would have been ID'd at some point anyway, so there's no point in hiding that," Lucas says.

160

I nod. It's a good point. "But that takes me back to the pieces of their bodies that are missing. Why cut into them like that?"

"Maybe he's doing something to the bodies that he's hiding. Maybe that's what the forensic countermeasure is," Mo says. "He's cutting into them to hide something he's doing. Maybe he's a biter and is taking those parts of the bodies to hide dental impressions and ensure no saliva can be pulled."

"That's a great thought," I say and start jotting notes down on the board.

"Damn, Mo. Look at you putting that big brain to good use," Astra chimes in.

"Okay, I like it. That all seems to track," I reply. "Now, let's focus on our offender. We're relatively certain he started killing in 2000. Let's say he was fresh out of high school when he started killing. That probably puts him in his forties?"

"Roughly," Astra says. "I'd say he's forty-five at most. There's a level of technique to his killings that suggests he was perhaps already in his twenties when he started to kill. I don't think a kid could have performed a clean disarticulation."

"Yeah, I think you're right," I confirm. "Not to mention the fact that kids are typically impulsive, and our guy is methodical enough to have avoided raising any red flags all this time. That takes skill and patience. A kid isn't going to be able to pull that off. And it's got to be somebody with some form of medical knowledge."

"Or access to YouTube," Lucas says.

Having looked into it after Astra made the same argument, I shake my head. "YouTube didn't start until 2005. Our guy was active five years before that," I say. "He didn't learn to disarticulate a body on YouTube."

"The internet was around in 2000 though. I'm sure there were sites where that sort of information could be accessed," Lucas argues.

Lucas isn't wrong, and it's a good thought. It's something else we need to account for.

"Rick," I say. "I want you to run a search for sites between, say, 1995–2000 that might have contained information about disarticulating human bodies. In those early days of the internet, I can't imagine there were many. It's a long shot, but see if there's any way at all to connect the names on that list with the sites that were available at the time. Comments or anything. I mean, they say the internet is forever, right?"

Rick grimaces for a minute, but nods. "Um. Okay."

"What is it?" I ask.

"Forever might be an exaggeration," he explains. "A site from that long ago is going to be a hell of a time to find. If a server went down or someone stopped paying for a domain name, it might basically be lost to the wind. And even if we did find the right place, it may have changed hands dozens of times with no way to trace the original source or whatever content the domain might have hosted decades ago. There are some pretty amazing archival efforts out there in this day and age, but a site like this would already have been pretty deep underground at the time. Combine that with two decades of digital detritus, and we just... no promises, okay?"

"Well, just do what you can, and we'll hope for the best that he left some sort of a digital trail," I say. "Like I said, I know it's a long shot. Just do what you can."

"We'll get to it," he nods.

I step back and look at the notes I've written down and let myself work through it all for a moment and decide how to attack this. I have a plan for Astra and me today, but I want to start winnowing down the list Nina and Rick are putting together. But to do that, I'm going to need to relinquish a little bit of my control. I'm going to have to trust Mo and Lucas to do something I have concerns about them doing.

Stepping back from the board, I pick up my coffee cup and take another drink—mostly to give me a few more moments to wrap my mind around it all. Eventually, I'm going to have to trust them to do the important things. I know they have the ability, but they lack the experience. And that's what worries me. I worry about something being missed and this guy having free rein to keep on killing. The fact that so many bodies are turning up that carry the same signature only underscores that point for me. Things got missed, and girls are dying because of it.

But I'm going to need to take the training wheels off at some point and turn them loose. I can't keep holding their hands.

They're eager to get into the mix. They're intelligent, capable, and solid agents. Both of them. And I need to learn to trust them.

"All right. Nina, Rick, of the list you've compiled so far, how many of those guys are over forty?" I ask.

"Thirteen of the fifteen," she answers.

"Any of them have any sort of medical training?"

"One is a nurse, two are biology teachers, and two others were pre-med but dropped out soon after starting classes," she replies.

"Okay, Mo and Lucas, I want you both to go and interview the names on that list," I tell them. "Focus specifically on those five who've got some degree of medical knowledge first. Look for any tells, microexpressions—it's important to hear what they're saying without their saying it."

Mo nods, seeming to pick up on how serious this is. "We'll handle it."

"Good. And Lucas, follow Mo's lead," I say. "She's the lead in these interviews."

"Copy that," he says, seeming to be excited to get to work. "What's your plan?"

"Astra and I need to take a ride." I tap on the photos of the two girls Paulson brought to my attention. "We've got people to talk to as well."

CHAPTER TWENTY-FOUR

Okala Family Residence; Cortland Township, ND

W E FOLLOW THE BLACKTOP ROAD AND PULL TO A STOP in front of a blue and white, double-wide mobile home that has most certainly seen better days. The paint is faded and peeling, and plants that are brown and dying—if not dead already—sit in a motley assortment of pots lining the outside of the mobile home. An eight-by-eight piece of Astroturf sits on the ground to the left of the front door. Judging by the number of toys sitting on the turf, there are young kids inside.

A breeze blows a cloud of dust across the open ground behind the mobile home as we get out of the car. There are a couple of dozen of these mobile home groupings clustered in this area, sitting on the sites of former small towns that never managed to take off. It's allowed the people who form these small townships to plop their mobile homes down and create a community of their own. It's probably not ideal, but who's going to stop them?

Cortland Township is tiny and made up of a dozen of these mobile home communities scattered over the remains of the small town that had once stood here. On our way in, we passed a tiny little area that I guess passes for a main street through their makeshift town. Not enough people live in Cortland to call it a proper town, and it's definitely not a city. It's not even a hamlet. Township is probably even stretching it. If I had to pick a word to describe Cortland, it would probably be commune. It's just a collection of like-minded people banding together to live and prosper as best as they can.

It reminds me a lot of the small artist's communes that dot the landscape of New Mexico and some of the southwestern states. Cortland is a patch of dirt and grass for people who want to get away from other people. It's an impulse I can understand sometimes. It's also a place for some indigenous folks who refuse to live on a reservation but don't want to live among the non-indigenous either. In a way, it's limbo for them. They're caught between two worlds and don't want to belong to either. It's a collection of people who, more or less, just want to be left alone and on the outside of so-called civilized society.

Still, as I turn in a circle and look around, I have to say, if you want to get away from people and modern conveniences, this is the place to do it. They're surrounded by absolutely breathtaking natural beauty. There is a profound sense of peace and calm in Cortland. This is the sort of place you come to when you just want to be able to hear yourself think.

"I think I could be happy out here," I say.

"Please," Astra replies. "The lack of wine shops out here alone would send you scampering back to the big city in no time."

"You have a point," I reply with a laugh. "But you can't say it's not beautiful and peaceful out here."

"Oh, it is. But you would be bored inside a week."

"Maybe."

"Definitely," she insists. "I know you better than you know yourself, Wilder."

As we stand there, the hair on the back of my neck stands up, and I can feel eyes on us. I look around and see a couple of kids peering at us from around the corner of one of the mobile homes. I see the curtains in another moving and know somebody's behind it staring at us.

"I don't imagine they get many visitors out this way," Astra notes.

"No, probably not. I've never enjoyed feeling like a zoo exhibit though."

"Yeah, me neither," she says. "Hey, you ever see that movie, *The Hills Have Eyes*?"

I shake my head. "Can't say I have. Why do you ask?"

"Well, you should Google it. Suffice it to say, I'm kind of catching that vibe," she says. "Let's go get this over with and get out of here."

"Agreed."

We walk up the three rickety steps to the front door of the mobile home and knock. It opens almost instantly, as if the woman on the other side was waiting for us. She's a short woman, no more than five-three, and sturdily built with wide hips and bust. She's got warm, tawny skin, and her black hair is shot through with gray and hangs to the middle of her back. The woman's face is etched with deep lines, and she's got a frown on her lips that seems to be her default expression.

Behind her, I see another woman—maybe in her mid-thirties—who looks a lot like the woman standing before us. Only younger. She looks at us with wide, curious eyes. But then the older woman turns and looks over her shoulder at the young woman and says something in their native tongue. The younger woman hurries away as somewhere deeper in the home, I hear the sound of two children crying. The older woman turns back to us, her expression hostile.

"What is it?" she demands.

Astra and I badge her, and the woman narrows her dark eyes, staring at us even more distrustfully than before.

"FBI," she says, her tone making it seem more like a curse than a fact. "What do you want with me?"

"Agents Wilder and Russo," I say. "We were hoping to talk to you, Miss Okala. We have some questions—"

"Questions about what?" she growls.

"It's about Samantha, ma'am," I say gently. "We've got some questions about your daughter. May we come inside and speak with you for a moment?"

The moment I mention her daughter's name, the woman's eyes fill with grief. The pain I see in her face looks as fresh today as it probably did the day her daughter went missing—and the day her body was discovered. But then her eyes harden again, and she clenches her jaw.

"I've got nothing to say. I've said all there is to say," she spits. "Talking about my Samantha isn't going to bring her back. It didn't even help when she was alive."

"I understand, Miss Okala, and I can't pretend to know your pain," I say. "But the man who took your daughter is still taking girls. And we were hoping—"

"That's not my problem. It has nothing to do with me anymore."

"No, ma'am, we're not suggesting it is your problem," Astra jumps in. "We were just hoping that you would be able to answer a few questions—"

"I've got nothing to say to you people. You people did nothing to help me when I came to you after Samantha was taken," the woman hisses.

"You spoke to somebody with the Bureau?"

"I spoke to that good-for-nothing Sheriff Barnes," she growls. "He didn't do nothing. I bet if the girl were pretty and blonde, he would have fallen all over himself to help. But for us? We get shown the door and don't hear from them again until they come to tell us our child's been murdered."

"Ms. Okala, I understand your frustration and sympathize with your pain—"

"How can you? Have you lost a child?"

"Well, no ma'am—"

"Then you don't know a damn thing," she snaps. "Now, go. I don't want you here. I have nothing to say to you. Leave us alone." She slams the door in our face, and I raise my hand to knock again but think better of it and stop myself. Our being here asking questions only dredges up the pain she felt on the worst day of her life—the day she was told her daughter was dead. Our presence is a reminder of what she lost. A reminder of the piece of her heart that was torn out and will never fully heal.

I feel bad for reminding her of that pain. I would never have dreamed of doing so if it weren't necessary to save the lives of other girls. But I can't blame her for slamming the door in our faces. In her place, I can't say I wouldn't have done the same thing. The problem is, we're leaving empty-handed. But I suppose that's our problem.

We climb back into the SUV and head out, driving along the blacktop paths that cut through the small community that will lead us back to the highway. As we're just about to pass through the two crumbling brick pillars that mark the entrance to the mobile home park, a woman steps out from behind one of them. I recognize her as the younger woman who'd been in the Okala family home.

I pull to a stop and exchange a glance with Astra. With a small shrug, we both climb out of the SUV and step over to her. Aside from the lack of grays and lines on her face, she looks like a carbon copy of the woman I assume is her mother.

"You're FBI, right?" she asks.

"Agents Wilder and Russo," I say. "And you are?"

"Monica," she says. "Samantha was my older sister."

"I'm very sorry for your loss," I say.

"It was a long time ago," she replies, though, like her mother, the pain in her voice still seems fresh. "Anyway, I can't stay long. My mother would kill me if she knew I was out here talking to you."

"Why doesn't she want you to speak with us?" Astra asks.

"She doesn't trust the police. When Samantha went missing, Sheriff Barnes laughed at her. Told her nobody cares if an Injun girl goes missing," she explains, her voice suddenly tight with anger.

"My mother moved us here because the people on the reservation could be just as bad as the people in town. She thought here, we could start fresh in a place where all people were equal. Turns out equality doesn't exist anywhere for people like us."

I want to say something that will make her feel better. That will make her believe that equality does exist. But I don't have the words. The truth is, the idea of equality is a myth. As long as there are people who have hate in their hearts for people just because they may not look like them, and those people are put into positions of authority over others, inequality will continue. As long as people are teaching their children to hate others because of the color of their skin or who they pray to at night, that fabled equality people dream of will remain forever out of reach.

That doesn't mean we shouldn't aspire to be better though—that we shouldn't do all we can to make our society better and more just for everybody. And I want to believe that as long as there are people who continue fighting to make that dream a reality, we might eventually get there. We might eventually win that fight. Or at least, get a lot closer to it than we are now. We might never completely eradicate hate and ignorance from the world, but we should always keep fighting like we can. I like to think if we do that, things will eventually get better for all, and we'll leave the world a better place for those who come after us.

"I'm sorry that you've endured so much," I say.

"That's the world," she replies with a shrug.

"What is it you wanted to speak to us about?" Astra asks. "Do you know something about your sister's disappearance?"

She nods. "Sort of. I mean, I don't know much, but I did see a couple of things," she says. "My mother has given up on ever getting justice for Samantha, but I will never stop believing we can get it. That we can take her killer down."

"I can promise you that as long as we're here, we're going to keep fighting to make that happen, Monica," I tell her. "We will keep fighting to get justice for your sister. She deserves it. And so do you and your mother."

Monica's big, dark eyes shimmer with tears. She bites her lip viciously to keep them from falling, but she's unsuccessful in the effort. A pair of large tears spill from the corners of her eyes and run down her smooth, russet-colored cheek. She wipes them away with the back of her hand and sniffs loudly.

"I'm sorry. It's just… there still isn't a day that goes by that I don't think of her," she says softly. "Sammy was the best big sister a girl could have. She always helped me with my homework, let me hang out with her friends—she even protected me. There was a boy who was picking on me, and when Sammy found out, she marched straight over to his house and punched him square in the nose. Broke it too. He never bothered me again."

The corners of her lips pull back into a sad smile at the memory, but the tears keep falling.

"Your sister sounds pretty incredible," Astra says gently.

Monica nods. "She was."

Silence spins out between us, and we give her a couple of moments to gather herself again. She reaches up and tucks her hair behind her ears. Monica's face is red, her eyes puffy, and her expression tinged with her pain. But she holds my gaze firmly with her jaw clenched, determination to get through this etched into her face.

"My sister was seeing a man from town," she says. "I don't know his name—she never told me that. But I saw him once. Sort of."

"Sort of?" I ask.

"It was dark out, and Sammy snuck out to go be with him one night. I followed her and hid in the bushes when she got to him," she tells us. "He was tall. Maybe six-two or three? He had brown hair that hung down to his shoulders, and he was wearing a black and red jacket. There was a picture of a pirate or something on the back."

I glance at Astra and nod. It's a description of a McCumber varsity jacket. So, at least that bit of information has been confirmed.

"Listen, I know this was a really long time ago, but do you remember seeing any numbers on the sleeves of that jacket?" I ask. "Right underneath the fleur-de-lis?"

"The fleur-de-what?"

"The flower on the jacket sleeve that's right up here," I say, touching my upper arm. "Do you remember seeing any numbers just below that?"

Monica screws up her face and looks off. Her brow is furrowed as she focuses and tries to see back in time to that night so long ago. Some of her hair comes loose again, and she idly tucks it back behind her ear, never seeming to lose her focus. She finally turns to us.

"I—I can't say for sure. I don't remember that bit," she says. "But I think it was like maybe twelve or fifteen. Maybe. I just don't know for sure."

"That's all right," I tell her. "You did great."

"Is there anything else you remember about that night?" Astra asks.

She nods. "He drove an old pickup truck. It was dark brown with a lighter brown stripe down the side," she says. "A Chevy... a Chevy Silverado. I want to say it was early 80's."

"That's specific," Astra notes. "That's a pretty good memory."

"I'm good with cars," she replies with a shrug. "Anyway, I saw her get into that truck with him before."

"And what makes you think this guy is the one who took her?" I ask.

"Because she told me she was going to meet him the night she went missing."

"You don't happen to remember a name for this guy, do you?" Astra asks.

She shakes her head. "Sammy never told me."

"That's fine," I say. "You've given us a lot of great information."

She puts her hands on her hips and stares at us with a barely restrained hostility in her eyes and a frown on her lips.

"I gave this same information to Sheriff Barnes. And he did nothing with it," she says. "Can you promise me you will?"

"I give you my word, Monica," I tell her, never breaking eye contact. "We are going to do everything in our power to get justice for your sister. And we will not stop until we're able to give you the answers you and your mother deserve."

She absorbs my words for a moment, then swings her backpack off her shoulders and quickly unbuckles it. Monica reaches in and pulls out a plastic bag with a pale yellow sweater inside. It's dirty. Dingy. It looks aged and weathered and has several brown spots I can see that could be blood—or might just be dirt. As I stare at it for a moment, I realize what it is I'm looking at. I raise my eyes to her.

"That's your sister's sweater, isn't it?" I ask.

Monica nods. "She was wearing this when they found her. Because Barnes isn't a real Sheriff, he has no crime lab. And the old Sheriff in Annenberg proper wouldn't do anything with it. He gave it back to us without doing any testing or anything."

She hands it over to me, and I look down at it, knowing the key to this entire case could be in this bag. DNA back in the early 2000s wasn't what it is today. It's much more sophisticated today than it was back then, and if there is so much as a hair on this sweater, the techs will find it, analyze it, and, so long as our perp is in the system, spit out a name.

I take the plastic bag from her as gently as I'd handle a holy relic. In some ways, this very well might be the grail of this case.

"Thank you, Monica. This is helpful," I say.

"I hope it helps."

"It might do more than help," I say. "It might be the key to justice for your sister."

CHAPTER
TWENTY-FIVE

The Mad Cow Steakhouse; Annenberg, ND

"I MEAN, I'M ALL FOR TAKING THE POWER BACK BY appropriating a name and all," Astra says. "But is mad cow disease really worth reclaiming?"

"Sheriff Paulson says this is the best steakhouse in town," I reply.

"Yeah? And which of his friends or family members owns it?"

I laugh as I climb out of the SUV. Astra falls into step beside me as we cross the parking lot. Overhead, the darkness in the east is creeping ever westward like a puddle of ink that's been spilled across the sky. I breathe deeply, inhaling the savory aroma of beef on the grill. My mouth is watering by the time we get through the front doors. I instantly feel something beneath my feet, and when I look down, see the peanut shells that litter the floor. They crack and pop as we walk across them to the hostess's station.

"What's wrong?" Astra asks.

"I don't like walking on things. It bothers me."

"You are a strange woman, Blake Wilder," Astra says. "I don't know that I've ever met somebody with more weird quirks and hang-ups."

"It's like you don't know yourself or something."

Astra laughs. "Shut up."

"Evenin', ladies," the hostess says. "Party of two?"

The hostess is a pretty girl of about eighteen or nineteen maybe. She's got long blonde hair and dazzling blue eyes. Her cheeks have a healthy glow to them, her smile is wide and warm, and she's got a thick, curvy build. In other words, she's exactly our killer's type. Astra cuts her eyes to me, and judging by the frown on her face, I see she doesn't miss it either.

"Actually, we're meeting our friends here," I tell her. "They should already be here. The reservation was under Wilder."

The girl consults the notebook on her desk, her brows furrowed. A moment later, her smile returns, and she nods.

"Right. Here you are," she chirps. "Your friends are already here. We have you all back in the Moo Room."

"Excuse me?"

"The Moo Room… it's a private room," she says. "My boss figured with you folks talkin' about all your secret FBI stuff, you might want some privacy."

"Right. That's very thoughtful," I reply. "Make sure to thank your boss for us, please."

"No problem. Just go ahead and follow me."

She leads us through the main dining hall, which is about three-quarters full. As Astra and I are paraded across the room, I'm consciously aware of the people staring at us. It's like some of them think just because we work for the Bureau, we're like alien beings or something, and they're just waiting for us to sprout a second head or hit them with a laser death ray. After being gawked at in that mobile home park in Cortland, the last thing I want is to be stared at here on top of it. But it is what it is, I suppose. Just another of those occupational hazards.

The hostess steps aside and holds her arm out, gesturing to the open doorway. Astra walks through first, and I hear the team loudly greeting her. I pause, though, and turn to the girl. She looks at me, that well-practiced smile still on her face.

"Was there something else I can do for you?" she asks brightly.

"No. No, I'm fine thanks. I just… just be careful out there," I say and quickly clock her nametag. "Don't go anywhere alone. Don't be caught alone anywhere. And always have mace or something with you. Be careful, Jessica. Please."

Her smile turns to a frown as she seems to gather what I'm talking about. She nods as a flood of emotion crosses her face.

"I will," she says. "And please… find the man who's doing this. Find the man who's destroying my hometown."

"We're doing our best."

Her eyes linger on mine for a moment, and she gives me a slow, uncertain smile. "Enjoy your dinner tonight."

"Thank you."

As I watch the girl walk off, I feel a wave of protectiveness. I want to catch this guy to avenge everybody he's killed so far, but to also keep that girl who led us to our room safe. To protect her. To keep her out of a killer's grasp.

"Blake, get your butt in here," Astra calls.

With one last look at the retreating form of the hostess, I turn and step into the room and take a seat next to Astra. Lucas and Mo are sitting across from us, and Nina and Rick are sitting at the head and foot. It looks like the others are already two beers ahead of us, so when the waitress comes in and greets us, we put in a quick order for a couple of drafts.

When she goes to grab our drinks, Astra and I quickly scan the menu. The waitress comes back a couple of minutes later with our beers and takes our orders.

"Astra, you should be ashamed of yourself," Rick says.

"Yeah? Why's that?" she asks.

"You order fish in a steakhouse? I'm pretty sure there's a law against that," he replies. "At the very least, it's an offense against God."

"If God didn't want me eating salmon, he wouldn't have put it on the menu," she counters with a laugh.

"I'm pretty sure that was the heathen manager of this joint," he says. "For shame, girl. Seriously, for shame."

"Says the man who orders tofu bowls for lunch pretty regularly," Nina says.

He laughs. "That's different. Seattle doesn't sit in the middle of beef country."

Nina waves him off. "Don't listen to him, Astra."

"Don't worry. I never do," she fires back. "Whenever he speaks, all I hear is the voice of Charlie Brown's teacher."

I glance over and see that Lucas is quiet, his face stony. He's just sitting there staring at the wall and sipping his beer.

"Lucas, you okay?" I ask.

He looks over at me and shrugs. "Yeah. I'm fine."

"That was convincing," Astra comments. "C'mon. Spit it out. What's eating you?"

He takes a sip of his beer and sets his bottle down with a sigh. "I saw some horrible things in counterterrorism. I honestly thought I saw the worst things people could do to each other," he admits. "But since I've been here, in this unit, I've seen how wrong I was. The things people do to each other, not for political or religious ideologies, but for fun or some personal satisfaction, are even worse. Sometimes... sometimes it just hits me kind of hard."

"We've all gone through that—still go through it. We all have the black moods and slip into a funk," I say.

"The nightmares are the worst," Astra adds.

I nod. "They are. But the point is, we all deal with what you're dealing with right now, Lucas. We've all been there before and we'll all be there again," I tell him. "It's one of the hazards of the job, I'm afraid. Some days you'll be fine. And others you'll have to force yourself to get out of bed."

"How do you cope?" he asks.

"Honestly, I see a professional. I talk things out," I tell him. "I also rely on my team. You guys are all part of the reason I can keep doing this. Don't be afraid to lean on any of us. You can call us any time, day or night, if you're struggling. You can't do this job without having a good support network, Lucas. And that's what you have here. We all rely on each other to keep ourselves sane and functioning."

"And as you can see, we all let Blake down when it came to keeping her sane," Astra says with a mischievous smirk.

"Not to mention that she's barely functioning most days," Mo chimes in.

"Oof," I groan. "Not you, too, Mo?"

"What can I say?" she says with a shrug. "I enjoy a good pile on."

"Yeah, I read that about you on the bathroom wall at the office once," Rick says.

Everybody—even Lucas—laughs at that. And it's like he pulled a cork out of the bottle and the tension begins to dissipate. Even Lucas seems to be loosening up, which is a good thing. The conversation is lively and light and sprinkled with a lot of laughter. It's as if by some unspoken agreement, we're all avoiding the topic of work right now and are focusing on getting out of our heads... if only for a little while.

As the appetizers come and are followed by our meals, we eat, drink, and rip on each other. Our room is filled with uproarious laughter, which is probably spilling out into the main dining hall. Given the reason we're here and the case we're dealing with, I have no doubt some people don't appreciate the mirth. But for us, it feels needed. It's like we're pulling the pressure release valve, blowing off the steam accumulated after a long, brutal, and darkly emotional day filled with horrors civilians will never know. You can't do this job without a sense of humor. Granted, our brand of humor is usually gallows humor, but as far as I'm concerned, being able to laugh and get out of our heads for a while is important.

It's why I run my unit the way I do. Why I try to keep it as loose and light as possible. We see the worst humanity has to offer, day in and day out. We see horrible things nobody should ever have to bear witness to. Those things leave scars. If you bottle it up and keep it all stuffed down inside, one day you're going to explode. It will damage your psyche in ways you might not be able to recover from. It can damage—if not ruin—your life.

I know some folks in the Bureau think we should all be stoics. Should all be emotionless robots who don't let the tragedies we see every single day affect us. That we should be able to just brush it off. But there's a reason suicide rates among law enforcement are as high as they are. It's because the one thing we're never taught at the Academy is how to cope with the awful things we see. There are no classes that teach us how to deal with the emotional fallout of the tragedies we're exposed to. We're simply told to handle our business. To be tough. Strong. To let it roll off us like water off a duck's back.

It's some of the stupidest advice I've ever heard. We're human. We have emotions, and the things we see are going to affect us. I know many people don't approve of the way I run my team. They think I'm too loose and too indulgent with my unit. But I've found that dinners out with a few drinks and a lot of laughs over the course of a case can be mentally and emotionally beneficial. Being able to connect with each other, remind ourselves that we're human, share the good and the bad, and talk about how we're feeling, has a hell of a lot more benefit to us than just sucking it up or burying it.

If encouraging my team to tell off-color jokes, swap inappropriate stories, and have a few laughs at each other's expense is wrong and means I'm not Bureau command material, then so be it. My team is more than a collection of parts to me. They're more than cogs in the big wheel of so-called justice. They're people. Friends. They're my family, and I would lay down my life for any of them. Protecting them is part of my job. And that includes protecting their mental and emotional well-being too.

I push the plate of half-eaten strawberry shortcake away from me and groan as I clasp my hands over my belly.

"I can't do it. I'm going to pop," I say.

"Lightweight," Rick chides as he slides my plate over to himself and finishes it.

The waitress comes through and cleans off the empty dishes then refills our coffee. And as she does, it seems that unspoken agreement has shifted. Now that the meal is over, we have to talk about the day and set our plans for the next day.

"We interviewed half the people on the list," Mo says. "I made sure to record it so you could follow up and make sure we didn't miss anything."

"I'll give it a listen, but I doubt you did. I have faith in you guys," I say. "Anything interesting come up?"

"Not really," Lucas says. "Most of them have easily verifiable alibis. And those that don't, just don't seem like our unsub. I didn't get much of a bad hit from anybody."

Mo nods. "I agree. Everybody was pretty solid. Normal. I didn't get red flags off any of them either."

Sociopaths are adept at blending in. They're chameleons and can hide in plain sight passing for normal among people. Most people wouldn't be able to pick a sociopath out of a crowd if they were given multiple opportunities. It's why men like Ted Bundy and Dennis Rader were able to operate unincumbered for as long as they did.

But we're taught to look for the small tells. We're trained to see those little details a civilian with no training wouldn't pick up on. We're not perfect, of course, but I like to think I would be able to spot the sociopath a pretty high percentage of the time. They just tend to give off a strange vibe. It's hard to explain, but there is always something just slightly off about the ones hiding something—especially when being questioned by law enforcement. Something that later on, well after the fact, people will slap their foreheads and wonder why they didn't pick up on sooner.

We're trained to pick up on those things. I think Mo and Lucas are intuitive enough that they would have caught that whiff off any of the guys they sat down with today. I'll listen to their recordings later on, but I trust them. I just have control issues— Dr. Reinhart is always on me about that. That's where my concern about their experience stems from, I'm sure.

In some ways, I exhibit sociopathic tendencies—like my unflattering need for control. Obviously, I channel it differently, but it's there. It's disturbing to know this about myself, but I also think it's why I'm good at my job. I can relate to those tendencies in some ways which allows me to anticipate them.

"Have we heard anything about where Paulson's guys are in searching for Brooke?" Astra asks. "Are they still out canvassing?"

"I haven't checked in with him on that, but I will," I say. "Last I heard, they were still canvassing but are coming up as empty on that front as they did with the others. It's like this guy grabs them and then just vanishes."

When we first arrived, Paulson and I had a conversation and decided that because he's got a relationship with the people in town, it would be best for him to continue searching for living victims. People in this part of the country tend to be distrustful of the feds anyway and are more likely to open up to him. So, we agreed that he'd canvass while we hunted the killer.

"He's a ghost," Lucas says. "He just materializes out of nowhere, grabs the girls, then vanishes with them."

It's not a description I like. Nobody is a ghost. Nobody materializes and then vanishes into the ether. But it's not entirely inaccurate in this case. The fact that nobody has seen or heard anything is insane. These are strong, young women. He blitzes them, that much we know from the blood at the Brooke Haverson scene. But the fact that he was able to get her to open the door in the first place keeps bothering me. It tells me she knew him. Trusted him enough that she opened the door to him. It disturbs me on a deep level. That he used that trust and then betrayed them in the way he did infuriates me.

"What did you guys find today?" Lucas asks.

Astra fills them in on what we found out in Cortland. As I look around the table, I see the glimmer of excitement in their eyes. They realize, like we did, that this could be the key that unlocks the case. I'm trying to keep myself from getting too excited. The sweater is almost twenty years old. I'm sure whatever DNA is on the fabric has probably degraded. It might be unusable. My hope, though, is that because it was kept in a plastic bag, away from the elements, and wasn't handled by anybody else, there will be something useable.

"That's fantastic. This might be what we've been looking for," Mo says.

"It might be. But we really should manage our expectations. It's a really old sweater that might have been contaminated," I say.

"We need to keep our heads in the game and focused on what's on our plates in front of us."

I look around the table and meet everybody's eyes. They give me a nod of understanding. I'm hopeful, but I won't let them see that. I want them focused on those things we can control, not on something that may or may not pan out. I don't want them standing around watching like some of Kobe Bryant's teammates would when he was handling the ball. I want them fully engaged in the game, moving without the ball, and trying to make a play.

"Okay, so what are the next steps?" Lucas asks.

"Tomorrow, I want you and Mo to go and interview anybody you didn't hit today," I tell him. "And if you have time after that, talk to Deputy Koda. See about getting her to talk to some of the families of the indigenous girls on the reservation. We have no standing there, so tribal police will give us the bum's rush no doubt. But she might be able to grease the wheels enough that we can get on the reservation. If she can get our foot in the door, go and talk to them. Get whatever you can on those victims. Sweet talk them into giving you case files if you can."

"Copy that," Lucas says.

"Rick and Nina, I have a project for you too," I say.

"Oh good, we were feeling left out," he says.

"First, I want you to compile a list of anybody and everybody in the area who owns or has owned a Chevy Silverado—made in the 80s," I say.

"Dark brown with a light brown stripe down the side," Astra adds.

"Right. That."

Nina looks at us. "This is North Dakota. I'm pretty sure there's a state law requiring everybody to own a truck."

"Be that as it may, we still need that list," I say. "The color should be a good way to narrow it down."

"You haven't seen the trucks tooling around town," Rick says with a laugh. "But we'll put the list together. No problem, boss."

"Good," I say. "Then cross-reference that against McCumber High grads, say, from the year 1995 to 2000. That'll be a good place to start."

"Copy that," Nina says.

"And then you can filter it down even further. Take whatever list you generate from that and cross-reference it against McCumber football players who wore the numbers twelve or fifteen," I continue.

"That's pretty specific," Rick says.

"Which should make it easier, right?"

"But it might not be football," Astra notes. "It could be any sport really. The numbers on the sleeves don't denote football only. The softball players wore them on their sleeves too."

"Good point," I acknowledge. "All right, expand that to include all sports McCumber offers—or offered in that time span."

"Oh, this is going to be fun," Nina says with a wide grin. "This kind of stuff fires me up."

Rick gives her a pointed look. "And she has the gall to question what I find fun."

"What are you guys doing tomorrow?" Lucas asks.

"We got a call from the field office in Minot," I tell them. "We're going down there, and they'll hopefully be able to test the sweater for DNA while we're there."

"And with any luck, we're going to have the name of our killer by the time we get back," Astra says. "Keep your fingers crossed, people."

For the first time since this case began, I'm starting to feel that sense of momentum building. And it's slowly starting to pick up speed. I'm optimistic about what we're going to find in Minot tomorrow, but it's best to avoid anticipating what we'll find out. It's just one more piece in the bigger puzzle. And though it feels like we're picking up steam, we're still a long way from the station.

All my years in the Bureau have taught me that just when you feel like you reach the summit, the ground beneath you can shift and send you plummeting all the way back down again. So, I'm optimistic. But I'm also doing my best to manage my expectations.

CHAPTER TWENTY-SIX

Medical Examiner's Suite & Forensics Lab; Minot Field Office, Minot, ND

"ARCHIE THAYER," HE SAYS ENTHUSIASTICALLY. The atmosphere in the ME's suite is cold and sterile. Everything is done in tile so white that it'll make you snow blind if you stare at it too long. On the back wall, behind Archie Thayer, is the bank of stainless steel refrigerated drawers used to hold the corpses. My case has seven of the twelve drawers currently in use. The tables, sinks, and other appliances in the suite are also stainless steel, and the air carries the faint odor of pine trees and bleach. Everything in the suite is so clean I have to wonder if it's ever been used before.

"Blake Wilder and Astra Russo," I reply. "It's nice to meet you."

"Yeah, you, too," he says. "Let me just say I am psyched to be working on this with you. As I'm sure you can imagine, there isn't a lot going on in North Dakota. Certainly nothing as exciting as what you two are working on."

Archie's smile hasn't dimmed since we walked in. He's a tall, lanky kid who can't be more than thirty. It's impressive that somebody so young is running a forensics lab—even if it is in North Dakota. That tells me Archie knows what he's doing and gives me a boost of confidence in him. I'm just hoping it turns out to be warranted.

Archie is six-three, at least, with cool, pale skin, a mop of shaggy red hair, and green eyes behind his black-framed glasses. He's got freckles splashed across the bridge of his nose and braces, which trips me out. I don't see many grown people wearing braces. They make him look even younger than he is. It's not nice, but Archie reminds me of the photos I've seen of that ventriloquist's dummy, Howdy Doody. He is a very friendly guy though. He's got energy and enthusiasm for days.

"Oh, before we start, I wanted to give you something," I say.

"And here I didn't get you anything. I feel terrible," he says.

His tone is serious, and when I look up at him, he looks positively tortured. But then he lights up the room with a smile, and his laughter echoes around the room. The smile stretches my lips before I have a chance to stop it, and before I know it, Astra and I are laughing along with him. It was just such a goofy thing to say, how could we not?

"I'm just kidding with you, of course," he says. "Just a little levity, you know?"

"Believe me, I'm a big proponent of levity," I reply.

"Then we are going to get along great."

I take the plastic package with the sweater out of my bag and hand it over to him. He turns it over and looks at it from the outside, taking it in from all angles.

"Appears to be yellow cashmere. Fading and aging make me think it's probably fifteen or twenty years old," he says.

"You can tell that by looking at it?" Astra says.

He gives her a sly smile then turns the package over and points to the small sticker attached to it. It's a small orange circle with "2005" written in faded blue ink. I shake my head but find myself grinning again.

"The evidence tag helps," he chuckles.

Astra and I groan as we roll our eyes. His jokes are horrible, but there is something intensely likable about Archie Thayer.

"Can we swap Rick out for Archie?" Astra asks.

"I'll have to check with personnel."

He laughs and sets the plastic bag down on the stainless steel autopsy table standing between us. Archie pulls the arm of the overhead light down and takes a closer look at it. His brows are furrowed in concentration, and he's humming a song to himself.

"Are you really humming a DMX song, Archie?" Astra asks.

"What? I love DMX," he says. "Helps me concentrate."

Archie is about the last man on the planet I would have expected to be a DMX fan. He just doesn't put off the hardcore-rap-fan vibe to me. But, hey, what do I know?

"Well, those brown spots appear to be blood," he says. "But I honestly don't know that we're going to be able to pull DNA out of it. I mean, it's old. Seventeen years in an uncontrolled environment isn't good. The plastic bag might have slowed the degradation, but I can't say yet whether it slowed it enough to give me a viable sample."

"We figured it was a long shot," I say.

"But a long shot is better than no shot," Astra adds.

He grins and gives her a finger gun which makes me grimace. I don't know why, but finger guns have always irritated me. It's irrational, I know. But seeing somebody doing the finger guns is like hearing fingernails on a chalkboard to me.

"That's a good attitude right there," he says. "I like that."

Astra laughs and Archie gives her a high five. She nudges me with her elbow, encouraging me to join in the fun.

"Lighten up, Blake. Live a little," she says with a mischievous grin.

"I think you're light enough for both of us."

Archie chuckles and straightens out his lab coat. "Sorry," he says. "I don't get a lot of visitors here, and I sometimes lose my head."

"It's fine," I say, smiling at him. "I'm all for keeping things light and having a laugh. We need it in our line of work."

"Don't I know it," he says, casting a meaningful look at the drawers behind him. "Without a little laughter, we'd go mad."

"Absolutely," I say. "Couldn't possibly agree more."

"Okay, well, I'm going to do my best to pull some DNA off these stains—assuming it's blood. Just because it looks like blood doesn't mean it actually is blood," he says. "Reminds me of a girl I went out with sophomore year at Boston College. She looked like—"

"Okay, I'm going to stop you right there," I say with a laugh.

"What? I was going to say she looked like a blonde. Turned out to be a brunette," he finishes with a smile. "Had me fooled for weeks, that one."

"You are too much, Archie Thayer."

"Better than not being enough, I suppose."

I nod. "I suppose you're right," I say. "So, tell me, why did we make the two-hour drive from Annenberg to Minot? Other than to drop off the sweater, that is?"

"Right," he says, snapping his fingers. "Come over here and take a look at what I've cued up on the microscope for you."

The microscope is sitting on a counter off to our right. Astra and I walk over and take turns looking through the eyepieces at the slide he's got prepped on the stage. Not coming from a scientific or medical background, I have no idea what I'm looking at. I raise my eyes to Astra who gives me a shrug, stuck in the same boat I am. We both turn to Archie, who's looking back at us with a satisfied smile on his face.

"What are we looking at, Archie?" I ask.

He cocks his head and looks at us like we're not seeing the literal elephant standing right in front of us.

"Field grunts," I say. "We kick in doors and leave the science parts to smarter people."

"Oh. Right," he replies, clearly deflated that we ruined his big show. "Sorry. I spend so much time in here and surrounded by other medical staff and scientists, I sometimes think everybody knows the same stuff. My bad."

He walks over and opens up the laptop situated next to the microscope and pulls up a photo that looks like what we just saw under the microscope. He turns to us.

"Okay, so this is a sample from one of the bodies you sent down to us," he says, then perks up. "And also, before I forget, thanks for sending so much work my way. I've been bored as hell, and this has been one fascinating case to work on. Unexpectedly challenging."

"Glad we could help," I say dryly.

He runs a hand through his shaggy mop of hair and gives us a boyish grin. Archie just gives off a vibe like a kid who's excited to show off his first science kit. His excitement and good mood are infectious. It somehow even manages to blunt the serious, grim reason for our visit to his lab.

"Okay, anyway, what you're looking at is a sample from Juliette Templeton's body," he says. "She's chronologically the oldest victim—well until you had the remains of Samantha Okala and Jennifer Rivers sent along. I haven't been able to examine them yet, but I don't expect to find anything different in their bodies."

"Well, can you tell us what you found in the four original bodies we sent?" Astra asks.

"Right. That cellular destruction you can see in that sample is consistent with being frozen," he tells us. "That cellular destruction is consistent through all the victims you brought in, save for Rivers and Okala, who I haven't examined yet. But if they are attached to your killer, I expect to find the same."

"Well, that makes sense," Astra says. "The first three victims were found in ground that was near frozen. They'd been exposed to near-freezing temperatures—"

Archie cuts her off with a shake of his head. "Exposure to natural elements isn't enough to do this—unless you're talking well below zero. It's been cold here, but it hasn't gotten cold enough to do that to the cells within those bodies."

Archie is talking quickly, almost excited to share his knowledge, and I can tell we're deep in his wheelhouse. This seems to be thrilling for him, which is kind of morbid. But I suppose in

North Dakota, he doesn't get a chance to show off like this very often. It's not exactly excitement central here.

He clicks a few keys on the laptop, and a split screen comes up showing the same cell on one side but another one on the other screen. He points to the new photo.

"I want to show you a visual comparison," he says. "The cell on the left is healthy... well, relatively speaking. It's still a cell from a corpse, but one that hasn't been frozen. You can see the differences between that and the cell from your victim."

Astra and I look closely at the two photos. I'm no scientist, but even my untrained eye can see what he's talking about. The difference between the two is obvious.

"Do you know how cold it would have to be for the bodies to suffer that sort of cellular destruction?" I ask.

"I'm going to say it has to be thirty or forty below," he replies.

"What about the latest victim—Emily Strauss?" I say. "She wasn't exposed to the elements for long—"

"Same thing," he confirms. "She's suffered from the same cellular destruction the others have."

"So, he's freezing them," I say. "That's new."

"I'm guessing it's a forensic countermeasure," Archie says. "Freezing the bodies makes it almost impossible to pinpoint a time of death."

"He's smart. Trying to confuse the investigation," Astra says.

I nod. "Yeah. Very smart," I add. "All right, let's set all that aside for the time being and circle back to it later. I know the bodies came to you in pieces—"

"Yes, complete disarticulation. It's quite impressive," he says, that tone of excitement back in his voice. "It takes some real skill to accomplish that."

"It does," I say. "But as I was saying, I know the bodies came to you in pieces, but have you been able to determine a cause of death?"

He shakes his head. "It's hard for me to say, given the condition of the bodies," he tells us. "But with Emily Strauss being in better condition than the others, I was able to observe wounds I did not see in the others. The decomposition was still too advanced in the others for me to say accurately."

"So, what did you observe in Emily that you didn't in the others?" Astra asks.

"Bruising around the neck. It's tough to see given the fact that the head was removed, of course, but it's there," he says. "That's suggestive of strangulation. I was able to see her eyes as well, which contained petechia, also suggestive of strangulation. However, I can't say for certain whether the hyoid bone was broken as she was being strangled, or if it occurred during the decapitation."

"So, you believe it was strangulation that killed her," Astra says.

"I'm not one hundred percent certain, but it's likely," he replies. "However, based on what I observed regarding the blood flow to the tissues and the wounds, I'm almost positive she was alive when she was being... cut."

My heart falls into my stomach at his words. "You're kidding me," I whisper. "She was alive when he was inflicting this torture on her?"

"I'm almost certain, yes," Archie confirms.

"Jesus," Astra mutters.

I brush my hair back behind my ear and look down at the white tiles on the floor, taking a minute to process everything Archie just laid on us.

"So, he tortured these girls, cutting pieces out of them, then strangled them to finish them off," Astra says.

"As I said, that's my theory," Archie says. "I can't confirm that with one hundred percent certainty, but it seems likely to me, yes."

My stomach roils with a sick, greasy feeling, and I can taste the acrid tang of bile in the back of my throat. I suddenly want to just go home, throw my blankets over my head, and shut the entire world out. We've dealt with monsters before, but this is a monster on a completely different and more depraved level.

"God, I hate this world," Astra mutters.

I nod, in complete agreement with her sentiment.

CHAPTER TWENTY-SEVEN

Anderson Realty Building; Annenberg, ND

"THAT SOUNDS LIKE SOMETHING OUT OF A BAD horror movie," Mo says. "That doesn't sound like something out of real life."

"Archie won't say it's one hundred percent accurate, but he says he's pretty sure that's how things went down," Astra says.

A grim, heavy silence has descended over the office as everybody soaks in what Archie told us. The looks of horror on their faces mirror the expressions on mine and Astra's. It was a long, quiet drive back from Minot. We both needed the time to process what we'd learned. We got back into town an hour ago, stopped for a quick bite, and called everybody back to the office to talk about the situation. These were the first words Astra and I have uttered since leaving the field office.

"Unreal," Lucas finally mutters.

"Unfortunately, it's all too real," I say.

"What else did he say?" Mo asks.

"He agrees with us that the killer has some surgical skill and that the disarticulation was perfectly done," Astra says.

I take a sip of my soda and then set the bottle down. "The reason he called us to Minot, though, was to show us something—"

"I think he just wanted company. He seemed a little lonely," Astra says.

"That too," I reply. "But he wanted to show us that the bodies had been frozen. He wanted to give us the visual and an explanation of what it was we were seeing."

"Frozen?" Lucas frowns. "That tracks with them being left outside, right?"

"I thought so too, at first," I reply. "But Archie said for that type of cellular destruction, we're talking about thirty to forty below zero. Being left outside wouldn't have had the same effect on the body or the cells."

"I learned more about the body in a couple of hours with Archie than I did in all the biology classes I took in high school," Astra says.

"So, we're thinking our guy has an industrial freezer?" Mo asks.

"He'd have to have one," I reply. "Or at least, have access to one."

"That should narrow down the suspect list," Nina offers.

"Considerably," Rick adds.

Rick and Nina exchange a glance, some silent bit of communication passing between them. They both turn to their laptops and start tapping away.

"So, we're thinking our guy froze the bodies to slow down the decomp, which would throw off all our timelines," Lucas says.

"That's the idea we came up with, yeah," I nod.

"So, our guy has medical knowledge, understands forensics, and is vicious as hell," Mo notes. "That's quite the trifecta."

I lean back in my chair and let it all run around in my brain. All of that is true, but there's something more. Something we're missing. The idea that there is a gap in the theory has been plaguing me since we left the field office. As monstrous as the man is, I just have the nagging feeling there's still something even more horrible that has yet to reveal itself. I don't know what it is, but I'm sure there's something about the killer we're just not seeing yet. And it's frustrating the hell out of me.

"Okay, we'll circle back to this," I say. "What did you guys find out today?"

"We found out there are a lot of people in Annenberg and the surrounding areas who own or have owned Chevy Silverado's of the 1980s vintage. And quite a few of them are brown with that light brown stripe," Mo tells us. "It's like the most popular color or something around here."

"It's like trying to find a needle in a stack of needles," Lucas offers.

"And how many of those attended McCumber High?" Astra asks. "And were members of a sports team?"

"Between 1995 and 2000, we have—get ready for this— sixty-two men who played sports at McCumber and owned Chevy Silverados," Nina calls out. "I didn't filter for the brown color scheme just because those can be changed easily enough. There were still thirty-nine men who had the stock brown paint scheme in the area during those years."

"We haven't been able to run the names of anybody within those parameters still in the area," Rick says. "We were going to get to that tomorrow."

"One thing I want to know in all of this is this guy's motive," Lucas says. "Why is he doing this? Why has he been doing this for the last twenty years?"

"That's unfortunately something we're only going to learn once we have him in custody and can ask him ourselves," Astra says. "It doesn't seem like there's a sexual component to this. Not one that's overt."

"How can you know that?" Lucas asks.

"It doesn't have any of the usual earmarks of a sexually-based crime," I tell him. "That's not to say this guy doesn't get off cutting these women into pieces, but sexual gratification doesn't seem to be his primary motive. There's a different need motivating our guy."

"And the chances are good that it's not going to make sense to you. Or to me for that matter," Astra says. "It's like Blake is always telling us—it only has to make sense to him."

"Speaking of suspects," Mo says. "We seem to be distinctly lacking in that department."

A wry chuckle drifts out of my mouth. "Yeah, I noticed that too."

There's so much noise in my head right now that I'm having trouble thinking clearly. As the rest of the team talks among themselves, pitching ideas and theories, I pinch the bridge of my nose, trying to stave off a screamer of a headache.

"Okay, let's cut this off for the night," I say. "Let's go get some rest and regroup in the morning. I feel like we're on the cusp of breaking this thing open, but we all need to be thinking clearly to sort through all the information we have."

"That's a good idea," Astra says.

"Agreed," Mo says. "I'm beat."

We all get to our feet and get our workstations squared away. Once we're set up for tomorrow, Mo, Lucas, Rick, and Nina head back to the hotel. I'm still keyed up, though, and nervous energy is racing through my body.

"You should get some rest," Astra says. "Watching you pace around the office so furiously is exhausting me."

"Yeah, sorry, I'm still pretty worked up," I say. "I need to burn off some of this energy before I'll be ready to sleep."

"So… you're going to pace it out of yourself?"

"Nah. I think I'm going to go for a run. I haven't been out for a run for a few days," I say. "That should help me clear my head."

"It's like thirty degrees outside."

"It's brisk. It'll be lovely."

She laughs. "You and I have different definitions of 'lovely,'" she says. "But you enjoy yourself. I'm going to snuggle under these thick blankets and stay warm."

"You enjoy yourself," I say with a laugh.

"Thanks. I will."

Astra laughs as she heads for the bathroom. I take the opportunity to grab my bag and quickly change into some leggings, a T-shirt, and a hoodie with reflective yellow panels on the back. After that, I pull on my running shoes and a beanie.

"All right, I'm heading out," I call through the bathroom door.

"See you in a bit."

I put in my earbuds and then head out, locking the door behind me. Once I get my playlist going, I drop my phone and keys into my fanny pack, zip it up, and pull my beanie down. I stretch out a bit and jog in place for a minute to get my body warm. And when I'm ready, I take off at a run, setting a good pace for myself.

It's not that I like running necessarily. In fact, I kind of hate it, truth be told. But it makes me feel physically good, and more than that, it helps me clear my head. I've had some of the biggest epiphanies of my life when I'm out on a run. And when I'm stumped on a case, I've found that some physical exertion helps clear whatever is clogging my brain and keeping me from thinking clearly.

Twenty minutes into my run, my legs and lungs are starting to burn, so I throttle myself down a bit and settle into a steady pace. The streets are dark and quiet. It's cold out, and my breath is coming out in steamy plumes; but it's peaceful, and I can feel my head already starting to clear. I'm already beginning to feel better.

As I run, I glance over my shoulder, and my sense of peace is shattered. About twenty yards behind me, a truck is driving behind me; its lights are out, and it seems to just coast forward to prevent me from hearing it. When I turn, reaching for the gun in my pack, bright headlights flare to life, completely blinding me.

The engine roars as the truck bears down on me.

CHAPTER TWENTY-EIGHT

Anderson Realty Building; Annenberg, ND

T HE MAN SAT IN HIS TRUCK ON THE DARKENED STREET A few doors down from the office the FBI agents were using. He'd seen them all go in a while ago, and though he had an idea to go in blasting and try to take them all out, he ultimately rejected the idea. It posed an unnecessary risk to himself. And he'd come close enough to disaster when he'd tried to break in the other night.

The man prided himself on his meticulousness and attention to detail. It's what had made him such a great athlete back in the day. He studied tape as hard as his playbook, and he was never

surprised by what a defense threw at him. But with that attempted
break-in, he'd been sloppy. Careless. He hadn't put in the necessary
work to be successful, didn't know they were sleeping there, and it
nearly cost him dearly.

*"I cannot begin to describe the hunger that I feel again. Run if you
intend to survive. For the beast is coming to life…"*

He sang along softly with Disturbed as he drummed his
fingers on the wheel, waiting for inspiration to strike. Music had
always helped him stay calm. In control. He could lose himself in
the lyrics, and it helped him stay focused on other tasks. It helped
keep that animal inside of him at bay.

"Music soothes the savage beast," he muttered, then giggled
maniacally to himself.

The door to the old realty office opened, and he watched as
the people filed out. He watched the heavyset guy with the bushy
beard, the tiny Hispanic woman, the butch woman with the short
hair, and the Asian guy climb into an SUV and drive away. The
man felt like it was a sign of his good fortune.

"And it's not even my birthday," he said to himself as a wolfish
smile crossed his lips.

With those four gone, that left only the dark-haired agent
who could be a model—Astra Russo, according to his buddy in
the sheriff's department—and the woman he was gunning for:
Blake Wilder. His buddy told him the tall strawberry blonde was
the leader of the team that was nosing around in his business and
making life harder on him than it needed to be. That made her the
thorn in his paw. The fly in his ointment.

The man reasoned that if he took out Wilder, the rest of
the team would fold. Cut the head off the snake, and the body
dies. It's an age-old saying for a reason. It might not shut down
the investigation completely, but it would sure put a crimp in
their plans. It would be enough of a setback to allow him to keep
working. To keep building up to the big reveal that would rock the
town of Annenberg to its foundation.

He was going to show them all. You don't just forget about
people. You don't discard them like trash. The man was going
to keep carving a bloody path through the town, dicing up the
children of those very people who'd cast him aside when he

needed them most. He was going to teach those people a lesson they would never be able to forget no matter how hard they tried. A lesson in loyalty. A lesson in being a good person.

It was why he'd turned his hobby, his passion, into his mission. He'd enjoyed the fruits of his labors and savored every last succulent morsel he'd carved out for himself over the last twenty years. It was his father who'd showed him the way. Who'd showed him how to navigate the waters of their particular form of amusement without being caught. It was his father who'd showed him how to be a Great White, smoothly sailing through schools of guppies without giving off a ripple that would send them scattering.

For his father, it had been entertainment. A leisure-time activity. For him, though, it was something else. It was a need. A deep-seated *need* buried deep down inside of him. He didn't want to do the things he did. He *needed* to do them because the hunger inside of him would grow so intense it would overwhelm him. There was only one thing that would sate that ravening beast inside of him.

His father knew he was different. Knew he didn't kill for the same reasons. There was something rawer, something more primal in his drive to take life. His father understood that and taught him how to survive and avoid being caught. And one of those first rules was that he was to never touch the people in his hometown. The site of his greatest glories. The place where people had worshipped him. The man had been a god in Annenberg once upon a time. People had revered him. That was a pond his father had said was to never be fished in.

And the man had obeyed that commandment. For more than twenty years, he'd done as his father instructed. But then the people of that godforsaken town had turned on him. They'd betrayed him. They'd turned their backs on him when he needed help. After all he'd done for them, all he'd done for the town, they had thrown him away like trash. The mere thought of it sent a flash of rage coursing through his veins. With a savage scream, the man punched the roof of his truck once. Twice. Three and four times, punctuating every punch with a howl of rage.

The man forced himself to calm down. To unclench his fists. He quieted his mind and focused on the music. The song had changed, and he moved his hands to the wheel, drumming along with the rhythm of an Alice in Chains song he'd always felt like he could relate to:

I'm the dog who gets beat, shove my nose in shit. Won't you come and save me, save me?"

"Focus. Focus," he muttered. "Get yourself back on task. Get your head in the game and focus on the next play. Get out there and make something happen!"

He repeated the words like a mantra. They were things his old coach used to say to the team during a game. He was a taskmaster, that one. Always on them about staying focused. Keeping their heads in the game and never looking beyond the next play. That mantra had helped him through the years. It helped him stay in the moment and keep focused on what was important: the next play.

By the time he looked up again, he was back on an even keel and had his head back in the game. He sang along with Alice in Chains until the song changed again, this time "Simple Man" by Lynyrd Skynyrd. His father hadn't just taught him to be an apex predator; he'd taught him a love and appreciation of all kinds of music. For those things, he was grateful. His father had made his life just so much more colorful.

As he watched the office, trying to decide the best way to dispose of two federal agents, the door opened, and the Wilder woman stepped out. She looked like she was about to go for a run. She pulled her beanie down over her forehead and did a little stretching to limber up. The man watched her, a wide smile on his face.

"I take it back. I think it is my birthday," he said.

He followed her at a discreet distance for a little while, waiting for her to get off the main thoroughfare through town. It took about twenty minutes for her to do it, but when she cut down a smaller street off Ralston, the man's smile grew wider. He was sure he looked like a Great White at that moment, ready to swallow a small fish whole. The man pressed down on the accelerator and the truck shot forward.

He watched as Wilder looked over her shoulder and then turned around as he approached. The man hit the switch that turned on his headlights as well as the rack of halogen lamps mounted to the roll bar in the bed of his truck. The woman was effectively blind, so the man stomped on the accelerator. The engine roared, and he picked up speed as he closed in on Wilder. The lights on his truck framed her perfectly. It was like she was caught in the spotlight, trapped by its radiance. Wilder looked frozen in the moment, with her hands up to shield her eyes and a growing expression of horror on her face. With a malicious grin on her face, the man closed in on her. He was fifteen yards away.

He was ten yards away.

His engine howled, and Wilder's skin seemed to glow in the halogen lights. The man let out a loud whoop he was sure she could hear over the growl of his truck.

Five yards.

Wilder threw herself to the side at the last possible moment, and the man swerved to try and clip her anyway. The crunch of broken glass and squeal of tortured metal as he scraped along the car parked on the street filled his ears. Rage setting fire to every cell in his body, the man locked up the brakes of his truck and brought it to a screeching halt of smoke. Grabbing the pistol off the seat next to him, he jumped out of his truck and came around, ready to be done with this once and for all.

He came around the car he'd sideswiped, expecting to find Wilder. Instead, he found nothing but an empty sidewalk. The sound of footsteps pounding pavement drew his attention, and the man looked up in time to see Wilder sprinting away. He raised the gun in his hand and squeezed off a pair of shots without hesitation. Sparks flew as the first bullet hit the concrete and the second hit a brick wall to her left.

He squeezed off one more shot, but she'd already disappeared around a corner. She was gone. He'd failed. Again. His coach would be on his ass, chewing him a new one right now. And his father would be slamming his fist into his head, telling him he was trying to beat some common sense into him. The man threw his head back and let out a scream of rage and frustration that echoed up and down the street.

His throat raw and his face red, the man jumped back into his truck and roared off into the night. He needed to regroup, break down what went wrong, and formulate another game plan. It was getting late in the fourth quarter, and all he needed was to punch one into the endzone. He was going to win. He was a god. And people would once again revere him in this godforsaken town. They were going to learn to fear him.

CHAPTER TWENTY-NINE

Anderson Realty Building; Annenberg, ND

IT'S NOTHING. I'M FINE," I SAY IRRITABLY. "I DON'T NEED a medic. It's a scratch."

The paramedic gives me a withering look. "The sooner you let me clean these and patch them up, the sooner I'll be out of your hair."

"Blake, let her do her job," Astra orders.

Grumbling to myself, I sit back in the seat and let the paramedic clean out the scrapes I got first from diving onto the concrete, then the chip from the brick wall that cut my cheek.

"Why in the hell didn't I take my weapon with me?" I mutter.

"That's a good question," Astra says. "Especially considering the guy already took a shot at you once. I should have insisted you take it. Or go with you."

"I thought it was in there," I tell her. "I must have just been so preoccupied that I forgot to pack it."

"Blake..."

"It's fine. I'm okay."

"But it might not have been," she insists.

"But it was, so let's move on."

The door to the office opens and Sheriff Paulson steps in, closely followed by the rest of the team. They all huddle around me, worried expressions on their faces.

"This your doing?" I ask Astra, annoyed.

"I thought they should know."

"There's nothing to know," I snap. "I'm fine."

"She gets a little cranky, doesn't she?" Rick notes.

"I would be too if somebody tried to kill me—for a second time," Nina says.

"Okay, you know what?" I say, shooting to my feet as the medic casts me a frustrated look. "There's no reason for anybody to be here. You all—"

"Should get to work," Astra says firmly. "We need to find out who this prick is. I don't plan on giving him another shot at Blake. So, start digging. I want a list of names before sunup."

Amazingly enough, everybody goes to their workstations, opens their laptops, and gets to work without a word. I stare at them for a long moment then turn back to Astra.

"They never do as I say that quickly," I grumble.

"They like me better."

The medic pushes me back down into the chair and quickly finishes her work. She tapes small bandages over the cuts then packs up her kit and leaves. Paulson steps over and looks at me with a frown on his face. It seems to be the default expression of the day.

"I have my guys searching the area—"

"What color is the paint?" I ask.

"Pardon?"

"Given how hard he hit that car, there's bound to be some transfer," I reply. "I need to know what color the paint is that was left behind on that car he mangled."

"Dark gray, I think. Why?"

"Nina," I call out. "Get a listing of everybody in this town who owns a dark gray truck. I don't have the make or model but do what you can."

"Copy that."

"Are you all right?" Paulson asks.

"I'm fine," I insist.

"She's cranky," Astra says. "You'll have to forgive her lack of proper manners."

Paulson chuckles. "I don't blame her. In her shoes, I'd be pretty ticked too."

"As long as you're here, we should bring you up to speed on everything we've found so far," I say. "Have a seat."

The door opens again, and Deputy Koda comes in carrying a tray of coffee cups and a box of donuts. She sets them down and everybody descends on them like vultures on a carcass. I grab a cup and a chocolate cake with sprinkles then sit back down.

"There is a special place in heaven for you, Deputy Koda," I say as I raise my cup to her. "Come sit with us. I want you to hear this."

She looks at me awkwardly, cuts her eyes to the sheriff, then gives me a meaningful look. I turn back to Paulson who's sipping his coffee.

"If not for Koda's determination, we wouldn't have what we have," I say. "She's an incredibly smart, insightful person. You'd do well to give her more responsibility around here."

He looks at Koda as if seeing her for the first time, his lips pursed.

"I'd like her to sit in on this briefing and hear what her hard work and persistence have given us," I tell him. "She's earned it."

"Fair enough," he says and gestures to Koda to come join us.

She grabs a chair and sits in our little circle, a look of surprise on her face. I can tell, though, that she's happy and proud of her own efforts, and she gives me a grateful nod. With everybody settled, Astra and I fill them in on everything that's happened and everything we've learned since going out to Cortland and Minot. Through the telling, both Paulson and Koda look equal parts shocked and disgusted. I can't say I blame them for that.

"I can't believe all that has been happening in my town," he says.

"I can't believe it's even worse than I imagined," Koda adds. "I mean, what I found was bad enough. This is… something else."

"Yeah, this is bad," I say. "But I have a feeling the worst is yet to come. There's something I can't see yet… something big. And I have a feeling we're not going to know what it is until we find our guy and get him into bracelets."

"Do you think he has a mass shooting or something like that planned?" Paulson asks.

"He will want to go out in a blaze of glory," Astra says. "What form that's going to take, we don't know. But the fact that he's moved his killing grounds into his comfort zone tells us that he wants the attention. That he wants people to know his name."

"The note he left in Emily Strauss's mouth seems to back that up. He feels slighted. He feels forgotten," I say. "He wants people to remember him. That's why we're leaning toward him being a former star athlete at McCumber. He got used to the adulation, and now he's not feeling that. He feels left out and alone. So, he's going to make sure people remember him."

"My God," Paulson says softly.

"What can we do?" Koda asks.

"You guys know this town. You know the people," I say. "I'd like you two to work with my team. They have a set of parameters they're working with to narrow down a suspect pool. I'd like you to sit with them and see if you can narrow it down even further."

"If he's brazen enough to attack Blake out in the open like that, it means he's getting desperate," Astra says. "He might be in his endgame already, and we need to put a pin in this guy before he explodes."

"We'll do whatever we can," Paulson nods.

"One other thing," I say. "I mean no offense, but you're the only two people I trust in your department. Keep the information you learn here under your hats. I have a feeling that information is leaking out and—"

"My department doesn't leak, Agent Wilder," Paulson says defensively.

"With all due respect, Sheriff, it does," Astra counters. "If it didn't, Kira Rice wouldn't have known there was nothing on the surveillance tapes outside the coffee house Emily Strauss worked at."

"But her sister is dating one of your deputies, so..." I say, not finishing my sentence.

Paulson's face darkens and grows tighter. He's not happy to learn that his deputies are leaking information and spilling department secrets during pillow talk.

"Yeah, that's a problem," he admits. "I'll be taking care of that pretty promptly here. I can guarantee you that."

"That's a problem for a bit later," Astra tells him. "Right now, go sit with our people and see about finding this guy. If he's ramping up to finish this—whatever his plan is—time is of the essence, Sheriff Paulson."

"Right," he says with a nod. "Come on, Koda. Let's see how we can help."

I watch as they walk over to offer themselves up to the team. Getting to my feet, I stretch myself out. Astra stands and motions to the door.

"Let's go for a walk," she says.

I arch an eyebrow at her. "You think we should be walking around town right now?"

"Normally, I wouldn't want to stand so close to you when somebody's tried to kill you. The last thing I want is to be collateral damage if they try again," she says with a laugh. "But I think every cop in Annenberg is out there right now. Our guy is ramping up, but I don't think he's looking to go out that way. I don't get the suicide-by-cop hit off him."

"No, I suspect you're right. It's not flashy enough. And he doesn't want his death to be the story," I reply. "He wants to be alive to see the chaos he's caused. He wants to watch the town tear itself apart whenever he finishes this."

"Agreed."

We move to the door and step outside into the cold pre-dawn air. Between the medics arriving and the deputies sweeping the area, the whole ordeal has taken hours. The sky in the east is starting to lighten, signaling the oncoming morning. Our breath trails out of our mouths in thick, steamy plumes, and I clutch my coffee cup a little tighter, trying to leech whatever warmth out of the cardboard that I can.

She's right about every cop in town being out and about. We had a deputy pick us up the minute we stepped outside, and he's trailing about twenty yards behind us. Apparently, Sheriff Paulson feels that we need a babysitter. Ordinarily, I would balk and send the guy away. I've got Astra, and I now have my weapon on my hip. I can take care of myself. But I'm not really in the mood to argue right now.

"How are you doing?" she asks when we're about a block away. "You okay?"

"Yeah, I'm fine."

"You're always fine, Blake. I know that. But how are you really?" she presses. "I know you better than anybody, Blake. I know you bottle stuff up. It's not good for you. I thought your shrink taught you that."

A rueful grin touches my lips. "It was close. It was really close," I relent. "I haven't been that scared in a long time. For a minute there, I thought that was it for me."

Astra is silent for a moment then looks over at me. "And how are you coping with that?"

I laugh softly. "You thinking about starting a second career as a shrink?"

"Well, I'm not going to lie," she shrugs with a smile. "Not being shot at or having some kook try to run me over with his truck is appealing."

"You'd be bored in a week."

"Probably true."

"Definitely true," I say. "Physically, I'm fine. I mean, I'm stiff and sore, of course. And given how bad my face feels after these last couple of days, I'm feeling like I went ten rounds with Mike Tyson, but it'll heal."

"And mentally?"

"Mentally, I'm pissed off at myself," I growl. "I should have picked up on the guy following me earlier. It's not like his truck was all that subtle. So, yeah. I'm pissed that I never saw him coming. I should have."

"Don't beat yourself up too much. Between Kit and the job—and all the insanity that comes with it—you've got a lot on your plate," she says.

"It's no excuse. I always tell you guys to keep your head on a swivel. I failed to do that, and it nearly got me killed."

Astra stops and turns to me, forcing me to follow suit. She looks me in the eye, her expression firm.

"Then do better," she says. "Don't beat yourself up and vow to do better."

"I will."

"You better," she demands. "I don't want to live in a world without my best friend. So get your head in the game, Blake."

"Will do, Coach," I say.

We turn and walk on a little farther, neither of us speaking. She was right though—a walk is exactly what I needed to decompress. To take my mind off what happened and refocus it on what's yet to come. Astra likes to say she knows me better than I know myself, and I suspect she's right about that. We've been friends for so long, she's seen me at my best, at my worst, and at every point in between. And I'm beyond grateful to always have her there to talk me off the ledge when I need it. I'm beyond grateful to have a friend like her.

As the sun starts to crest the mountains in the east, it sets the sky on fire in shades of red and orange as it spreads its sparkling golden rays across the land. I have no reason to believe it other than that building sense of momentum in my belly, but I feel like today's the day this all comes to a head. Today is the day the dam is going to crumble, and all hell is going to break loose along with it.

I take a quick glance at Astra and her face is pinched, her expression sober. As usual, we seem to be in sync, and she looks like she's thinking along the same lines I am.

"You feel it?" I ask.

Astra nods. "I do."

"Then let's get to it."

CHAPTER THIRTY

Anderson Realty Building; Annenberg, ND

O NE OF PAULSON'S DEPUTIES BRINGS IN A BOX OF sandwiches and chips. Given the withering glare, the sheriff shoots at his subordinate, I have to assume it's the deputy who leaked information to Kira Rice's sister. Mo walks over and thanks the man, then starts handing out everybody's lunch. We've been at this all day, and though our scope is narrowing, we're not where I want us to be yet.

I stand at the whiteboard looking at the notes I've scrawled down. Aside from going back to victimology, I'm going back to our profile and trying to refine that. If we can nail that down, I think we'll have a better chance of pinpointing our guy.

"What is our suspect pool looking like?" I ask.

"We've got fifty-seven names on the list," Nina calls back. "They all fit some portion of the profile, but nobody fits it completely."

I tuck a strand of hair behind my ear and keep looking. Not fitting the entire profile isn't the problem. Most suspects will have an outlier or two that doesn't fit in with a profile. Age is the most common piece of data that's incorrect, simply because it's almost impossible to determine that. Defense attorneys love to use the age range we ascribe to their clients as proof that profiling is nothing but pseudo-science and can't be trusted. After all, if we can't get their age right, how can anything else we say be right?

Age is impossible to get right. But there are markers we follow that lead us to determine the range of a given unsub. A younger offender often lacks the maturity and sophistication that older offenders do. Younger killers are often frenzied and unorganized. They lack the discipline to cover their tracks properly. Older offenders—serials, in particular—tend to be more methodical. Their crime scenes are typically organized and clean. They have the sophistication younger killers lack. And unlike their younger counterparts, they're patient. They take their time and don't rush things. Most of the time, they make fewer mistakes.

For this unsub, we thankfully have a frame of reference to assign an age range. With his first kills dating back to 2000, assuming our offender started killing right after high school, that puts him in his forties. Because of how the bodies were discovered—the first three in challenging terrain—it's unlikely he's much older than that. It's not easy to carry dead weight down the slope in that first park. Not even if the dead weight is cut up and put in a bag.

If the girls had been spread out through multiple bags, I might argue that our killer could be older. But because they were cut up and stuffed into one bag, that tells me we're in the right age range. But that's only one part of the profile. Other variables might point us toward a particular person and lead us down a wrong path. I feel like the clock is ticking, and we don't have much time if we're going to find this guy.

"What do you think the odds are that Brooke Haverson is still alive?" Astra asks as she steps up beside me.

"Honestly? Probably not very good," I reply. "The fact that he's freezing them makes me think he's not keeping them alive as long as we thought. But it's not impossible."

Astra frowns. "I kind of figured you were going to say that."

"I'm trying to be hopeful. I want to be wrong and find her when we find him. Alive. I just don't have a good feeling about it," I say.

"This is one of those rare times when I hope you're wrong. I don't think I've ever wanted you to be wrong more in my life."

"Yeah, that makes two of us."

We both stare at my notes on the board for a minute, each of us trying to put all the puzzle pieces together in a way that forms a coherent picture. The right picture. There is a young girl's life hanging in the balance who, if she's still alive, doesn't have time for us to be wrong.

"How do we winnow down fifty-seven names?" I ask. "How do we cut the list down to get our guy?"

"We can't go knock on all those doors. It'll take way too long," Astra says. "And if he feels us getting close, he might just kill Brooke to keep us from winning. That is… if he hasn't killed her already."

"That was my thought too—"

Before I can say more, my phone rings. I pull it out of my pocket, see that it's the Minot field office, and feel a flash of hope. With a cautious smile on my face, I show Astra the caller ID and then gesture for her to follow me outside. It's too loud in the office, and I want to be able to hear Archie's words. As we step into the afternoon sun, I see the two cars Paulson has positioned at either end of the block, his men stationed there to keep an eye on us.

"Cross your fingers Archie has a name for us," I say.

"Consider everything crossed. Twice."

I connect the call and put it on speaker so Astra can hear. "Archie, hey," I say. "I wasn't expecting to hear from you today. Hopeful, but not expecting it."

"Well, you know me. I like to be like Santa Claus and obstetricians—always delivering good surprises," he replies.

I laugh despite my grim mood, and Astra rolls her eyes, but she can't hide her own smile. Archie just has a way of lightening the room.

"How are things going up there in Annenberg?" he asks.

"Other than somebody trying to murder Blake? Twice? Everything's been peachy keen up here," Astra quips.

"Twice? What? Really?" he asks, sounding scandalized. "Jeez. Hearing stuff like that makes me super glad I work in a lab. I don't think I'd do well with people trying to murder me all the time."

"It was twice. It's not all the time," I reply.

"It's a lot," Astra adds. "Like, I don't know anybody who's almost been murdered as much as Blake."

"That's… disturbing," he says.

I laugh softly, the banter lifting my mood. But there's only one thing that's going to put me in a good mood.

"Listen, Archie," I say. "We're kind of spinning our wheels here. We're kind of stuck in the mud. I'm hoping you can help get us unstuck. I'm assuming you're calling about the DNA on that sweater. So, what do you have for us?"

"Gosh, I hate doing this, but I'm not calling with good news," he replies. "I wish I were and that I could help get you unstuck, but I'm unfortunately not."

I sigh and lean back against the wall. Astra and I share a look of pitiful commiseration. I shouldn't have gotten my hopes up.

"Our luck never runs that smoothly." Astra says exactly what I was thinking.

"Was there anything on that sweater?" I ask.

"I found no hairs or fibers," he says. "But we were right, those brown stains were blood."

"Too degraded for DNA, huh?" I ask.

"Well, the blood wasn't human," he clarifies.

"It wasn't human?" I frown. "Then what was it?"

"It was a mixed sample, actually," he says. "I found cow, pig, and chicken blood mixed into the samples on the sweater. I'm assuming the contamination came from wherever she'd been buried."

I lean my head back and look up at the sky, feeling my frustration building. Another dead end. More ticks of the clock that Brooke Haverson doesn't have.

"I'm sorry, Agent Wilder," Archie says. "I wish I had better news for you."

"Thanks, Archie. I wish you did too," I reply. "But you have nothing to apologize for. I appreciate your help."

"You bet. And if there is anything else I can help you with, please don't hesitate."

"You can count on it," I say.

"Take care of yourself and try to avoid being murdered."

I laugh. "I'll do my best."

I disconnect the call and drop my phone into my pocket. The optimism that had filled the air just a moment ago fizzled out like a deflating balloon.

"Back to square one," Astra grouses. "Do not pass go, do not collect two hundred dollars. God, this sucks."

I keep staring at the sky, watching the clouds lazily drifting by. All these disparate pieces of information are bouncing around in my head, but none of them seem to be fitting together into any coherent pattern. But just as I'm about to throw in the towel on finding my way back to square one with Astra, something in my head clicks.

I stand up and feel my veins filling with electricity and fire as a thought occurs to me. It's one of those feelings I get when I know I've stumbled onto the right answer. As I think about it and turn it over in my mind, scouring intently for any holes in my theory, I don't see any. I may be stumbling down another blind corridor, but I don't think I am. Everything inside of me is telling me I've got the right answer.

"You have that look," Astra says. "You just put something together, didn't you?"

"The disarticulated joints, the frozen bodies, the mixed blood sample," I list off. "We've been looking at this the wrong way."

"How's that?"

"We're not looking for somebody with medical knowledge. We're not looking for a doctor," I explain.

"Then what are we looking for?"

"A butcher."

"You're kidding me," Astra says.

"Think about it. Butchers have to disarticulate the bodies of animals all the time. It's not very different to pull a cow's leg apart from a human's. Then, to preserve the meat, you have to freeze them, right?" I postulate. "And then you have the blood. How likely is it that the girl would have been buried in a spot that contains cow, pig, *and* chicken blood?"

Astra chews on her lower lip as she thinks about it. The more I think about it myself, the more convinced I become. Everything fits. More than that, not only does everything fit, that feeling I've been carrying around that I've been missing something vanishes. All the pieces in my mind have fallen into place and have formed a complete picture. Now, all we need to do is find out whose face belongs in that frame.

"Come on," I say.

We walk back into the office, and I step over to the whiteboard. My body is vibrating with electric excitement, and that feeling of momentum has reached a fevered pitch in my mind. This is the right path. I know it is.

"Okay guys, stop what you're doing," I announce.

Everybody stops and turns to me, plunging the office into silence.

"Sheriff Paulson, how many butchers do you have in town?" I ask.

He screws up his face and thinks about it for a minute. "Three," he says. "Well, soon to be two now that Jay Scopes is going under. Damn shame. He's got some of the best barbecue in town. But once his dad died, he kind of went off the rails."

"When did his father die?" I ask.

"Oh, a couple of months ago now," Paulson replies. "Drunk driver. Nasty business."

Astra and I exchange a look, and I see that she's finally convinced that we're heading down the right path. Before I can issue orders, Nina and Rick are already banging away at their keyboards. A buzz of anticipation descends over the room, and I see Paulson and Koda give each other quizzical looks. Before I explain, though, I wait for Rick and Nina to work their magic.

"Jay Milton Scopes, forty-two years old, graduate of McCumber High, class of 1999," Nina reads off. "Was a four-year athlete. Played football, baseball, and hockey. He wore jersey number twelve."

"Yeah, he was McCumber's starting quarterback all four years. Made varsity as a freshman, which was unheard of," Paulson interrupts. "Had a full ride to Notre Dame but blew out his knee in the state playoffs. Wrecked his knee, in fact, and he was never able to play again. It was really a shame. He had what it took to have a great pro career."

"And what happened after that?" I ask.

"He went to work at his dad's butcher shop," Paulson replies. "A couple of years ago, he expanded and built his barbecue joint. Developed a barbecue sauce all his own. Patented it and I thought he was making a killing with it. It came as a surprise to everybody when we found out he was going under."

"Bad investments and a pretty bad gambling habit drained him dry," Rick jumps in. "Looks like all his cards are maxed out, he's got two mortgages on his house—he's bleeding money every way a person can bleed money. The man is broke. He's also not making as much money on his barbecue sauce as you think. Though I will agree with you, it is *amazing*... thank you, Lucas, for bringing those sliders back to us."

Lucas nods. "Right? Incredible flavor."

"It looks like he set up a GoFundMe campaign just after his father died. He was trying to raise fifty grand to save the shop," Nina says.

I think back to the day of the search and recall the man. He was wearing his letterman's jacket—something he took great pride in. He was the one regaling the football team with stories of his glory days. He'd walked with a slight limp—a memento of the injury that had taken everything from him.

"How much did his campaign raise?" I ask.

"Just under three thousand," Nina reports.

"That explains why he feels left behind and forgotten," Astra says. "Nobody was willing to pitch in when he needed their help the most."

"He used to be a god. People used to revere him," Mo says. "And now he's learned the world has moved on without him."

"And it pushed him over the edge," Lucas adds.

Paulson shakes his head. "But you said he's been killing for twenty years. I don't understand how his father's death has anything to do with this. Or why he's suddenly killing girls from good families in town."

"He has been killing for twenty years," I offer. "But he's been tightly controlled. He's been methodical and cunning. He learned how to avoid detection and has been operating for two decades. I'm going to guess since he started so early, it's something he learned from his father. I'm willing to bet that if we go back further, we're going to find that his father was killing girls too. But they were careful. They stuck to their game plan."

Paulson shakes his head, trying to deny it. "That's preposterous. Merrill Scopes was a good man. Kind. Generous. He—"

"Was a sociopath and knew how to blend into any and all social situations," I counter.

"But his father's death, combined with the closure of his family business, the mounting bills, and the lack of help from a community he used to be revered in all came crashing down on him at once," Astra adds. "It was too much, and he decided he was going to make a stand. That he was going to do something to punish all the people who didn't help him. All the people he feels turned their backs on him. He was going to do something to make them remember him."

Paulson's legs seem to give out under him, and he drops heavily into his chair. He runs a hand over his face, unable to wipe away the expression of disbelief. Koda stands to his right, her face stony and dark. I can't tell what she's thinking. She's almost impossible to read.

"This is our guy," I say. "I will stake my badge on it."

"He doesn't have a gray truck though."

"That you know of," I point out. "Maybe he bought it from somebody and never filed the registration. Maybe he stole it. We're going to find that truck out on his property though. I guarantee it."

"Why does he kill?" Koda asks.

I shake my head. "I can't answer that. Only he can," I tell her. "But killing fulfills some need inside of him. Maybe it was for his dad's approval. Maybe he just likes it. I don't know. All I do know is there's a hole inside of him, and killing these girls is the only thing that fills it."

Koda looks at Paulson. "He does tick off all the boxes," she tells him. "The profile they came up with sounds almost exactly like him."

"I knew his father. Hell, I knew him," Paulson replies, his voice thick with emotion. "They were good people. They were important members of this town."

"Which is why their refusal to help him hit Scopes as hard as it did," Astra says. "It's why he's punishing everybody by killing their daughters."

"This is unreal," Paulson mutters.

"This is about as real as it gets," I say, then turn to my team. "Let's strap up, guys. Make sure you put on your tactical vests. We're going to bring him in."

"I want to come," Paulson says.

"So do I," Koda adds.

"Fine," I nod. "Just make sure to stay back. The situation is going to be tense and emotional enough as it is."

I look around at the team. "All right, let's roll."

CHAPTER THIRTY-ONE

A Cut Above, Scopes's Fine Meats & BBQ; Annenberg, ND

W E HIT HIS HOUSE FIRST, BUT SCOPES WASN'T HOME. I fear that he knows we're closing in on him, so he took off and is in the wind. That's not how I profiled him, but he could have bolted. My profile, though, says he's not going to run or go out in a hail of bullets. I believe he's going to want to witness the fallout from what he's done and will stick around to see it. But that doesn't mean he's going to make it easy for us to find him.

Because he's still got a young girl we are still considering alive until we have proof otherwise, I want to keep the situation from escalating. I don't want him doing something rash. If Brooke Haverson is still alive, I want to do everything I can to keep it that way. That's why I told Paulson to keep his men away. He wanted to storm the shop, but I quickly vetoed that idea and told him to deploy his men back to Scopes's house to look for evidence. He reluctantly agreed on the condition that at least he and Koda could accompany us.

I still don't think Paulson is totally on board with the idea that Scopes is our guy and wants his men there to make sure we're not pulling something over on him. Even though he's been helpful, the distrust of the federal government is strong here, and he just wants to make sure we're not railroading an innocent man. I get that. And frankly, I admire his dedication to protecting his people. I can't fault him for it.

On the other hand, though, I'm not going to let him interfere with our apprehension. Scopes's guilt or innocence isn't up to us to decide. It's for the courts to determine. It is our job to follow the evidence and follow all leads. And right now, that's leading us straight to Jay Scopes. We're going to bring him in, question him, and let the chips fall where they may.

I deployed Mo and Lucas to the front of the shop and told them to take Paulson with them. Astra, Koda, and I are pulling up behind the shop.

"He's here," I say, pointing to the open rear door.

"Looks that way," Astra nods.

We get out of the SUV and pull our weapons, and I key open my microphone.

"Sheriff Paulson, Scopes is here," I say. "I'm looking at the gray truck that tried to run me down last night."

"Are you sure it's the same one?" comes his reply.

"Judging by the damage to the front passenger's side, I'm going to say yes," I reply.

There's a long pause as he absorbs the information. I'm sure it can't be easy to wrap your mind around the fact that somebody you've known your whole life isn't who you thought they were. It can't be easy to find out somebody you thought of as a friend has this dark side to them. To find out they're a monster.

"Copy that," he finally says.

"Sheriff, are the two businesses on either side of Scopes's shop occupied?"

"The one on our right is not; the one on our left is—it's an accounting firm," he replies.

"You might want to get them out of here. I don't think this is going to turn violent, but I don't want to take any chances," I tell him. "I don't want any collateral damage."

"Copy," he says.

"Let me know when we're clear to enter."

Astra and Koda are standing on either side of the open door, weapons drawn, bodies taut and coiled, ready for action. I stand by the ruined side of the truck and recall just how close a call it was. Just how narrow my brush with death had been. It makes me shudder to remember it.

"Agent Wilder!"

A man's voice—presumably Scopes's voice—drifts out of the open doorway. I exchange glances with Astra and Koda. They both give me the same shrug. I step up beside Astra and lean over so I can shout through the open door.

"Jay Scopes?" I call back. "Why don't you come on out here?"

"Why don't you come on in here and have a chat with me?"

Astra gives me a small shake of her head. "No way. You can't go in there," she whispers. "What if he has the place wired to blow? What if he's sitting on a machine gun and lights you up the minute you step into view?"

"What if he just wants to talk?" I counter.

"Blake, he's killed a bunch of girls—"

"Girls. Not women," I say. "I don't fit his preference."

"Preferences change. Desperation and realizing they're facing the end of the line can make these monsters change anything and everything. He might kill you just because he can. Need I remind you he already tried twice," she hisses.

"I'm not armed and I'm going to give myself up when we're done talking," he calls out. "Just you and me. I give you my word."

A bitter laugh bursts from my throat. "And I should take the word of a man who's murdered thirty young women?"

"Thirty?" he asks with an ominous laugh.

I know he's baiting me. I know he wants me to walk in there. Whether it's just to talk or whether he's got something planned, I don't know. But my profile doesn't suggest he's going out violently, which makes me lean toward thinking he just wants to talk. But what could he possibly want to talk to me about? I'm not from this town. I'm not one of his people. If there's somebody he should be wanting to speak with and explain himself to, it's Sheriff Paulson.

"Buildings are clear. You're good to go," the Sheriff's voice crackles through the radio.

"Blake, don't," Astra urges.

"We profiled that he's not going out in a blaze of fire and bullets," I say. "If we don't trust our own profiles, what are we doing? What can we trust?"

Astra grimaces, but she knows I'm right. She knows there's nothing she can say. It's not that I want to walk into that room necessarily. It's stupid to walk into a room with a killer without backup. But I'd be lying if I said there wasn't a morbidly curious piece of me that wants to go in and see about having a chat with him.

"He's offering to talk," I say. "It might be our only chance to get some answers."

Astra looks down at the ground and then back up at me. "I don't like this."

"I'm not a big fan either, but I want answers."

"Keep your radio open. I want to hear everything," she tells me. "And call out the instant you feel this thing going sideways—which, for the record, I'm ninety-nine point nine percent sure it's going to. I want to be the one to save your butt because I intend to lord it over you for the rest of your life."

"I would expect nothing less," I reply with a grin.

"Good luck," Koda says. "And if the opportunity presents itself, don't hesitate to put one in his forehead. Maybe two."

She gives me an awkward smile, and I can't tell if she's kidding or not. My gut tells me no. Having murdered as many indigenous girls as he has, I'm sure there's a big part of Deputy Koda that wants some primal vengeance. And I can't blame her for it.

"All right, Scopes, I'm coming in," I call out. "If I even smell something off, I'm going to put a round in your face. Maybe two." I glance at Koda, whose smile looks a little more real this time. "I just want to talk. That's all," he calls back. I key open my mic. "Everybody, hold positions. I'm going in," I say. "Stand ready, though, just in case."

Keeping my gun out in front of me, I walk into the dim interior of the shop. I come down the hallway, passing a time clock, an open door that leads to a bathroom, and stacks of cardboard boxes that hold supplies. The hallway opens up into the shop which is about fifty feet long and forty feet wide. It's not a big place, and it has a homey feel to it.

The walls are a pale blue, the tile on the floor is blue and white, and along the wall across from me are large, refrigerated cases that still hold a variety of meats. There are three large blackboards hanging on the wall behind the cases that list out the day's specials and the different meats for sale. The air is fragrant with the aroma of the same barbecue sauce I smelled the day we held the search for Brooke Haverson. On the far end of the counter are several large pots filled up with sauce simmering on top of small, lit flames. For a shop that's supposed to be going under, it sure seems like a business-as-usual sort of day.

Scopes is sitting on the counter next to the cash register looking at me with an amused smirk on his face. As promised, he's unarmed. He's just sitting there wearing a pair of blue jeans, dark work boots, and a red-and-black checked flannel with the sleeves rolled up. Kansas's classic song, "Dust in the Wind," is playing from a boombox on the counter behind the cases, and Scopes is singing along with it.

"It's nice to meet you face to face, Agent Wilder," he says.

"So? I'm here. What do you have to say?"

"Are you always so abrupt?"

"I just don't feel the need to make pleasant conversation with a man who tried to shoot me, then run me down with his truck. I'm quirky like that."

He laughs softly. "I hope you're not expecting an apology. We're adversaries after all."

"I'm not expecting anything from you. Except for your surrender," I say.

"Of course. But before we get to that, I want to talk to you."

"So? Talk. I'll give you two minutes."

"We'll see."

"Where is Brooke Haverson?" I ask.

"She's here."

"Let me see her."

"In time."

"Is she still alive?"

"Do you know why I'm turning myself in to you?" he asks.

"Because you realize there's nowhere for you to go and that the game is up?"

He shrugs. "We were getting there. We had entered the final act. But, no," he says. "I'm turning myself in to you because you are the final piece I needed to finish what I set out to do. I'm only just now realizing it. But you ever get that feeling when you think about something, you just know it's true?"

"More than you know."

He nods. "Then you get it. When I thought about you after I tried to run you down—and I thought about you a lot—I realized that instead of killing you, I needed to *use* you. It hit me that you're here for a reason. And that reason is to help me."

I lower my weapon to my side but don't holster it, then begin to walk around the shop, never taking my eyes off him.

"And how am I supposed to help you?" I ask.

"You're my final act," he replies. "It's far more fitting for me to be taken in by a fed than some small, Podunk town sheriff. Don't get me wrong. I like Sheriff Paulson well enough, but he kind of makes Barney Fife look like a Rhodes Scholar. Know what I mean?"

"I don't. Sheriff Paulson is a good man. He's intelligent, and he cares about the people in this town," I reply. "He even cares about you."

"I didn't say he wasn't a good man. But he isn't savvy to the ways of the big, bad world outside of this little, old place," he says. "But you… you're a fed. A celebrated FBI agent. I hope it's not too strange that I looked you up online."

I shrug. "No stranger than anything else you've done," I say. "Now, take me to Brooke."

"Don't you want to know why I've done all this?"

"It all boils down to your ego," I say. "You felt bad about yourself because the town wasn't helping you keep your shop open. You used to be the big man on campus, but after you blew out your knee, you became a mortal again. The world has gone on without you, and that's pissing you off."

He grimaces, and I can tell I hit a nerve. "It's a little more complicated than that."

"It's really not. At the end of the day, this is all about you not getting the attention you think you're owed. The attention you think you deserve. You peaked in high school and now you're mad because you never amounted to anything else in your life."

He jumps down from the counter, his face red and twisted with rage. I bring my weapon up and point it straight at his face. He lets out an indecipherable howl of outrage and reminds me of a kid throwing a tantrum. It's so pathetic it's difficult not to laugh.

"Blake!" Astra calls.

"I'm fine," I call back. "Stay out. It's all good."

Scopes smooths down his hair and takes a deep breath, then he exhales slowly. He takes a couple of beats to calm himself down and then raises his eyes to me once more.

"You have no idea what you're talking about. My family did a lot for this hellhole of a town. We helped so many people," he says, his voice still trembling with rage. "And when *we* needed them, they turned their backs on us. When *we* needed help, where were *they*?"

"So, you feel wronged by the people of Annenberg. You feel like they betrayed you," I tell him. "I get it."

"Do you?"

"I do. And because of your family name—because you used to be revered—finding out that adulation had a shelf life, and it expired long ago, must have really hurt. Right?"

"My family needed them. When my father got sick, nobody stepped up to help," he goes on, irritation flaring through his eyes. I can tell, though, that it's not irritation at me. It's the rage he's been carrying for his whole adult life. "My family's business, which has been a part of the fabric of this town for sixty years, is going under because I didn't have the money to care for my father and nobody stepped up to help. And then he got hit by a drunk and the damn Sheriff's department didn't even have the decency to catch the man. But I did. And I made sure he suffered."

"So you feel betrayed because of what happened to your father. And you took it upon yourself to take your revenge?"

"That's right."

"But your father only died a few months ago, Jay. What about all these other victims? These girls?"

"They had what was coming. Ain't my fault they were in the wrong place at the wrong time."

"And I'm guessing all of your bad investments and all that gambling you've done isn't your fault either?" I ask. "Because it looks to me like you're asking everybody else to pony up for your own mistakes."

"That's not true."

"I've seen your financials. It's kind of true."

He falls silent and glares at me, the hatred burning in his eyes.

"You and your father have been killing for a long, long time," I press. "I can put bodies on you as far back as twenty years ago. Why? Why did you start killing?"

His grin is malicious and is as close to the embodiment of evil as I've ever seen. "Call it a family business," he shrugs. "I learned from my father. He learned from his."

So, at least that much is confirmed for me. "So, you started killing because you wanted your father's approval."

He shrugs. "Once again, it's more complicated than that," he says. "But you seem to like simplistic answers. So be it."

"Explain it to me."

"You're the vaunted FBI profiler. I'll leave it to you to figure out."

"Fine. You made it sound earlier as if you've killed more than thirty girls."

"Many more."

"Where are the bodies?"

"All over."

"I'm sure if you are willing to work with the US Attorney, they will be willing to work with you regarding your sentence. They might take the death penalty off the table," I say.

"Do you think I care about the death penalty?"

"I do, actually," I say with a wolfish smile. "I think you want to stick around and see the fallout of what you've done. I think you want to read all the papers, see all the talk shows. Hell, I don't doubt that deep down, you're hoping to be interviewed yourself."

The faint smile on his lips sends a chill down my spine. It's his eyes. They're vacant. Totally devoid of all emotion. I've only just noticed that about him and think that's the creepiest part of the man.

"Perhaps," he says.

"All right, let's finish this," I say. "Where is Brooke Haverson?"

"As I said, she's here. But before I let you see her, I want to show you something."

He reaches behind him, and I bring my weapon up again, my body taut, my jaw clenched, and my finger poised over the trigger.

"Stop moving!" I shout.

He stops and looks back at me. "Relax, Agent Wilder. I promised you I had no weapon, and I don't. I'm not reaching for one either," he says. "I just think there's something you need to see if you hope to understand me. Understand what it is I'm doing."

"Blake," Astra calls. "You good?"

I hesitate and Scopes holds his hands up, showing me they're empty. "I only want to show you something."

"Blake!"

"I'm good, Astra," I call. "I'm good."

I want to understand. I want to see whatever it is that Scopes has to show me. Licking my lips nervously, I nod.

"Slowly," I tell him. "You move too quick, and I swear to God I'll put a bullet in you."

"Fair enough."

With exaggerated slowness, Scopes reaches behind the counter and comes out with a blue, three-inch, three-ring binder. It's faded and aged and stuffed with plastic sheets. The binder has obviously been handed down through the generations.

"What is that?" I ask.

"It explains everything."

"Then, are you going to let me see it?"

"In time," he says with a grin, holding tightly to the book. "I don't want to spoil the surprise just yet."

"I'm done with this. Give me the binder or—"

"Just… indulge me. For two more minutes. Tops," he says. "There's just one more thing you have to see. Please, Agent Wilder. Two more minutes. You can keep your gun on me the whole time. I swear to God I'm not trying to hurt you. I just want you to see."

I look at him for a long moment, and though I see unadulterated evil in his eyes, I surprisingly don't see any hint of deception. If anything, I'd say he looks… excited.

This is his plan, and I have no choice but to follow it to the bitter end.

"Fine," I say. "Show me."

"Follow me."

He turns and walks behind the counter, then pushes through the swinging doors that lead to the back of the shop. Staying a good ten feet behind him, I follow, my gun at the ready. When I step into the back of the shop, I see Scopes standing at the door of one of the two industrial-grade freezers, turning the dial on the combination lock. It pops open a moment later, and Scopes pulls it off then tosses it aside. He turns to me with that eerie smile on his face.

"Are you ready?" he asks.

"Before I do anything, I want you to put your hands out," I demand.

He does as I say, and I step over to him. With the barrel of my Glock pressed to the side of his face, I give him a quick pat-down and don't find a weapon on him.

"I gave you my word," he says.

"That you did."

Taking him by his right wrist, I walk him over to a steep bar mounted to the wall. I clasp one of my handcuffs around his wrist, then lock the other to the bar. I give it a couple of firm tugs, and it holds fast. He's not going anywhere. Scopes doesn't offer any resistance. He just stands there with that smirk on his face, and it's creeping me out.

"Binder," I demand.

"Freezer first," he counters. "See what's in there, then I'll hand over the binder."

I'm not necessarily in the mood to indulge him, but I'm not in the mood to get physical with him and tear the book out of his hands. This is one of those times when the path of least resistance is the better choice. It's not a choice I make often, but I'm going to make an exception in this case just because I want to get this over with.

Grumbling under my breath, I step over to the freezer he'd just unlocked and pull the door open. And when I see what's inside, my legs give out under me, and I fall to my knees. The sound of Scopes laughing hysterically echoes around the room but sounds like it's a thousand miles away.

"Astra, get in here," I say, my voice choked and barely more than a whisper. "Get everybody in here."

CHAPTER THIRTY-TWO

A Cut Above, Scopes's Fine Meats & BBQ; Annenberg, ND

ASTRA STORMS INTO THE BACK ROOM AND RUSHES OVER to me. She steps over and helps me to my feet, then turns to the freezer and stops. Her entire body tightens, and her eyes grow wide. Koda, who's on the other side of me, has the same reaction. And through it all, Scopes is standing behind us, cuffed to the wall, still cackling like a lunatic.

"Dear God in Heaven," Astra whispers.

There are two rows of hooks hanging from the ceiling, and each row has four hooks. They're all currently in use, and on each hook hangs the body of a young girl. The first one I see is unmistakable. Brooke Haverson.

I stare into her glassy, frost-covered eyes and feel like sobbing. Like all the others, her skin is blue and crusted in ice. Her mouth is hanging open, and there's a look of agony twisting her features. And like the others, Brooke has had large sections perfectly excised from her body.

All at once, I realize it's not a forensic countermeasure. He's not cutting out those sections from their bodies to hide the impressions on his jaw. He's not a biter. These girls have been carved up not to throw us off his scent and muddy the waters of our investigation. Not for pleasure or excitement. Not even for the thrill of a kill. But for consumption. Scopes cut them up the same way he would carve a side of beef. Or a hog.

I'm so stunned that I can't move. I can barely breathe. So, when Koda turns and rushes across the room, all I can do for a moment is stand there and watch as she delivers a flurry of blows that rock Scopes's head back and to the side. Astra is the first to react. She manages to break her paralysis and runs over to Koda. She wraps her arms around the deputy's body, pinning her arms to her sides, and yanks her back.

Scopes is bleeding from the nose and the mouth. There are abrasions on his cheeks, and his left eye is swollen and starting to close already. But he's still laughing like this is the funniest thing he's ever experienced. I force myself to walk away from the freezer, tearing my eyes away from the bodies of those girls hanging from the hooks. I need to move. I need to do something to keep myself from focusing on them. From obsessing on them.

"Jesus Christ," Paulson shouts when he steps into the room.

Mo and Lucas are stone still, staring into the freezer, wearing matching expressions of shock and disgust. Paulson turns away, his face red and clouded over with emotion. But I see him bury his face in his hands, and his body shakes as he sobs. We need to call somebody. We need to call everybody. The problem is, I'm so freaking rattled right now, that I don't know who to call. Paulson's guys aren't equipped to handle this. Hell, I'm not sure the Bureau is either.

But I know my team is looking to me to guide them. To lead them. I know to some extent, Paulson is too. He's in uncharted territory here and way out of his league. When he says nothing like this happens in Annenberg, I believe him. The sense of shock and disbelief in that back area of the shop is palpable. It's a heavy weight that's pressing down on all of us. It's choking us. It's making it difficult for us to breathe let alone think.

But somebody needs to step up. Somebody needs to seize this moment and take control. And I know it has to be me. This is my team. This is my job. And I can't let the situation get this deep beneath my skin—no matter how monstrous it is.

"Sheriff Paulson. Deputy Koda," I say. "I need you to take Mr. Scopes into custody. Make sure you read him his rights. More than that, I need you to remember he has rights."

I look at Koda pointedly, and to her credit, she looks away, the shame of losing control of herself in that moment painting her features.

"We don't want Scopes getting off on a technicality, a trumped-up charge of brutality, or anything like that," I remind them. "I know how close this hits to home and how emotional this is for you all. But you need to keep your heads about you. Now more than ever. Don't give his defense attorney any ammunition. Do not let him win. Do not give him that."

Scopes is still cackling as Koda and Paulson somberly cuff him. Koda is reading Scopes his rights, her voice robotic and her face expressionless. As they lead him out of the shop, I pull my phone out of my pocket, dial the number, and press it to my ear. He picks it up on the first ring.

"Agent Wilder. Nice to hear from you again," Archie says. "How's your case going?"

"Archie, we need you in Annenberg. As soon as you can get here," I tell him. "Bring your entire crime lab. We need everybody."

"Is everything… okay?"

"It's not. It's really not."

"We're on our way."

I disconnect the call and then send a text to Rick and Nina, telling them to bring their gear and get over here. There's a lot we can do before the team from Minot arrives. That done, I drop the phone back into my pocket and turn to my team. Their faces are drawn and pale, and their movements are stiff and wooden. They look shell-shocked.

"I know this is hard, guys. In many ways, I know this might be the toughest case we've ever had," I say. "And when we get back to Seattle, I'm going to tell Ayad and Stone we need at least a week out of rotation. I want to give you all time to deal with what we're seeing here right now. But until then, we've got a job to do. If you can't do it, I understand. There's absolutely no shame in saying you can't. If you want to go back to the hotel and don't want any part of this, now's the time. And again, there is no shame."

I exchange looks with everybody and see the firm resolve in all their eyes. I didn't expect that anybody would go, and they didn't let me down. But I wasn't lying. If any of them wanted out, it would have been fine. But they're going to stick with this until the bitter end—and the end will be bitter. I've never been prouder of my team than I am right now.

"All right. Let's get to work," I say firmly. "The team from the Minot field office is on their way. Let's start bagging everything we can find."

Nobody says a word, but everybody gets to work searching the place from top to bottom, looking for evidence. As they bag things up, I walk over and pick up the binder Scopes dropped. As I start flipping through it, my heart drops into my stomach.

"Jesus," I groan.

The pages are filled with recipes, each of them incorporating the name of a girl into the title—presumably the names of his victims. I turn to the last page to confirm my theory and grimace when I see the title, "Sweet and Sour Brooke." It's got three stars beside the title and some handwritten notes scrawled across the page.

I close the book and try to control the churning in my belly. I glance at my watch and say a silent prayer that Archie and his team arrive quickly. The sooner they get here, the sooner we can process the scene. And once we have it processed, we can close out the case. The agents from Minot will take custody of Scopes, and we will be free to go home and try to forget everything we've seen here.

I just need Archie to get here. Soon.

"We've got about two dozen boxes stuffed with evidence," Archie tells me. "And that's not including what your people boxed up before we got here."

"And there's still the residence to process," I tell him. "According to what Scopes told me, this is a tradition handed down through the generations. At the very least, his father was doing the same thing. Maybe even his grandfather."

"Wow. That's... awful," Archie says grimly, but he quickly brightens again. "Do you think cannibalism is hereditary? Or do you think it's learned? It makes the whole nature versus nurture thing a whole lot darker, doesn't it?"

"Yeah, you could say that," I reply, my tone grim. "Sorry, I guess I'm just not really in the mood for witty banter today."

"Sorry," he says. "I'm usually a little more on when I'm dealing with something horrible. Though, to be fair, this level of horrible is unprecedented in my life."

"Mine too."

"So, I'm terrified to ask, but what did you find?" I ask.

"Well, we still don't have the ID's on the seven girls in the freezer with Brooke Haverson," he admits. "Your techs have been running their prints and photos through every database, but have come up empty so far."

"We know they're not from Annenberg. But we don't know where Scopes picked them up or how long he's had them," I muse.

"They're indigenous. That much I can tell you. I just can't tell you anything more than that, I'm afraid."

Deputy Koda flashes through my mind. Another seven indigenous girls nobody is looking for. Another seven girls whose disappearances aren't being investigated. I scrub my face with my hands and try to control the anger that surges through me.

"I can also tell you that you are correct about Scopes—consuming these girls," Archie tells me with disgust in his tone.

"And if I had to guess, based on that recipe book you found, he's been doing it for a long, long time."

"I'm pretty sure that book started with his father. At least."

"It's going to take some time to determine the age of some of those—God, I hate even saying it—recipes, but I suspect you're right. A quick look through, though, makes me think it goes back even farther than that. But we'll have somebody analyze it to be sure," he says.

"Unreal. At least three generations of cannibals. How does that happen?"

"God knows," he says. "But that's not the worst part of this story."

"It gets worse?"

He nods. "Yeah. It does. A lot worse."

"What is it?" I ask.

I don't know that I want to know what his answer is going to be. Especially since I have a feeling I already know what he's about to say. But I vowed to see this case through to the bitter end. If my team can handle it, I can as well.

Archie grimaces. "The meat in his cases is human," he says. "We haven't tested all of it yet, but so far, everything we've looked at is human. There's no reason for us to believe the rest of it isn't the same. We'll test it all, of course, but my best guess is that he's been selling the meat from those eight girls in his freezer to the people of Annenberg."

"Dear God," I mutter.

Lucas had been walking by us, but he stops and looks at us with wide eyes and a face etched with a growing sense of fear and disgust. I know what he's thinking. He's thinking about the sandwiches he and Mo ate—and took back for Rick and Nina—on the day of the search.

"What about the barbecue?" Lucas asks. "Was that made with—people?"

Archie frowns. "We tested the meat in the barbecue pots, and yes, it's confirmed to be human as well."

Lucas turns green and looks like he's about to be sick then walks away briskly. I can't even begin to imagine what that has to be doing to his head right now. But we'll deal with the fallout once we get back to Seattle. Right now, we need to finish up here.

"We still have a lot of testing to do and pieces of the puzzle to sort out," Archie says. "I'll be in touch with you as soon as I have more information."

"Thank you, Archie."

"Listen… I can't even begin to imagine how bad this is going to warp the minds of your people. This is going to take them some time to deal with," he says. "I hope you guys can all find a way to do that. To deal with it."

"Thank you, Archie. I'm sure I'm going to be following up with you plenty in the coming days," I say. "So, it looks like we're going to be getting to know each other pretty well."

"See? There's a silver lining," he says, offering me a small smile. "If you'll excuse me. I have lots of work to do."

As he walks off, I can see a slight spring in his step. Archie's disgusted by what's going on here, but it's not difficult to see that he's also excited to delve into this mess. I'm sure this is the most exciting thing to hit the Minot field office… ever, maybe.

"Agent Wilder?"

I turn around to find Sheriff Paulson standing there. The look on his face is one of excruciating agony. As difficult as this is for us to deal with, I have a feeling it's ten times worse for him. A hundred maybe. These people were his friends. Neighbors. Knowing what went on here has to be the most difficult and traumatic thing he has ever experienced.

"How are you holding up?" I ask.

"About as well as can be expected," he replies.

A moment of awkward silence passes between us. Paulson looks exhausted. Wrung out. The toll this is taking on him is obvious, and I feel awful for him. We stand there looking at each other in silence. The tragedy and suffering within these walls are so profound that it seems to have stolen our voices. But Paulson clears his throat and clenches his jaw, determined to go on.

"The story's already out," he says. "People already know what Scopes was doing here."

"We figured it would get out eventually. Though granted, I didn't expect it would be this quick," I say.

"The city is in shock," he says. "If Scopes was trying to shake Annenberg to its foundations, he succeeded. It's going to take the town a long time to recover from this. Frankly, I'm not so sure we ever will fully recover. What Scopes did was evil. Plain and simple."

"You're not wrong about that," I reply.

"And in the end, he's getting what he wanted. People will remember his name," Paulson says. "They're never going to forget it."

"Infamy has a way of lingering on. No doubt about that."

I glance over at Deputy Koda who's standing off to the side, filling out some paperwork. Turning back to Paulson, I frown.

"Listen, I don't want to step into your business and all, but you've got a really good one in Koda," I say. "Smart. Intuitive. She's passionate and determined. I think she'd be an asset to your department if you gave her a chance and a little more responsibility."

He follows my gaze over to her and nods. "She's shown me something with this whole thing," he acknowledges. "And she opened my eyes to the disparities within my department. I'm going to make some real changes—make sure nobody's getting overlooked."

"That's good, Sheriff," I say. "That's really good."

"Anyway, how are your people holding up?" he asks.

"It's going to leave some scars, no doubt about that. It's going to take some time for them to process everything," I say.

"I can imagine."

Another awkward silence settles down over us, and we shift on our feet.

"Well, it's time for me and my team to head back to home base," I say. "But we're leaving you in good hands with the team from Minot. They'll be able to answer any questions you have. And you have my card, so feel free to give me a buzz as well."

"I appreciate it, Agent Wilder. I appreciate everything," he says. "So, don't take it the wrong way when I say, I genuinely hope I never see you again."

A laugh bursts from my throat. I cut it off quickly, though, knowing how inappropriate it is given how much death we're surrounded by.

"Believe me, Sheriff Paulson," I say, shaking his hand, "I feel exactly the same way."

CHAPTER THIRTY-THREE

Office of SSA Wilder, Black Cell Alpha Team Bullpen; Seattle Field Office

AFTER LANDING IN SEATTLE, I SENT MY TEAM ON HOME. I wanted to give them some time away from the office with their friends and loved ones. I urged them all to talk to one of the many therapists the Bureau provides. Or to talk to their own. Or to just talk to somebody. Anybody. I begged them to do something other than keep it all locked away inside.

What we saw out in North Dakota was monstrous. It's going to take some time to fully wrap our minds around it—if we can ever fully come to grips with it. But one thing I do know is that trying to bottle that up and hold it all down inside is a recipe for disaster. Holding something like that inside will eventually make them spin out and explode. It will eventually exact such a heavy toll that it will turn their lives upside down.

Despite my eagerness to see my sister, I had to come into the office to fill out a few reports. I probably could have waited until tomorrow, but the truth was, I wasn't ready to see Kit yet. I wanted a little time to myself. A little time to unwind and decompress. I don't want to see Kit when I'm as wound up as I am right now.

"I didn't expect to see you here today."

I look up to see Ayad standing in my doorway. He's leaning against the frame with his hands in his pockets and a concerned look on his face.

"I figured I'd get a jump on the after-action reports," I tell him.

"Those could have waited."

"I know how you like promptness with our reports."

He gives me a wry smile then walks in and sits down on the chair in front of my desk. He crosses one leg over the other and folds his hands in his lap. Ayad is nothing if not prim and proper. But it's probably good that he's here, since I needed to talk to him anyway.

"I heard your case was rough," he starts with something that sounds like actual concern.

"Yeah. It was bad," I tell him honestly. "Which is why I want my team to have the next week off. I want them to have a little time and space to get their heads cleared."

"Done," he says. "In fact, tell them they've got the next two weeks off."

I look at him, surprised by how agreeable he was to that. It wasn't what I expected.

"I would also encourage you to tell your team to avail themselves of the counselors the Bureau provides—"

"I practically got on my knees and begged them to see somebody. I don't want them locking this away inside," I say. "What we saw out there was beyond belief. They need to see somebody."

"I can make that a condition of their return," he says.

"I don't want to force them. But I'll keep a close eye on them," I tell him. "If any of them start to spin out, you'll be the first to know."

"If that happens, I'll have to take them off rotation and make their return conditional on a shrink's sign-off."

I nod. "I know. I just want to give my team every chance to get themselves right on their own terms," I say. "Forcing them into therapy can be counterproductive."

"Agreed," he says. "You know, you and I didn't get off to a great start."

"No. We didn't."

"It's as much my fault as it is yours," he admits. "I think we were both too busy trying to mark our territory that we didn't see how we can benefit each other."

I sit back in my seat and purse my lips. He's not wrong. I know I can be stubborn and set in my ways; this whole change and transition haven't been the easiest on me. And I know that I can sometimes be difficult. And it seems like he's offering a tentative olive branch, so the least I can do is meet him halfway.

"You're right," I say. "And I apologize for being a pill. I promise I'll do better."

"We don't have to be best friends to work well together—and I, too, will work on being better as well," he replies.

Détente. This is not what I expected from him when I stepped into the office today. But it's not an unwelcome development. Maybe this is the silver lining in the dark clouds we've all been living under.

"You are one hell of a leader, Blake. You and your team get results," he begins. "I might not always like how you get those results and will occasionally push back on you, but you are doing good work out there. I had misgivings, but I am impressed with you. With your skill and your leadership. You're making us all look good. And I admire the way you protect your team and push them to excel."

"Thank you, Chief."

We lapse into silence for a moment. This sense of peace between us doesn't feel bad. I still don't think we'll ever be best friends, but I think we can learn to co-exist. And that's good enough for me.

He gets to his feet. "Well, I just wanted to come by to congratulate you on closing the case," he tells me, "and to let you know that I'm here for whatever you and your team might need. All you have to do is ask."

"Thank you, Chief Ayad. I appreciate that."

He shakes my hand then turns and walks out of my office. I watch as he steps through the bullpen and then out the doors, leaving me alone again. Despite the good feelings left in Ayad's wake, there's still some small piece of me that remains wary. And though I hope this détente between us is real, I can't help but hear an old phrase I learned a long time ago rattling around in my head... *Timeo Danaos et dona ferentes.*

I fear the Greeks even when they're bearing gifts.

CHAPTER THIRTY-FOUR

Jade Moon Apartments, Pike Market District; Seattle, WA

SITTING IN A CHAIR BESIDE KIT'S BED, I HOLD HER HAND, gently squeezing it. April left for a couple of days to see to some business of her own but vowed to come back. She and I have spent the last couple of days getting to know each other, and despite my early misgivings, I've come to like her a lot. And I'm thankful she's been there for my sister.

I feel a hand on my shoulder and reach up to take it. Looking up, I squeeze Fish's hand and give him a smile. His smile is dazzling and warm, and he looks at me like a favored child. Fish is known for his flamboyance, and today isn't doing anything to diminish that reputation. He's dressed in a metallic blue suit with a white shirt, red tie, and matching pocket square.

"I wish I had the confidence you have in that suit," I say.

He holds his arms out and turns in a circle, giving me a good look. "Pretty suit, right?"

I laugh softly. "It most certainly is."

Fish is going legit, but he's still dressing like one of the villains from Batman's rogue's gallery. It's kind of charming. It makes him unique.

"You look troubled, my dear," he says, his voice soft.

"Just a rough case."

"All your cases are rough."

A wry smile touches my lips. "This one was rougher than most."

"But you're all right?"

I nod. "More or less. I feel like I'm going to be sitting down with somebody to talk about it pretty soon though."

"Then that's what you should do. The sooner the better," he tells me, sounding genuinely worried about me.

"I will. I promise."

"I hope so. Your job leaves scars. Deep scars," he says. "You need to take care of yourself so you can take care of your sister."

"Speaking of, how has she been, Fish?"

"Kit woke up briefly—"

Hearing that Kit had woken from her coma sends a bright jag of excitement racing through me. I sit up straighter, a smile on my lips.

"She did? What did she say?"

"All she said was *Stone*," he says.

I frown. "Stone?"

He nods. "According to April, yes. She said Stone, and then slipped back into her coma again." He produces an envelope from his pocket and presses it into my hand. "April left this for you. She said Kit wanted you to have it."

"What is it?"

"A safe deposit box key, I believe," he says.

I look in the envelope and see that it does indeed look like a safe deposit box key. It immediately piques my interest. I have no idea what she might have stashed away.

"What did the doctor say about her waking up?" I ask.

"He is optimistic that she will wake up—and stay awake. It's simply a matter of time," he says. "He believes her waking up is a good thing and just thinks we need a little more patience."

I look down, frowning. I was hoping by the time we got back that Kit would be awake and talking. The fact that she's still in a coma worries me—despite what the doctor says. Fish's hand falls onto my shoulder again, and he gives it a gentle squeeze.

"Kit is like you—she's a fighter, my dear," he says. "She will come out of this and will be back to normal before you know it."

I nod, but my mind is spinning. What did she mean by saying *Stone*? What does she know about my boss's boss? It sends a bolt of worry through me. I know she's been working on finding out the true head of the Thirteen. Was that supposed to mean that Stone is the head? Was she trying to warn me?

"You should get some rest, Agent Wilder," Fish says. "You look exhausted."

"I am exhausted."

"Well, it is a good thing I had the guest room made up then," he tells me. "Why don't you go crawl in for a couple of hours. I promise you she's not going anywhere."

Fish is right. I need a little sleep. Lying down for a few hours isn't a bad idea. I get to my feet and throw my arms around him and give him a tight embrace.

"Thank you for taking such good care of her, Fish. And for protecting her."

"You're family. Therefore, she's family. I take care of my family."

"And I'm grateful for it."

Fish takes both of my hands in his and squeezes them tight as he looks deeply into my eyes, his expression firm but kind.

"And I'm grateful to have you in my life, Blake. You are my moral compass. I can always count on you to point me in the right direction," he tells me. "If not for you, I might still be running my empire instead of turning over a new leaf."

"I doubt that. I may have given you a nudge, but you're a good man," I tell him. "You would have gotten around to going legit eventually."

"Well, you certainly expedited the process."

"We're good for each other," I say.

I look down at my sister again and frown as a million different thoughts collide in my head. But as I think about what she's been through, about what landed her in that bed, I feel my heart fall into my stomach. She'd woken up from her coma to utter one word. Stone. But was it a warning? What did she find out about him? And is that information in the safe deposit box down at the bank? The mere thought of it sends a chill through me.

My phone buzzes in my pocket, so I pull it out and look at the screen. When I see Max Stone's name pop up, my veins fill with ice water. It's as if thinking about him prompted him to call me. A worried look crosses Fish's face when I show him the phone.

"What if Kit was trying to warn me about Stone?" I ask. "What if he is the head of the Thirteen she's been looking for?"

"Then it's all the more important for you to answer that call," he says. "You don't want to give him the idea that you're onto him. It could be fatal for you—and for her."

He's right. But the thought of Stone, a man I look up to and trust, being the head of the Thirteen, fills me with an anxiety I've never known. More than that, the idea that he could be responsible for what happened to Kit fills me with rage. I remember seeing him with Kathryn Hedlund, and that tide of rage and anxiety rises even higher. I don't know that I'm going to be able to talk to him without giving myself away.

"Blake, you need to answer the call," Fish presses. "I know it will be difficult, but you must act as if everything is all right. That everything is normal. Your very lives could depend upon it."

"Yeah. Yeah. You're right."

Closing my eyes and steeling myself, I connect the call and press the phone to my ear.

"ADIC Stone," I say.

"Blake, I just heard you were back in town," he replies. "And I heard you're coming off a traumatic case."

"It was difficult. Yes," I say. "You heard correctly."

"I'm sorry for what you went through," he replies. "And I don't mean to pile on, but there's something we need to discuss."

"All right. What's up?"

"Not on the phone," he says. "Meet me at the Nakamura Sculpture Garden in an hour."

He disconnects the call before I can reply, leaving me standing there looking at my phone. I slip my phone into my pocket and then look at Fish.

"I'll send somebody with you," he says.

I shake my head. "He'll sniff them out in a second. It's a relatively public place. I'll be fine," I say. "Besides, I need you to look after Kit."

"Blake—"

"I'll be fine."

I look down at Kit and take her hand again. She looks so small and frail beneath the blankets, and it makes my heart hurt just to look at her. I hate seeing her like this. But what I hate even more is the idea that Maximillian Stone is responsible for her current condition.

Fish is right. I have to play along for now. But if I find out Stone is the head of the Thirteen and that he is responsible for Kit being shot, there isn't anybody on this planet who will be able to protect him from me.

CHAPTER THIRTY-FIVE

Nakamura Sculpture Garden, Capitol Hill District; Seattle, WA

THE NIGHT IS DARK, AND THE SKY OVERHEAD IS LITTERED with patchy clouds, making the moonlight slanting down from above intermittent. When I pulled into the parking lot for the sculpture garden, I found it empty, which I found odd. There's usually somebody in the gardens. Even at night. It's a peaceful place. A good spot to come and think.

But as soon as I catch sight of the closed sign on the gate, I know why Stone wanted to meet here. It's guaranteed to be empty. And as I step through the gate and look around at the positions I know hold surveillance cameras, I don't see any of the red lights indicating they're functioning.

"Yeah, this is going to go well," I mutter.

I briefly consider turning around and driving away, but Fish is right. If I don't show, I could be signing not only my own death certificate but Kit's too. Clenching my jaw, I pull my weapon out of its holster and follow the path down through the park. The sculptures all around me, mixed with the trees and tall bushes, are dark and foreboding. I've been here many times, but tonight it's taken on a dark tone. It looks like some terrifying landscape from a child's nightmare.

Swallowing hard, I walk on, searching the shadows for signs of movement, searching the park for any sign of Stone at all. The silence is so thick I can barely breathe. My stomach churns, and there's a sharp anxiousness that ripples through my heart as I walk along the darkened path.

As I walk, I silently chastise myself for being so stupid as to show up at a park in the middle of the night to meet a man who may be responsible for my sister being in a coma and could quite possibly want me dead as well.

As I pass a tall, abstract sculpture, I hear the scuff of a shoe on the concrete path behind me. I wheel around but feel a hard body slam into me hard enough to knock me off my feet. I land on my back with a thud and groan as the breath is driven from my lungs. My gun is knocked out of my hand, where it hits the ground with a clatter. Knowing I have scant seconds to act, I start to scramble to my feet only to feel a heavy foot driven into my midsection, slamming me back down to the ground.

I raise my eyes and see a dark silhouette looming over me. He's wide and bulky, and the deep shadows of the hood he's got pulled over his head keep me from seeing his face. Not that I would have seen it anyway because as the man brings his arm up, all I can seem to focus on is the yawning, black maw of the weapon being pointed directly at my face…

AUTHOR'S NOTE

Thanks for reading *The Missing Girls,* book 12 in the *Blake Wilder FBI Mystery Thriller series.* If you want to read something really fun and thrilling until the next Blake Wilder book, may I suggest - *Murder on the Astoria* featuring FBI Agent Olivia Knight. Just read the description, that's going to be a fun one! You can also checkout the rest of the *Olivia Knight FBI Mystery Thrillers* if you haven't read them before.

My intention is to give you a thrilling adventure and an entertaining escape with each and every book. Being a new indie writer is tough. However, your support has helped tremendously. I don't have a large budget, huge following, or any of the cutting edge marketing techniques.

So, *all I kindly ask* is that if you enjoyed this book, please take a moment of your time and leave me a review and maybe recommend the book to a fellow book lover or two. This way I can continue to write all day and night and bring you more books in the *Blake Wilder series.*

By the way, if you find any typos or want to reach out to me, feel free to email me at egray@ellegraybooks.com

Your writer friend,
Elle Gray

P.S. I'm working hard to bring you more books and also squeeze in a mini summer vacation :)

ALSO BY
ELLE GRAY

Blake Wilder FBI Mystery Thrillers

Book One - The 7 She Saw
Book Two - A Perfect Wife
Book Three - Her Perfect Crime
Book Four - The Chosen Girls
Book Five - The Secret She Kept
Book Six - The Lost Girls
Book Seven - The Lost Sister
Book Eight - The Missing Woman
Book Nine - Night at the Asylum
Book Ten - A Time to Die
Book Eleven - The House on the Hill
Book Twelve - The Missing Girls

A Pax Arrington Mystery

Free Prequel - Deadly Pursuit
Book One - I See You
Book Two - Her Last Call
Book Three - Woman In The Water
Book Four- A Wife's Secret

ALSO BY
ELLE GRAY | K.S. GRAY

Made in United States
North Haven, CT
13 September 2023

41506365R00141